Acts of God

Also by Mary Morris

PICADOR USA   NEW YORK

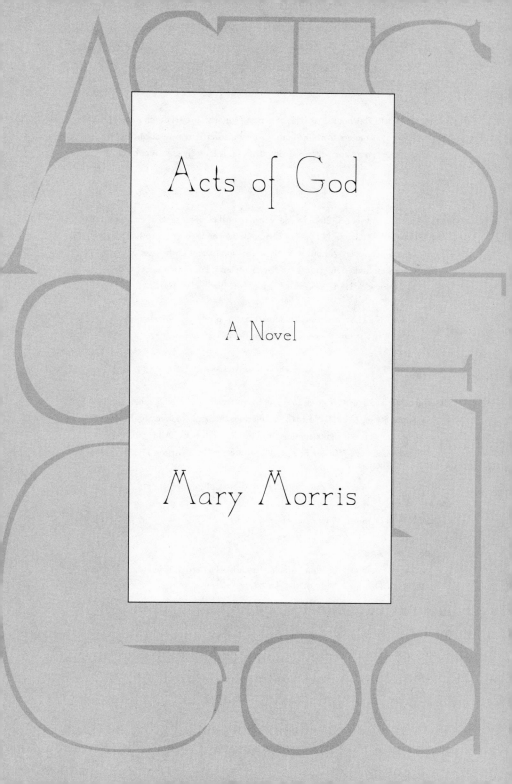

Acts of God

A Novel

Mary Morris

ACTS OF GOD. Copyright © 2000 by Mary Morris. All rights reserved. Printed in the United States of America. No part of this book may be used or reproduced in any manner whatsoever without written permission except in the case of brief quotations embodied in critical articles or reviews. For information, address Picador USA, 175 Fifth Avenue, New York, N.Y. 10010.

Picador® is a U.S. registered trademark and is used by St. Martin's Press under license from Pan Books Limited.

Book design by Victoria Kuskowski

Grateful acknowledgment is given to quote from "Small World" by Stephen Sondheim and Jule Styne. © 1959 Norbeth Productions Inc. and Stephen Sondheim. Copyright renewed. All rights administered by Chappell & Co. All rights reserved. Used by permission of Warner Bros. Publications U.S. Inc., Miami, Florida 33014.

Library of Congress Cataloging-in-Publication Data
Morris, Mary.
    Acts of God : a novel / Mary Morris.—1st ed.
        p. cm.
    ISBN 0-312-24663-3
        1. Family reunions—Fiction. 2. Suburban life—Fiction. 3. Friendship—Fiction.
    4. Women—Fiction. I. Title.
PS3563.O87445 A615 2000
813'.54—dc21

00-033986

First Edition: September 2000

10   9   8   7   6   5   4   3   2   1

This book is dedicated to the Elm Place Gang and Jane Supino

and Paige Simpson—Illinois girls all.

To D.R. for the memories, to Miss Dorsch for the lessons,

and Larry and Kate for the rest.

In little towns, lives roll along
so close to one another;
loves and hates beat about,
their wings almost touching.

—WILLA CATHER, *Lucy Gayheart*

My father used to say that sometimes you think you know a person, only to find out that you don't. That life, when it comes to people, is full of surprises. I've found this to be true. You think you understand someone, only to realize that you didn't. That you were wrong all along. Perhaps this is why I have chosen to live in such a remote place—a ramshackle house on a spit of land on the Pacific Coast.

Friends who live elsewhere tell me—and they may be right—that this California coast isn't a place where anyone can live. That it is meant to slide, collapse, or drift out to sea. But I'm not uncomfortable on the edge of disaster; I'm not uneasy being where it might all fall apart. My father, who sold insurance for a living, also had a sense of taking risks and this was one of the things he imparted to me.

For years I've led a straightforward life. No wild parties, no mad flings. Still, sometimes I drive too fast along the Coast Highway. And I run in the mountains where cougar roam. Cougar, my son, Ted, likes to remind me, are predatory animals and they will stalk you to your front door, knock it down, and eat you in your own kitchen. I know I shouldn't drive fast or run alone where cougar dwell, but I take these small chances—these little risks. They don't seem so bad and, after all, this is why I have chosen to be in this part of the world.

Otherwise my life has been stable. One marriage, one divorce, two kids. Until recently I didn't seem to want anything big to happen, having felt that enough had happened to last me a lifetime. What I needed now was peace and quiet. I was fairly close to this California version of Nirvana when the first invitation arrived. It was slipped under my door on a sun-drenched morning when I was out on my run. I must have stepped over it as I came in.

The air had a sweetness to it that day and I'd gone way up into the hills, then jogged down to the shore, where the yellow ice plant bloom. I followed the beach for a mile or so, the waves crashing at my feet. Then I climbed the dunes home. I have my routine. Walk in the door, grab a water bottle from the fridge and a towel from the drawer. Cool off, then shower.

I was taking gulps of cold water and wiping my face when I noticed the envelope lying on the floor. The envelope had a cat's face printed in the upper-right-hand corner and in blue lettering, "Home of the Winonah Wildcats." The mail doesn't come until after noon so I knew it must have gone to Betsy, my nearest neighbor. I hardly know Betsy except to wave, but often, for reasons neither of us can comprehend, we get each other's mail.

It was handwritten (a nice touch, I thought), addressed to me— Theadora Antonia Winterstone. A mouthful, I know. More name than a person like me needs but there you have it. When I was growing up, nobody called me by all those names. I was Theadora to my teachers, Tess to my acquaintances, Tessie to my friends, Squirrel to my family.

In my family we all had nicknames. We were, looking back until a certain moment, a happy family. When my father wasn't on the road, selling insurance or settling claims, we had our meals together. At night we were tucked into our beds. In the summer there were barbecues, a ball tossed around. Dogs, report cards, food fights. Normal things. I have no doubt when it all changed. But before, before that, Jeb was Trooper and Art was Squirt and I was Squirrel. "Trooper, Squirt, and Squirrel," our father called when he was back from his days on the road.

Why was I Squirrel—a name some family members still call me affectionately or if they want to tease me; why Squirrel? In part because I scurried about, and still do, dashing from here and there, but mainly because I collected things—hoarded them, wouldn't let anything go. My pockets were filled with feathers and bones, stones and coins, stamps, seed pods and bottle caps—whatever I found on my way home from school. Leaves I pressed between wax paper, doll parts, ribbons. Whatever I found in the Cracker Jack box. Grudges. And my share of secrets too. I've held on to these as well. Stuff, my mother called it. Squirrel and her stuff.

My mother, Lily, was always checking my pockets when I came home from a walk in the woods, trying to toss out whatever she could. For God's sake, she'd tell my father or my brothers, "Don't give her any more stuff." There was a certain dread when it came to cleaning my room. But my room was not a hodgepodge of these things. No, it was a carefully arranged place, museum quality, with everything neatly ordered, dusted, labeled on my shelf. Bird feathers, shells. Periwinkles, scallops, cockleshells. Souvenirs from outings we went on—a star key chain from Starlight Lake, a small wooden carved bear from the Dells.

Anything ever given to me, anything ever found, if anyone ever said, "Here, Squirrel, you can keep this," I kept it. It was mine. I kept things for a long, long time and when I outgrew something, I put it in a box, labeled and tucked away, until Lily, on one of her massive cleanups, would go into the basement and throw it away.

Because of this side of my character, there were many speculations about what I'd grow up to be—a rag picker at rummage sales or a researcher for the CIA were among my less flattering prospects, but my father was sure I'd become a great collector and classifier—a biologist who discovered new species like that tiny East Indian owl, believed until recently to be extinct. Or a curator of ancient objects, a lawyer with a genius for precedents. Chief librarian at the Library of Congress. My father had great dreams for me and it was a known fact among the members of the Winterstone family that I had an archival mind.

But in fact I did not become any of these things. Nor much else, for that matter. I suppose I've been a bit of a professional dilettante, dabbling here and there. Though many things in life have interested me, I never landed on anything that would really matter very much. Looking back, I know that there are reasons for this—moments I can pinpoint in time.

Nothing ever came of all the stuff I collected until now. It is the remnant of my archivist's nature. I know how to put things in order. Every fact, every date, who was where and when.

This is what enables me to tell this story now. I know where everything is.

I examined the folded sheet with its goalposts and letter sweater with a big "W" for Winonah emblazoned across the front. As I headed to the shower, I tossed it into the recycling bin. When I left home to go to college, I had my reasons—and they were good ones—for going away. I thought one day I might return to the Middle West to live, but I never did. Twice a year I flew to Chicago to see my parents, but I never drove up to Winonah. I kept my distance. I stayed away.

I moved as far as I could and still be within the continental United States. I went to college in Berkeley. Then I married Charlie and had two kids. After my marriage broke up, I moved down the coast just below Santa Cruz, where I now live. I bought a stone house, built by Francis Cantwell Eagger, the poet whose work has had a recent surge of renown. It is the second place I've ever called home, and I intended it to be the last.

I tossed away the next invitation, which arrived a few months later, as well. I didn't even have to think twice about it. I wasn't going and that was that. It was my daughter, Jade, who dug the third and final reminder out of the bin. Pack Rat Jade, we call her, always rummaging in the trash. The apple didn't fall far with this one. Snooping through my things. We are alike in this way, my daughter and I. Jade is great at flea markets and in musty basements. "Wow, Mom, look at this," she'll say, holding up an old doorknob, the cuffs of a long-gone fur coat. Jade can find a use for anything or can just sit for hours reading my old letters; nothing I'd ever meant for her to see.

It's pointless for me to buy lipstick because she'll snatch it, or have a private life because she'll uncover it as well. My daughter, the sleuth. So when she found this paper, she put it in front of me as if she'd just discovered evidence of some heinous crime. She pointed a bitten fingernail at the page.

"What's this?" Jade asked, hovering beside me, running her hand—another nervous habit of hers—through her close-cropped hair.

"It's an invitation to my thirtieth high school reunion," I said, snatching the paper from her.

"Wow," she said, "that's so cool," as if she thought it really was. She looked at me, defiant almost, as if it were a dare. "Well, you're going, aren't you?" It was inconceivable to her that I would not. But in fact I wasn't. Winonah, for me, wasn't a place to go back to.

"No," I said, "I'm not."

"Not going where?" Ted put in, walking out of his room. From the corner of my eye I could see his door open. On the door the words "Clato Verato Nictoo" appeared. I didn't know what these words meant and Ted wouldn't tell me. I tried dozens of times to unscramble them as if they were an anagram, to read them backward, to extricate their meaning. "If you have to ask . . ." Ted said whenever I wanted to know. Clato Verato Nictoo. Just one more thing that keeps me from my son.

"It's an invitation to Mom's thirtieth high school reunion." Jade snatched it back and held it up as if she were dangling a dead rodent by the tail.

"Oh, Mom, you've got to go," Ted said, swinging the peace medallion with the shark's tooth he wore over his surfer's shirt. His buzz-saw cut revealed the pink of his skull. "It will be fun."

"It will be boring and probably sad," I told them but they continued to protest.

"You might have a good time; you'll see everyone again. Besides," Jade said, giving me a wink, "you never know."

For years now they'd been trying to get me to go out, meet someone new. We live south of Santa Cruz, where a cool, winter mist makes this the artichoke capital of the world. It is true our house looks on to the sea and I can tell you a million things to do with an artichoke, but it's not as if I live in the Bay Area or even Marin or Sausalito, where I might get a chance to meet someone new. I've had a few relationships since my marriage ended, but nothing has really stuck.

I suppose the end of my marriage stunned me. Charlie sat across the table one evening while I was clearing the dishes away and said he wanted a divorce. It was a Thursday night in summer and the kids were playing outside. I could hear their voices, calling to friends in the yard. A ball bounced in the street. When I asked him why, he replied, "Because I don't really know you. You don't give anything away."

I looked around, thinking for a moment that he meant my stuff— the hats and jewelry and antique coffee grinders that cluttered our house. "We could have a garage sale," I said.

Charlie shook his head. "That's not what I mean at all."

We went back and forth, breaking up, staying together for several months, and then it was over. There have been a few others— briefly—since. I dated a psychologist from UC Santa Cruz the longest. When he drove off after our last date, a pebble hit me in the head. Since then, when the kids ask how a date was, I reply, "Pebble in the head." Now I can just point to my forehead and they know what I mean. I suppose Charlie was the one I really loved. At least, looking back, I recall it as a true passion. The kind where you think about this person all day long and when you lay down beside him at night you feel like you've been plugged into an electric socket. But in the end Charlie saw it more accurately than I. It was never quite right. There was something missing. There always seems to be.

I have no idea what has drawn me to one person and away from another. I've never been the most insightful person about myself, not like some people I know. Once or twice I've gone for counseling, but it never added up to much. It helped me get some new hobbies, though, that sort of thing. But it didn't enable me to understand what pulls me in one direction as opposed to another.

Probably what I do with my time doesn't help either. I always seem to be running around. First there's the kids, the house, and my plans, once the kids are out on their own, to turn it into a bed-and-breakfast.

A few days a week, to make ends meet, I work for my friend Shana, a real estate broker, where I show time-shares and seasonal rentals in Carmel. And in my spare time I volunteer for a wildlife rescue league.

I didn't go to school to learn how to do this, though I have studied on and off. Before I had a family, I worked for Fish and Game. They sent me to some remote locations where I counted salmon swimming upstream. I watched them shattering their bodies against the rocks to feed their young; this gave me lots of ideas. I even began to write a little book of aphorisms about this experience called *Reflections from the Salmon Counting Tower,* but nobody wanted to publish it.

After a while mammals became my focus. I seem to have become a kind of local expert on beached things—whales, dolphins, orphaned otter pups. They bring them all to me. The whales I can do little about, but I've been surrogate parent to a number of sea otters. I am convinced that what makes a creature beach itself isn't a suicidal tendency as some experts claim. I think it's a blip on the radar screen, a sonar misfiring that sends the wrong message.

Who knows why the message goes wrong—a virus, noise pollution, a genetic flaw—but the animals turn mysteriously in the direction of their ruin. I am left with the remains, with what has washed up on the shore.

I had no intention of going to the reunion or anywhere else, for that matter. Over the years I have tended to stay put, not to wander far from this coast. Besides, I didn't want to see people I hadn't seen in thirty years and would probably no longer recognize. Or open the proverbial can of worms. But the morning of the reunion Jade and Ted appeared at my room with my bags packed, a plane ticket which they'd charged on my Visa in hand. "Surprise," they said.

"I'm sick," I told them. I'd been fighting a cold. But they had the Tylenol ready. They looked to me as they once had when they were small on my birthday or Mother's Day, standing with a breakfast tray in hand, a pleased look on their faces.

"You're going," Jade told me. "We want you to." It was a fait accompli, they said.

2

As I flew home for the reunion, it was the summer of the great floods. The Missouri and the Mississippi had left their banks, burst their levees. So much for the Army Corps of Engineers, my father would have said. Below me, what had once been a great river appeared as a series of lakes with channels connecting one to the next.

From what I'd read in the newspapers I knew that people had drowned. A family went for a boating expedition as the waters rose; all were lost. Two boys had tried to go fishing; their bodies were found in a tree. Houses sat like little islands in the midst of these pools. As we flew over them, it was a clear day and on the roofs of some I could see the numbers of their insurance policies scrawled. This would have driven my father wild. He'd be racing from farmhouse to farmhouse, helping the farmers file their claims.

Before I was ten, I knew how to read a disaster, how to calculate the loss of life and limb. I understood what landfall meant, what an 8.2 on the Richter scale was; I knew the damage an F5 tornado (inconceivable) versus an F6 (unimaginable) could do. Debris paths, flood basins—none of this was news to me.

And I'd learned a few things about odds. "What are the chances?" my father used to say. "If it's three to one a tornado will blow through southern Illinois during the tornado season, then what're the odds it will blow through the Loop?" Actuarial statistics were the subject of family dinners. The death of a child wasn't worth a fraction of the death of a working spouse. Loss of income was greater than loss of consortium (the word my father used when he referred to companionship). Property costs more than grief. Dollar signs lurked behind every heartbreak. Over dinner I heard tales of farms foreclosed, policies lapsed.

From an early age I came to associate my father with bad weather. I developed a fear of oncoming storms—a phobic dread of wind and rain. I can't say I've ever gotten over it completely. When thick black clouds gather over the Pacific, I have to brace myself. When my father was on the road or even when he was home, I listened obsessively to weather reports, scanned the skies for that blue-gray sky that threatened snow, a yellow-green cast that foretold a tornado touchdown. It all meant claims. It meant that once again my father would be taken from me. I had no idea how much or how far, though in the end it wouldn't be the weather that took him away.

Now as I flew home, the flooded plain stretched below me. My father had always been opposed to the levees. He knew the rivers. He'd been born near them, grew up along their banks. He said when it came to rivers, and I suppose to anything else, for that matter, let them flow. Don't try to contain them.

A river will find its own shape and direction. There are two hundred sunken steamboats from the Missouri River that now lie at the bottom of plowed fields. This is because the river has chosen to go its own way. You can't trust the river; you never know when it will burst its banks and reroute itself.

My father knew better than to tell the farmers not to live on the silt-rich soil that lined the floodplain. Along the riverbanks you could reach your hand into the dirt and pull up the richest black earth in the world—fistfuls—and my father wasn't one to tell anyone to live elsewhere. But he did try to convince them to build on higher ground.

If my father were flying in this plane, looking down at this water-clogged land, if he were looking at what I saw from this height, he would have felt very sad and very vindicated. He would say, "They should've asked me. I would've told them."

3

I spy, what do I spy, something that is yellow. Is it a truck? I asked my brother Jeb. Is it my father's shirt or that yellow jacket that flew into the car? A freight train car, a street sign, that stripe down the center of the road? It's corn, Jeb shouted back at me. It was the summer I turned nine as I gazed at fields and fields, but I didn't see any yellow. All I saw were flowing carpets of pale green. But it's in the husk, I said, and Jeb just threw up his hands.

It didn't seem quite fair, the rules my brother played by, but still it was all around us. Miles and miles of corn. I'd never seen it before. For years I'd waited for this. My father was letting me go with him for the first time to the floodplain. Jeb was twelve and he'd been going with for the past two years. You had to be ten to go along, that was the rule. But since I was almost ten, my father made an exception for me. That was how he put it, "I'll make an exception for you, Squirrel," and even though I didn't know what an exception was at the time, I was happy to have one made for me.

Art cried because he was only six and had to stay home and Lily tried to explain to him that when he was bigger he'd go. In the end she had to pry his fingers from the car door. "Another year or two, Squirt," our father said, but Art just screamed that it wasn't fair and in the end our father had to agree with him. "You're right, son," he said. "Life isn't fair." Lily stood in the driveway, in an apron, holding Art back with one hand, blowing kisses with the other as we drove away. Her skirt caught in the wind and she pushed it down.

My father blew kisses back, a smile on his face, but the minute we turned north on Lincoln and drove under the railroad trestle, he put the radio on loud and started to croon. My father sang at home, but never loudly. Lily came from a big family and she didn't like noise. "But it's music, Lily," he'd argue with her, but she didn't agree. No shouting; no doors being banged. No music played loud. If you slammed a door behind her, my mother jumped in the air.

My father moved silently through our lives, but as soon as we were past the railroad tracks, heading west, he was tapping his fingers, humming along. We weren't half a mile from the house before we were all singing along to "You Ain't Nothing but a Hound Dog." We sang for miles at the top of our lungs.

When we stopped for gas, I slipped into the front seat, but Jeb complained. "Trooper," our father said, "you always get to sit there. Give Squirrel a chance."

It was hot even with the windows rolled down. The air smelled of pigs and fertilizer. The sun was boiling, heating up the vinyl seats of the car, but I didn't care. This was an adventure. Where we were going there had been a flood. Last year it was drought; this year it's flood, my father lectured us as we drove. Now the Everly Brothers were singing "Dream" and my father sang along. Though he was a little off-key, I was surprised he knew all the words.

My father had a deep baritone voice that would sound good on the radio, I thought. I could imagine him announcing things—the weather, the news, sports. Sometimes when I listened to the radio, I pretended it was my father's voice coming to me from far away. Now it almost made the car shake. I had only heard that voice at night when he sang to put me to bed, but it wasn't this big. It seemed to take up all the farmland that stretched before our eyes. For the first time I saw the land as he did—wide and empty and flat. Every Monday he drove out this way and every Thursday he came home. "Get a whiff of this, kids." He rolled down his window as we passed a pig farm. We held our noses, groaning, and our father laughed.

There were dozens of things my father could have done with his life besides sell insurance and settle claims. He had a keen sense for business and as he grew older, he constantly chastised himself for the mistakes he'd made. He was always kicking himself for not giving a few thousand bucks to the friend who came to him with a new invention—a little spray gadget you put on the top of bottles for hair spray and household cleaners. He and Lily had sat, watching the little demonstration. "No," she'd said afterward, "we can't take the risk." Aerosol cans. My father missed his opportunity to invest in aerosol cans. "I could've made millions," he muttered as he patched the roof or fixed the plumbing on Saturday afternoons.

His ambition once had been money—to make lots of it and get rich, then do what he wanted with his life. But he fell into the insurance line through a distant relative of my mother's, a man who said that insurance was a good, steady way to lay your foundation. In the end all the schemes for getting rich fell through and insurance was what he did. He learned to take pleasure in it as he took pleasure in most things.

Though he was a city boy by birth, he came to love the loamy smell of soil, the rich, earthy odor of dirt being overturned, of the freshly planted fields. Even the piquant odor of fertilizer or the stench of a pig farm was somehow pleasing to him. It was not what he ever expected to come to love, but then there were other things Victor Winterstone had not expected he would love. For example, our mother, Lily, the plain, freckle-faced girl who made a beautiful home and ran it like a tight ship.

He was a claims adjuster who adjusted. That's what he was, my father who chuckled to himself as he drove; that's how adjustable he'd become. He was happy as he drove, whistling, two of his children at his side. Head tossed back. He listened to the radio, tapping out the rhythms. Rolling down the window, he got a smell of the fetid earth. Compost. Dead things decaying out there in the fields. The promise of new life.

In the city he'd never felt the cycles of life. He'd felt the bars he frequented and the music and the parties and the girls who clung to him, but he didn't feel this. The way life moved on from one moment to the next. Seasonal change, things growing and dying. He wanted to reach out and grab it. Take what was left, hold it by the throat. And never let go.

I stuck my face out the window like a dog, breathing in the air my father breathed. In the backseat Jeb groaned, "Dad, I'm gonna be sick." He was mad that I'd displaced him.

"Jeb," my father said sternly, "cut it out." Jeb had a turkey feather he'd found in the gas station parking lot and he kept tickling my ear. I stuck my tongue out at him in the rearview mirror.

Illinois was flat. No one had ever told me this before but it was very flat. Sometimes there was a hill or two but then it was flat again. And green, but mostly it was corn and soy. Wheat. The wheat bent in the wind. I waved at farmers on their tractors. If they saw me, they waved back. Some kept waving until we were far away.

It took all day to get to where we were going and when we got there, it was all lakes. I'd expected rivers, running streams, but it was as if people were living in the middle of lakes. A cow floated on her back in one. Someone's bed was in the middle of another. "No one should live here," my father said under his breath and I knew we'd reached the floodplain.

My father had an office to go to in town that had the name of the company he worked for on it. Farmers Protection. He said he didn't just insure farmers, but that's how it began so they called it "Farmers." He insured all kinds of people for fire, theft, life. But in the office, people who looked like farmers were sitting, waiting for him. Men in overalls. A woman in a smock was in tears; a boy gripped her arm. Everyone looked weary.

My father was a practitioner of sleight of hand—small magic tricks he did to amuse children, mainly his own. He pulled quarters out of ears, turned a silver wand to gold. He could cut a rope in two, then make it whole. He made eggs disappear. Jeb told me on previous summers when he'd gone from farm to farm with my father that this was what he did to entertain people who'd lost everything they owned.

I kept expecting him to do one of his tricks—pluck a quarter from the ear of the boy who wouldn't let go of the woman in the smock. Instead my father sat at a desk. "Crop insurance," I heard him say, "that's what these farmers need." Then he told me and Jeb to go out-side. He gave us money to buy a hamburger and a milk shake. "Now you watch out for her," my father told Jeb. The river had left its banks.

As we wandered out into the street, people started shouting at my father. The woman in tears cried harder. We found a drugstore and sat at the counter. We ordered cheeseburgers, fries, shakes, but I didn't eat that much. Afterward we walked around town. It was a small town, but we found a playground. Jeb and I got on swings and pumped our legs harder and harder until we were swinging way up, then came way back down again. We swung until our legs ached.

Then Jeb took me down to where the river had burst its banks. It was only four or five blocks from where we were, but even as we walked there, I could see the strange sight of streets filled with dark ooze. A rushing stream of roiling water pushed just ahead of us. Houses sat in the middle of it with water up to the first-floor win-dows. In one house a dog barked mournfully on the roof.

Jeb stood, staring at the water. At its dark, brown color, churn-ing, angry as Jeb's face. Why should my brother look so angry? So responsible, as if he were the cause of this flood? He picked up a stick and hurled it in with all his might and we watched the stick being car-ried along with the current. Then he hurled another. Then he pre-tended to walk toward the water, to put his foot in and I screamed, holding him back. But he pushed me away and started to walk again toward the water's edge and this time I grabbed his shirt. Real tears came down my cheeks and when he saw my tears, he stopped. He laughed at me. "You didn't think I would, did you, Squirrel?"

I was still pulling on him, afraid to let go, until he stepped back from the river's edge. When we went back to my father's office, the people were gone. My father looked weary. We'd been thinking of driving straight back, but my father said he was too tired. He decided we should spend the night so we drove for an hour or so, which our father said was all right because it was on our way home.

When the air cooled and it began to grow dark, we stopped at a roadside motel that was mostly a parking lot. A big neon vacancy sign

blinked on and off and the "V" was burned out so it read "acancy." I
don't know why, but Jeb and I found this word very funny. Acancy.
The motel was painted turquoise on the outside and had a TV in the
room, and a small pool with lots of dead bugs in it.

The room was plaid and smelled of stale cigarettes, but we swam
in the pool, though I was more tentative about water now than I'd
been before I saw the flood, the water rising to the windows of
houses. My father used a strainer to get the bugs out of the pool. Then
he let us swim in our T-shirts and underwear. In the morning we had
to put on wet clothes.

Then my father took us out for steaks and French fries. We ate in
a restaurant that had green and pink Formica tables and a steer's head
over the door. I got to eat my steak with a serrated knife and it cut
smooth as butter. That night in the room we watched TV and Jeb and
I jumped from bed to bed, pretending that below us there was a roiling sea. We had a pillow fight, something we could never have at
home, while our father sat watching the news. We didn't go to sleep
before we were tired.

When it was time to go to sleep, Jeb grabbed some covers and
headed for the floor, but our father stopped him. "No way, young
man. Only Indians or barbarians sleep on the floor." After some back-
and-forth, they eventually shared the bed. I got the bed closest to the
window, where the amber light from the parking lot shone in. It was
a big bed but with scratchy sheets. It was also soft, not like my bed at
home, which was harder. I found a cozy place to slip into. Jeb and my
father both fell asleep right away, my father sputtering in his sleep,
and I drifted off, listening to the heavy breathing of men.

In the morning we drove back to Winonah. It was a long, hot drive
and the way back looked different from the way there. It was flat farmland, but as you got closer to Winonah and the lake it closed up on
you. The trees made the landscape thicker. They broke the flatness,
but I felt as if I couldn't breathe. I missed the open stretches of road.

When we got home, Lily-was sitting on the front porch, crying.
She looked like one of those farmer's wives from the floodplain.

When she saw us, she dashed off the porch. "Oh, I expected you last night. You should have called," she scolded my father, shaking a finger, but she was hugging us. I thought my mother was going to be angry. Instead she held us very tight.

That night as I was going to sleep, my mother came into my room. I had heard my parents arguing downstairs. Now she looked tired, but she didn't seem so upset anymore. She sat on the side of my bed. "So how was your trip?"

I told her I'd seen a cow floating on its back and a bed drifting down a stream. She seemed to like this so I told her more. I told her I'd seen a dining room set in the middle of a lake and a family picnicking on the roof of their house and when we'd driven by the waters had parted like the Red Sea.

Now she seemed a little annoyed with me. She ruffled my hair and rose from the bed. "No fibs, Squirrel," she said, pulling the covers to my chin. "Always tell the truth. Don't tell stories."

4

I never thought I'd be driving down this road again, but suddenly there I was, following the shore, on my way to Winonah. I followed the dips of the old Hiawatha trail that the Potawatomi had blazed a century ago when they traveled these bluffs. The steel-blue lake was to my right and I caught glimpses of it as I took each turn. I drove by the dome-shaped Bahai temple that my brother Jeb christened "God's orange juice squeezer" when we were kids, hot and bored in the backseat. After that we laughed whenever we passed it, making slurping noises until our father told us to pipe down.

I careened through the twisting section of road called the Hills, carved by Ice Age glaciers, and took the turns as if I were driving the bumper cars at Riverview. As a child, the Hills seemed to promise some kind of adventure. When I drive along the Coast Highway where I now live, I get this same surge—as if anything is possible. Above me loomed maples and oak, the sturdy trees I'd grown up with. I eased the car around each turn on the narrow road I knew like the back of my hand.

We used to take this road all the time when I was a girl and we'd visit our grandparents "in town." My father preferred the highway because it was faster, but my mother always said, "No, let's take the Drive." "The Drive" was slower with its winding turns, but there were things to see—stone houses where rich people lived tucked behind blooming shrubs. Famous houses designed by Frank Lloyd Wright. When we passed one of those, my mother pointed. "How'd you like to live here? He made everything small, like he was."

It had been almost three decades since I'd gotten on the Drive and headed north. But I wanted to go this way and not the highway. I wanted to come back slowly, to take my time. But still Winonah came upon me suddenly. When I crossed the town line and saw the sign, I felt a twinge as if I'd taken a wrong turn. But there was no wrong turn. It's the way Winonah is—a town where it seems as if you can't go wrong. But, of course, you can.

As I came into town, even in the dark I could see how Central Avenue had changed. A Gap was at the corner where we used to buy school supplies. Coffee bars with green awnings dotted the main drag. A fancy restaurant with curtains inhabited the spot that had once been Irv's Deli. Irv and his wife, who both had numbers tattooed on their arms, had shouted at each other day and night.

Some things hadn't changed. Crawford's Clothing was still there— the dresses in the window looked as if they were frozen circa 1970. The old drugstore was the same as it had been the last time I chained my bike to the rack and walked in to buy Prell shampoo. The big and brassy clock on the Bank of Illinois building told the time as it always had.

I'd arrived in Chicago that afternoon, stopped home to see my mother, Lily, who had a tunafish sandwich with chips on the side and a Coke waiting for me, as if I'd just walked in from school. Lily looked the same—her nose still turned up with freckles along the bridge, her hair streaked with gray, her green eyes watery. She was too thin, perhaps. Her hands felt cold, her skin was pale. I wanted to open the blinds, air out the place. I never liked being in my mother's apartment. It seemed as if she'd never unpacked, never quite settled in. The furniture from the old house was crammed into three rooms. My baby brother, Art, who lived nearby, tried to get her to sell some things, but she wanted to hold on to most of what she had.

The apartment was dark, slightly overheated, and smelled of cigarettes, though she swore she'd quit years ago. In each room was a copy of the *Comprehensive Crossword Dictionary* next to a pair of store-bought reading glasses. While my mother shuffled between the kitchen and the dining room with my sandwich and Coke, I opened to a random page: "*Continent.* 1) chaste 2) land mass as in Africa 3) legendary or lost as in Atlantis." She put the sandwich in front of me, removing its Saran Wrap cover, and watched as I ate it and sipped my Coke.

We talked for an hour or so about the kids, the weather in California. She listened as intently as Lily was able to before she began her list of complaints about her back, her sinuses, her cleaning woman, always prefacing her remarks with "Now, I don't want to complain" or "I don't want to pry, but . . ." and then she'd complain, bouncing from one subject to another.

When it was almost dark, I'd borrowed her car and headed north. I'd left later than I should have, but I didn't care. I wasn't in a hurry even though the party had begun without me hours ago. I knew how to get there, but I took my time. Now I drove slowly through Winonah, like a policeman on his evening rounds.

The streets lined with maples and elms shimmered in the heat and the air was hazy. Fireflies whose green lights flickered like fairies danced in the tended gardens and the song of cicadas filled the air.

Casting a ghostly light upon the houses, mist rose from the trimmed blue-green lawns. I could almost see my father coming out of that mist, pushing the mower up and down in even rows.

I steered past houses where friends once lived, looking into homes where I'd spent half my youth, though this gave me an eerie feeling, as if I could look inside the houses and still see their mothers stirring a pot on the stove; fathers, who had moved to Winonah to give their children a better life, reading in the den. But, of course, nobody I knew lived in those places anymore. They had not lived there for a long time.

Somewhere in the night a train whistle blew. I rolled down my window to listen to the *Milwaukee Road* making its last run. When I was growing up, we lived about a quarter mile east of the tracks. At night from my bed I could hear the trains—their horns and even the ringing of the gates as they went down. I knew that the whistle we heard on our side of town was the same whistle they heard on the other side of town and this has always been a humbling fact to me.

Winonah is a town that divides itself in every sense along its railroad tracks. The side closest to the lake is the right side and the side farthest away, heading out toward the farmland, the cornfields, and the highway, has always been the wrong side. A lot of people got rich on things you wouldn't think you could get rich on—gift cards, car parts, coffee cake—and they lived closer to the water. Many were Jews such as ourselves or wealthy Protestants. The Catholics—the Irish and the Italian—they lived on the other side. There were no blacks then in Winonah, though there are now.

We lived on the right side, but it was close enough by some standards to be considered the wrong side. We lived near the intersection of Dearborn and Lincoln. From my bedroom I could hear the sound of the cars driving across the wooden boards that lined the tracks, so different from the sound a car makes on pavement. That steady *thump-thud*. I must have heard it a million times when I was growing up. Even now in the night, though I live two thousand miles away, I wake up thinking I've heard that sound.

We barely made it, though we did; that was what mattered most to my parents, especially to my mother, who saw great value in such things. My mother who liked the table set just so, everything in its place. We had been secure enough to "keep the wolves from the door." This was an expression my father used, and when I was small I thought he meant real wolves. Many nights I drifted to sleep thinking I could hear them howling.

Actually what he meant was disaster. My father who sold insurance for a living in the floodplain of the Middle West had a clear sense of what disaster was. He'd seen lifetimes obliterated with the flash of a flood, a twist of wind. I was raised with the first law of insurance pounded into my head: You can't protect anything that really matters. You can't insure love or health. You can't guarantee peace of mind or your place in the world.

I hadn't thought much about my father's advice to me in a long time, but as I drove through Winonah, heading toward the railroad tracks, I began to think once more of what he was trying to tell me. Pausing at the tracks, I crossed into Prairie Vista. Here it was less pristine. Beer bottles and trash lined the tracks. Flashing neon signs lay ahead.

Prairie Vista was on the wrong side of the tracks, but that's where I was going that August night. We called it the land of a thousand bars—the only place where our parents could sip a little wine or go for a good time, and when we got older, it was where we went as well. For some reason, after Prohibition was repealed the towns along Chicago's north shore decided to remain dry. Winonah was famous for its music festival, for the invention of the hearing aid, and for the fact it was dry. But if we wanted a drink, we just drove across the tracks into Prairie Vista.

It was a hot night and the humidity made my spaghetti-strap dress stick to me. I drove with the skirt hiked up my thighs, the radio on an oldies station. It made sense that the reunion was being held at Paradise. Where else would they have it but in Patrick's bar?

It was as sweltering a night as any I can remember in Illinois. Sometimes on a night like that you can get a whiff of the alewives that coated the shore in late summer, their bodies sucked dry by lamprey eels. When I rolled down the window, things smelled rotten and dead.

5

Paradise was located on the strip of bars that lined the railroad tracks on the Prairie Vista side. I recognized it right away by the Christmas lights strung up and the hokey sign of heaven with little angels above the door. Dozens of cars were parked out front and a lot of them were cop cars. The music blared from the patio, which was also decorated with lights. Each light had a tin halo over it.

As I walked up, a Motown CD—Diana Ross and the Supremes—played, but a local band was warming up. They were very noisy and already the crowd was begging them to stop. The air smelled of ashes and beer. Polyester shirts clung to men's chests, revealing hairs. These men were ragged; their bellies, once taut and the color of bronze, rolled across their belts. They had elastic in their waistbands.

At first glance the women looked better. They smelled of almond soap and avocado cream. Hair concealed the lines of their face-lifts. Some had the fine-toned muscles of women who ride a treadmill all day, sipping mineral water through a straw. There was a well-preserved look to them; others did not look so well. But it didn't matter because I hardly recognized a soul.

In the entranceway someone took my ticket and stamped my hand with the letter "W" for Winonah High. Then she looked at me. "Tess," she said, "Tess Winterstone?"

Discreetly I glanced at her badge. "Penny, how are you?" She was Penny Wilcox, who'd been in my homeroom for four years, the one who married Gus Garcia. In high school she'd been a petite girl but now she'd puffed out (she'd puffed out in high school but there had been other reasons then). I reached for a name tag. It was clear I was going to need one. I looked around a room of strangers.

"Would you like the commemorative blanket?" Penny asked.

"The commemorative blanket?"

"Yes, from Winonah's centennial. It has all the historic sites on it. The proceeds go to the high school development fund. It will be mailed to you."

I was looking around to see if there was anyone I knew. "Sure, I'll take the blanket," I said, distracted, checking the box.

"Hey, Tess." A tall, middle-aged man hit me on the back. Who was he? The quarterback of the football team? The class president? Some people asked how my brother was. A woman I didn't know asked how my sister was doing. I replied fine, even though I don't have a sister.

Someone grabbed me from behind. "My God, Tess." It was Maureen Hetherford, whose hair had turned pure white since her divorce a decade ago. She looked like a very old woman with a very young face, like someone out of Shangri-la who would crumble once the spell was broken. "You're here."

"I am," I said.

"Hey, Tess, you made it," the Dworkin twins said in unison. I still couldn't tell them apart.

Most of the old gang was there. Though my father called us "the girls," to ourselves we were "the gang." There were ten of us and we moved like a herd of sheep in one smooth motion across a hill. We wore pleated skirts and bobby socks rolled down, cardigan sweaters buttoned up the back, saddle shoes. We bought our clothes in matching sets at Crawford's Clothing. After school we went to one another's houses and put on lipstick and danced to *American Bandstand*.

We knew all the dancers. We knew what it meant if Francis danced with Bobby, if Bobby danced with Charlene. Sometimes before we put on the lipstick, we practiced kissing, just to see what it felt like. We curled up in beds in each other's arms, lips touching. Never with our tongues.

Now Grace Cousins, who'd married a plastic surgeon and resembled Cher with her high cheekbones, was giving me air kisses. She wore a silver lamé strapless and told us to all come by for a swim in her checkerboard pool later. Samantha Crawford rushed over with her husband tagging along, the way he had since the day she married him, like a puppy dog. No one ever got to see her alone. Wendy Young gave me a hug. She looked the same as she had before she joined the itinerant religious sect.

"I think I want some pictures," I said. I had brought a new Olympus point-and-shoot with me and began snapping.

"Better take them fast," Lori Martin, who'd been head of the Winonah Wildcats cheering squad and president of the student council (no one had ever done both in the same year), said, mugging at the camera. "This is the last reunion we'll look good at."

"Oh, I wouldn't say that," Grace Cousins said, sucking in her cheeks. Suddenly Vicky was there, sweeping me into her arms. "I knew you'd make it."

"I didn't know myself until this morning," I told her.

"It's so good to see you. You look great, Tess." Vicky had been my best friend during high school. It was to her house I ran when I had to get out of mine and vice versa. We'd seen each other sporadically over the years, usually for lunch downtown.

"So do you." She clasped me with her long white fingers, those hands that opened aspirin bottles and tied ribbons on TV. Vicky had wanted to be an actress, but ended up as a fairly successful hand model. ("Well, at least part of me is acting," she liked to say.) For years her hands had been insured with Lloyd's, though she'd never disclose for how much.

"Well, what do you think of this?" Vicky asked, her seagreen eyes gazing around the room. Her strawberry-blond hair fell loosely across her face and she kept brushing it away. Her arms were bare in her thin rayon dress. Her gymnast's body was still firm and taut and she had freckles everywhere—like a farm girl, my mother, who also had her own share of freckles, used to say.

"I think I don't know anybody anymore."

"Oh, you know them. You just don't recognize them." She seemed to be making eye contact with someone. "But I see someone you'll recognize."

"Who?" I asked.

"Oh, you know who," she said.

I suppose Patrick had been staring at me for some time when I turned. Even before I saw him, I sensed that he'd seen me. Of course, it was his bar so naturally he'd be there. "I thought you'd come," Patrick said when he walked up to me. "I was sure you'd make it."

"Why is everyone so sure about what I'd do?" He looked the same. He was a little gray around the temples and maybe he'd put on a few pounds, but none the worse for wear.

"It made sense that you would. So how are you? How have you been?" I started to reply when the band struck up and it was impossible to talk.

"Let's go somewhere else," Patrick said, taking me by the arm. He walked with me over to a corner of the bar, looking at me askew, but that had to do with his bad eye. Basketball was supposed to be his way out. He would have gone to college on a sports scholarship and maybe even become a coach. He could sink anything from half court and slip in and out of guys twice as tall. Then someone put an elbow in his eye and he never went to college. He never left Prairie Vista.

"You look good, Tess, you really do," he said. He stared at me at an angle so he could get a look at me. I rarely gave much thought to how I looked, but as Patrick gazed at me, I suppose I did look good. I stayed out of the sun. I ran four times a week. We lived in the artichoke capital of the world and the mist that keeps the artichokes firm had also kept the wrinkles from my skin. My body had stayed small and compact. My hair had stayed dark auburn, thanks to a bottle, and I had let the curl go natural. Tonight I'd pulled those thick curls back with a silver scrunchie.

"Well, so do you," I told him, "you've hardly changed." It was true. He looked the same. Before Patrick and I ever dated, my parents went to a costume party at their club dressed as moving men. Patrick's father had a moving company and my parents borrowed Hennessey Moving and Storage overalls and cardboard boxes. I have a picture of them in overalls with strained looks on their faces as they pretended to move the giant boxes.

"Oh, but I have," he protested. "I'm not what I once was. But you look like you take good care of yourself."

"I run a lot and probably the place where I live is good for my health. And you?"

He was about to answer when I heard a laugh, sweet and smooth, except that it was too high pitched, almost shrill, like an opera singer's laugh. Only Margaret Blair had a laugh like that. It would have been one of the beautiful things about her, like her hair and her skin, except for its high pitch and the fact that it came too often.

Margaret stood just ahead of me, her black hair spilling down the back of a creamy satin dress. It was the color of pearls and hugged her breasts and her hips. It was as if thirty years had not happened to her. I dodged left, then to the right because she was the last person I wanted to run into now. "Come on," I told Patrick, "let's go over here." But when I turned, she was in front of me—her head tilted back, surrounded by a clutch of admirers, men I didn't recognize, though I'd probably once passed notes to them in study hall.

Patrick touched my elbow as he tried to steer me toward the bar, but it was too late. "Tess," she called. "Tess, is that you?"

Margaret came over, tottering slightly, holding a glass of wine. As she hugged me, her breasts pressed against mine. The chill of her wineglass against my bare shoulder sent a shiver through me. Then she stood back and looked me up and down. "You look the same, Tessie, except for your lipstick." Patrick turned toward the bar, a quiet gaze settling over his features. I kept thinking he'd drift away, but he didn't.

"My lipstick?"

"You used to wear red. But this peach color suits you."

My hand instinctively went to my lips. I didn't remember wearing red. "Well, you look the same too." It wasn't what I wanted to say. Many times I'd rehearsed this meeting in my head. How I'd tell her what I really thought. But now that I actually stood before her, I found her still beautiful, but rather pathetic, and myself almost speechless.

"You never answer my letters. You never return my cards."

"Oh, but I think about you," I told her, which was true in its own way. "I'm bad about answering my mail." I thought about the seasonal letters Margaret sent each winter. Those cheery Xeroxed epistles that outlined her family's accomplishments and failures—Nick's rise in his father's real estate business, Danielle's knee surgery, from which she'd recovered brilliantly; Margaret's small decorating business flourishing. It was inscribed for all to read, copied on red paper and stuffed into green envelopes, where she'd put stickers of reindeer and Santa Claus.

At the bottom of each seasonal letter, Margaret drew a smiling face and wrote, "Why don't I hear from you anymore?" The fact was I didn't want to know anything about her. I didn't want to hear from her ever again.

"Well, I think of you all the time," she said with emphasis, as if she were accusing me of something. "You were always nice to me." A somber look crossed her face. "Not everyone was, but you were. That meant a lot, you know, when I was the new girl."

"Well, I'm glad if that's how you remember it."

"It is. It's how I remember it." She took a long sip of her white wine, then pressed the glass to her cheek. "So tell me. What have you been up to all these years? Are you still living on the Coast?"

"Oh, you know, same place. Divorced, a couple of kids." I laughed, but she gave me an odd look as if she was sorry for me, and that made me angry. I'd always felt sorry for her because of where she lived and because her father never came and took her back to Wisconsin, the way she said he would.

The wineglass teetered in her hand and she took another sip from it. Her face was flushed and I thought that she'd already had too much to drink. "Well, you must come by. Nick and I would love to have you over." She rested her hand on my shoulder. "Come by and see us." Then someone pulled her away and I was happy to move on.

Patrick was waiting for me and he told the bartender to give me a beer. "She used to be my girl," he said, patting my arm. The bartender said the beer was on the house and Patrick found us two stools off to the side. "I'm sorry if she upset you," he said after a while.

"Just because she took you away from me . . ." I teased him.

Patrick grimaced, staring down into his beer. "You know it wasn't just that, Tessie. Things happen when you're growing up, things you can't quite understand."

"It's all right," I told him. "I forgave everyone long ago."

"We were young."

"I wonder what my life would have been if I'd stayed here and married you," I said with a sigh.

"You'd be divorced with two kids and I'd be running a bar." Patrick and I spent much of high school driving around in his father's car. I'd rest my head on his knee and stare up at the passing trees as he rubbed my head, my neck. The trees in Winonah arch so gracefully over the roads. The wind off the lake keeps their branches rustling, and I'd watch the branches from the vantage point of Patrick's lap as we drove. Sometimes his hand slipped to the side of my breast and then I felt that sweet awakening, a kind of ache that is more memory than anything else now.

Often he came to my house and we watched television in the finished basement my father built or sat in the den. There was something about him—a kindness that I carried with me over the years. His touch was light, as if it fluttered over me, and I imagined I'd find that same gentle hesitancy everywhere I went in the world.

Patrick and I, heads bent together, talked about this and that. He was estranged from his wife, though they were trying to work it out. Basically for the kids. "You know, Tessie, whenever I don't have anything to do, I drive by your old house. I just look at it and think to myself, Tessie lived here."

"Do you? That's nice."

He nodded, sipping his beer. We were silent for a minute. Then the band came blasting back on and we could hardly hear ourselves think. "Let's get out of here," Patrick said. "Let's go somewhere where we can talk."

We were heading outside to get some air when we ran into Nick Schoenfield walking in with a younger crowd. He wore a Hawaiian shirt open to his chest, which revealed a slight paunch. He was wide, built like a safe, and boisterous. Giving a wave to his friends, telling them he'd see them inside, Nick looked at us with his dark blue eyes, and laughed as if he'd just heard a great joke. "Tessie," he said, recognizing me right away, "It's good to see you."

"Well, it's good to see you, too."

He and Patrick exchanged a series of male pleasantries—slaps, handshakes, and locker-room jabs. "Just like old times. You two back together?"

Patrick laughed with him as if I were somehow their private joke. "How ya been, Tessie?" Nick said.

"I've been good. I'm still living out West."

"Well, the Coast agrees with you." He nodded, looking me up and down. "I always think of you as the one who got away."

"Did I?" I asked.

"Well, you give the impression you did. I thought you'd end up a star out there. You know you were voted 'The girl the boys were most likely to be secretly in love with.' "

"I was? By whom?" Nick opened the reunion brochure, pointing. There it was. Tessie Winterstone. "I had no idea. When did all this voting take place?" I wiped the back of my neck with a cocktail napkin.

"The ballot was in one of the invitations." Patrick laughed. "You probably threw it away." Nick smiled, his blue eyes piercing as if they could see through steel doors. His grin was warm and he hadn't lost his looks. He had been a beautiful boy and the years had been kind to him.

For a time when they played varsity, my brother Jeb and Nick had been friends. When Jeb first started bringing Nick around, that was the way he smiled at me—the wide, confident grin of a boy who is sure of himself. His boldness unnerved me. I had a crush on him, but then all the girls did. I used to bring them tunafish sandwiches and Cokes on Sundays when they watched football games in the den. If I asked questions, they ignored me. Sometimes I stood in front of the television just to annoy them.

My last memory of Nick was when he intercepted a pass and scored the winning touchdown in a game that made the Winonah Wildcats first in the state, beating Evanston. Evanston had huge, black players. (The joke used to be "Why did Evanston get the blacks and Winonah get the Jews?" And the punchline: "Because Evanston got first pick.") It was a big deal for the white boys to win. Nick rode around town, waving from the back of a convertible while the town cheered.

Larger-than-life caricatures of him were painted on the picture windows of all the big stores. Though he never realized his athletic promise, everyone believed he'd grow up to be just like his father. Mr. S., as his father was called, had once been a star quarterback for the Chicago Bears. He was a beefy man with knees so bad he wobbled, but he'd given the Bears some of their finest victories. In local restaurants people asked for his autograph.

Nick was being groomed for something big. That much you could see from the start. His father rooted for him at every ballgame and chided him whenever he missed an easy pass, a basket, a pitch, depending on the season. He was always coaching his son from the sidelines. On Saturdays Mr. S. made Nick work at Prairie Visita Automotive, a business he owned a share of. Nick didn't like to go, but his father insisted because it built character. All through high school Nick had grease under his nails. Now I noticed that they were manicured and buffed.

Nick paused, his head cocked, a frown on his face. He seemed to be listening for something, like a distant train. "Lousy band," he said at last. Patrick shrugged and said they were local and he couldn't afford better.

"Well, tell them to get a new bass player." Nick ruffled my hair as if he was really glad to see me. He had that same wide grin he'd always had, though his features were puffy like those of someone who didn't sleep much or did his share of drinking.

"So is she there?" Nick asked Patrick, an almost pathetic but slightly bemused look on his face.

Patrick nodded. "She's there."

"Well," Nick said, "is she behaving herself? How drunk is she?"

"Drunk enough," Patrick said.

Nick dropped his head down and shook it, the way I'd seen him do when a pass wasn't received or his team had lost an easy point. Then his smile came back and he slapped me on the arm. "So, Tess, what do you hear from Jeb?"

"Oh, the usual. He's still making out like a bandit." My older brother had, in fact, done exceptionally well for himself. He worked on Wall Street, had three kids, an apartment on Park Avenue, a house in the Hamptons, an impenetrable wife. We rarely spoke, though he sent me money from time to time, with a note, saying it was a gift for the kids. But it was always too much for a gift and more than the kids needed. He and I knew that.

"And you?" he asked. I told him it had been going great.

"Oh, less of a bandit."

I laughed. I told him that I had two terrific kids, and I worked for a real estate broker near Monterey. I got divorced a few years back but it was all right because I liked my freedom.

Nick listened intently, taking this in. "Well," he paused, "you always did." I wasn't sure how he knew this or if it was even true, but he said it in such a way that it seemed to be so. It left me feeling strange, as if this person I hadn't seen in years and who hardly knew me then was aware of something about me that I didn't quite know myself.

Nick heard someone call his name and said he had to get going, but it was great running into me. He told me his business took him west from time to time, and I gave him my card from the real estate office, scribbling my home phone on the back. Then he ruffled my hair again, gave Patrick a fake punch, and walked inside.

The houses get bigger as you drive down to the lake. It wasn't anything I'd ever really noticed before, but I noticed it late that night as I drove down to the shore. I took Lake Road and watched as the small brick- and wood-frame split-levels near the railroad trestle turned into sprawling ranch houses, which we called prairie houses, and then as I got nearer to the lake those houses built close to the ground rose into the two- and three-story mansions made of stone where the rich people lived.

I passed the old Everett Log Cabin, which had been my favorite house when I was growing up and for which Mr. Everett himself had chopped and honed the big trees and where his son still cut his lawn with a scythe, which my mother for years considered to be an abberation. And the Frank Lloyd Wright house on the corner of Laurel. Then I came to the old fairy castle where a princess was said to live.

I paused here, gazing down the long driveway at the house with its huge castle-like structure with turrets, a round tower, a big circular drive, and a fountain that poured around an arched cupid. The gates were looming, black wrought iron, and the huge front door was made of glass and wrought iron. From the road you could look down the long drive and see into the marble entranceway.

My mother liked to walk me down to this house when I was little. She'd stand with me at the wrought-iron gates. Sometimes she'd wrap her fingers around the iron as if she were trying to get in. I didn't usually feel sorry for my mother, but I did when she brought me here because I could tell there was something she wanted that she'd never have. Everytime we came here she told me the same thing. That the family was reputed to come from an obscure branch of Hungarian aristocracy and a real princess lived inside. Years later when I grew up, I learned that she was not a real princess at all but the heiress to Princess Pat cosmetics, but my mother—who knew the truth—liked to pretend we had royalty living in our midst.

When I was a kid, I tried to imagine what it was like to live in this castle. I envisioned myself dancing on its marble floors, sleeping in a canopied bed. But no matter how often we came here we never saw anyone waltzing inside, and we never got a glimpse of the princess. Still I imagined for her a happy, wonderful life.

The road down to the lake was dark and winding, black really, but once I got beyond the twists and turns of the old Indian trail, the moon was out and the beach shimmered a hot bright blue. I pulled up so that the car faced the lake and sat with the windows rolled down. The moon sent a trail of gold out across the water. The water lapped the shore peacefully, though I have known Lake Michigan to be not so peaceful.

The thing about Lake Michigan—what makes it a dangerous lake—is that it has a pretty shallow shoreline, then it takes this big drop about a mile out, and it's about as a deep as a lake can be. In the middle nobody knows how deep it is. It's also true that there's as much magnetism on its shores as on the North Pole, so it is very diffi- cult to navigate by compass when you're out in the lake. A lot of ships have gone down over the years, and almost everyone who goes down in them is lost. It's a dangerous place that looks nice and safe, which is what in part makes it so dangerous.

Tonight it looked peaceful. For a few moments I sat, enjoying the view. Other cars were parked nearby with their windows down. A pair of legs stuck out of the backseat of one. I used to come here with boys and kiss in the backseat of their cars. Now I was gazing out at the lake, alone. I sat for what seemed like a long time, half an hour or so, not wanting to leave. But then I forced myself to turn on the ignition, which seemed so loud in all that quiet, and drive back toward town.

In town I turned left instead of going straight to the highway. I knew I should be heading back, but there was one more thing I wanted to do. I took a detour down Dearborn to Sandburg, then crossed Lincoln, following the railroad tracks to the trestle. Driving under the trestle, I made a right and went a block or two until I came up to 137 Myrtle Lane.

I pulled over and got out of my car. It was still a hot night, but there was a breeze now coming off the lake. I stood under the sycamore and maples as the branches rustled. The house was dark, but in the moonlight it seemed to glow. I hadn't stood in front of this house since I'd left for college. It still had the white picket fence around it, but the old rose bushes had been taken out. There was a thick, unsightly hedge now. Heavy white wrought-iron furniture lined the front porch and a flagpole was spiked in the lawn.

Once I went with my parents to the house when it was being built. It smelled of fresh paint and sawdust. The toilets had no walls around them and the bowls were filled with cigarette butts. My father walked around with a set of blueprints in hand. My mother wanted a closet somewhere and my father stared at the blueprints, shaking his head.

When they weren't looking, I found a razor blade. I'd never seen a razor blade before and I drew it across the skin of my forearm, cutting a line. Blood flowed, soaking into the unfinished wood. It wasn't a very deep cut, but my parents screamed, horrified. It left a thin white scar. When I touch it, I think of home.

I used to imagine that I'd live in this house again one day and I was furious with my mother when she told me she'd sold it. "What do you want me to do," she shouted at me into the phone, "keep living in the past?" She moved into a condo in town and neither of us went back to Winonah again. There was no reason to, really.

But for years I used to dream of going inside the house once more. In the dreams there were doors I'd never seen before that opened into secret rooms. One room opened into the next until I found myself in a completely different house—a place I'd never been. Now I stood looking at the house in the moonlight. It made me feel odd to know that other people were sleeping inside. I'm sure if they'd seen me, they would have phoned the police.

I don't know how long I stood there before I got in my car. I decided to take the highway home. I put myself on automatic, turned the radio on high, and tore down the road like I was a kid again and my curfew was coming up fast.

6

Horse chestnuts come in hard shells with pointy thorns, looking like instruments of medieval torture. When they split open, out slips the smooth, dark seed, like polished stone. I didn't know what it was, this sharpness and this smoothness, but in the fall of the year they held infinite interest.

The best place to collect them was in front of the old Episcopal church, where the flowering chestnuts bent with bursting white flowers in late spring, cool shade in summer, and the chestnuts in their green, thorny pods in the fall. On my way home for lunch I paused there, scooping what I could, filling my pockets with prickly pods or, when I split them, with the wondrous polished seeds. I would spend my lunch hour collecting them.

If Jeb saw me, he'd shout, "Hey, Squirrel, last one home's a rotten egg." That's when they really started calling me Squirrel. When they'd find me under these trees.

I didn't care if he beat me home. I was always late, wolfing down the peanut butter and jelly sandwich with chips on the side and chocolate milk that waited for me in the breakfast nook. But during chestnut time it didn't matter to me if I got home for lunch or not. I couldn't get enough of these seeds, couldn't slip enough into my pocket. I was greedy for their touch. I never ate them or asked my mother to cook them, but I wanted to have them in my pockets, or on the shelves in my room.

Vicky and I and the rest of the gang found endless things to do on our way to and from school. We took this walk four times a day. Up and back, up and back. Sometimes we got a ride, if it was very cold or inclement, but mostly we traveled on foot, books strapped to our backs. We liked to kick leaf piles, taking care that no smoke came from them. If there was smoke, there was fire. We gathered gold and scarlet maple leaves, pressed them into our math books, and had our mothers iron them between sheets of wax paper. We put them in the windows of our rooms where the light shone through as if they were stained glass. And we collected horse chestnuts.

Now suddenly a new girl was there with a paper sack, digging under the leaves. She'd grab a pod, split it open with her bare fingers, hold up a shiny chestnut. "Look," she'd say, that wide grin on her face, "I got one." Her black hair tumbled over her shoulders and leaves got caught in its thickness. Her blue tweed coat was frayed. When she stooped down, I could see where the lining was torn.

I don't remember when anyone else came to town, but I remember when Margaret Blair did. Like magic, one Indian summer morning she suddenly appeared, sitting at the desk I coveted in Mrs. Grunsky's fifth-grade homeroom—the one in the sun, a little off to the side, not far from the turtle's bowl.

She didn't come at the beginning, but almost in the middle of the first term with her neat pile of pencils and books. Already the sugar maples were golden and there she was with her thick black hair and her rosy cheeks, her round body, her face that smiled as if she knew us already, as if she'd always been there.

Mrs. Grunsky said, "This morning we have a new girl." And that's what she'd be from then on. She'd always be the New Girl. What is she? we wondered. Spanish or Italian? Eastern European? Our parents spoke of Gypsy blood. The boys called her a spic or a wop. A dago or meatball or just the girl from the other side. She was trash or beautiful. Strange or mysterious. She'd be whatever we wanted her to be.

The year when Margaret appeared, I had the best homeroom in the world. Our gang formed a neat, little clique. Ginger Klein, who told great jokes, was there and Samantha Crawford, who lent me her clothes, and, of course, Vicky Walton, and we all sat near one another. Lori Martin was just down the row. The year Margaret Blair arrived was the one when we got to move from classroom to class-room and carried our books.

And now this new girl was here, walking between classes, waiting for us after school. Thinking she could just be one of us, but, of course, she couldn't. We wouldn't let her.

We called her Wishbone. Not to her face, though sometimes we did. We called her that because of the way her legs shaped themselves into those smooth, arching curves you felt you could just snap in two. Bow legs, my mother said, from a vitamin deficiency or from sitting on a horse.

Later we liked to taunt her. Make a wish, Wishbone, we'd shout, and we'll break you in two.

I'd never seen hair so long and thick, or the color, almost blue black. We weren't even sure it was real. During recess some of us placed candy bar bets, daring one another to go up and tug on that hair. Some of the boys raced behind her and tried to grab it, but I just went right up and asked. "Can I touch your hair?" I said. In the corner of my eye I saw the gang, huddled, giggling.

"Sure," Margaret said, giving me a wide smile, the way you do when you think someone's going to be your friend. I reached out and touched it. It felt like a horse's tail and was wavy as a snake. I thought it would turn itself into a serpent and wrap itself around my neck, but it didn't. It just lay there, compliant, agreeable in my hand. It was smooth as silk and, though I was only doing this on a dare, I kept on holding it like a rope you could use to slide down the castle walls. To escape with. "You can touch my hair whenever you want," Margaret said.

"It's like a horse's tail," I announced when I got back to the huddle of the gang. "It's real." Still nobody believed me.

She'd never catch up. How could she? She'd missed fractions and pioneer history. Half the social studies curriculum on petroleum. We'd already read three books for English, so we knew she couldn't catch up. But she did. The first question Mrs. Grunsky asked, her pale hand shot up.

She'd never be one of us. She'd never belong.

We didn't know anything about Margaret. Who she was or where she came from. We didn't know how she got to and from school. She just appeared out of nowhere on a street corner and walked with us before we even asked her. We assumed she lived with her family in a house on the Winonah side of town—our side. For in Winonah we all had our visible histories. We had our families, our brothers and sisters. People by whom we located ourselves in space and time. We knew who we were. We never had to ask. Until Margaret came to town, there were no question marks after our names.

Then one day my mother asked Elena, the Italian woman who ironed my father's shirts, if she knew anything about the new family and who they were. Because that little girl kept coming around. And Elena told my mother that they'd moved into an apartment above Santini's Liquor Store in Prairie Vista. Elena told my mother that there was just the mother, who dressed in short skirts that were too tight, and there was talk about her. Just that woman and her daughter. No man in sight.

My mother was shocked, not because there was no man or because Mrs. Blair wore short, tight skirts, but because it was so rare that a child from Prairie Vista crossed over to Winonah. The lowest place you could live was above one of those stores across the tracks in Prairie Vista. And my mother made it clear, though I don't remember how, that it would be better if I didn't have much to do with someone who came from that part of town.

On weekends we went to one another's houses. Vicky lived in a one-story ranch, like the one we first lived in before we built our two-story white Colonial. I didn't know what any of this meant, but I knew that's how our parents referred to our houses—ranch, prairie, Colonial. Colonial was best, I knew that. Vicky's father was a CPA and every morning he took the same train and came home on the same train like clockwork. Her mother had pure white hair even when we were small.

We cut pictures out of magazines and glued them onto paper, making collages. We could do this endlessly. Time had not occurred to us yet. It was amazing we ever got from A to B, as Vicky's mother liked to comment. Vicky's mother was a large woman with square bones. I was afraid of her. She never hit us or yelled at us, but she just looked at us in a way that was frightening.

Vicky was afraid of her as well. Vicky's mother had little china things all over the house. Bone-china plates and china statues—dogs and one statue that we always laughed at of two lovers in an embrace. You had to be very careful when you played in Vicky's house. Vicky had a big garden and once we got in trouble for eating green beans on the vine. We loved the taste of those green beans that we plucked, snappy and sweet. One day when we were eating beans, Vicky's mother came outside. We tried to hide in the vines near the corn, but she found us. She stood in front of us, shaking that big finger of hers, telling us never to eat beans out of the garden again.

Then Margaret showed up at Vicky's uninvited on a Saturday morning and broke a porcelain dog. "My mother will kill you," Vicky said, but Margaret just went calmly into the kitchen where Mrs. Walton was, the fragments of the porcelain dog in her hands. I'm not sure what we expected—screaming, Mrs. Walton's shouting. We hovered by the kitchen door and I heard Mrs. Walton say, "That's all right, dear. Accidents happen. You did the right thing by telling me." When we peered into the kitchen, we saw Margaret munching on fresh-baked cookies and drinking milk.

The next Saturday she showed up at my house. My father must have answered and let her in. He didn't even ask who she was. He just assumed she was one of the gang, which she wasn't. I don't know how she knew the others were at my house, but she did. The gang and I were in the upstairs playroom, eating chips and drinking tall glasses of chocolate milk.

The playroom was above the garage and in it there was the cedar closet. My mother was adamant about putting the summer clothes in the cedar closet during the winter, and winter clothes in the cedar closet during the summer. Inside it smelled like forests, the deepest parts of forests and ravines, the places you have to walk a long way to get to. There were shelves and cabinets inside the cedar closet and they made very good hiding places. When we played hide-and-seek, I always hid there.

It was one of the rules of the gang that we made ourselves at home in one another's houses. I could open a dozen refrigerator doors in Winonah and take anything I wanted and no one would think twice about it. Margaret wasn't one of the gang, but still she was eating chips, changing stations on the radio.

"Let's play hide-and-seek," Samantha Crawford said.

Lori Martin wanted to play too and said she'd be it. She started counting to ten, but when I went to my spot in the cedar closet, Margaret was already hiding there. I looked at her, shocked. "Who said you could hide there?" I spoke in an angry whisper.

She just shrugged. "It seemed like the best place," she said. Then I hid behind the sofa and was found right away.

When the gang went home, my sweaters lay on the bed; books had been taken down from the shelf. My collections so neatly arranged on the shelves were suddenly in disarray. Feathers were where the shells should be. I had a cardinal feather and a bluejay's which I couldn't find. None of the gang would do this. I yelled at Jeb and Art. "Did you guys go in my room? Did you mess up my stuff?"

"Take it easy, Squirrel," Jeb shouted back at me. "Who'd wanta mess with your things?"

7

Jade was waiting at the airport when I arrived. Her hair was cut short and she'd spiked it with goo. She wore ripped jeans that were much more expensive than jeans you just buy and rip yourself. She had four rings in each ear and a new one in her nose. The blue lipstick gave her face an eerie, spectral air and I tried not to look at this concoction that was my daughter as she told me that our house was slipping down the cliff.

It isn't anything noticeable, she assured me as she stood there, tugging at the crystal amulet around her neck. She informed me matter-of-factly that the insurance company had sent an appraiser by while I was away who noted that the northeast corner of our house needed to be shored up and that the foundation seemed to be giving way.

Under normal conditions I would have considered this news very bad, but Jade is such a warm, friendly girl and she greeted me with a great big hug and a no-big-deal smile on her face. Smacking her gum in my ear, she said, "Don't worry, Mom. Like you always say, there are only solutions. No problems. How's Grandma?"

"The same."

"How about that old boyfriend of yours? Did you see him?"

"Oh, we spent some time together. He's on his second divorce."

"So you have things in common." Jade gave me a big wink. I stared at my daughter with her close-cropped hair, her sharp, bony body.

On the way home we stopped at Half Moon Bay Diner, a little cappuccino and sandwich place I'd stop at for the name alone, perched up high on the edge of the road so you can look down at the Pacific. It's a place where I love to sit and Jade knew that, which is why she stopped there.

Since I first saw it, this part of Northern California has always been just right for me, with its dramatic vistas, its crashing sea. But

now as I munched on an avocado and sprout sandwich on pita, I felt
distracted the way you do when you think you've left home with the
coffee pot on.

"So, Mom," Jade said, "did you see anyone? Did you do anything?"

"Of course, dear, I saw lots of people and we did lots of things."
She sighed and I realized this wasn't the kind of answer she wanted to
hear. She wanted to know that something exciting had happened in
my life, that I would be a different person now that I'd been away for
a few days. I was afraid that once more the ordinariness of my life was
a disappointment to her. Jade was young enough to still believe that
you can walk into a room and a sea change will occur; that the earth
will move.

I'm the one who named her Jade. The Orient had once been a
passing interest of mine, one of many passing interests, I might add. A
place I wanted to visit. When I was younger, I'd sit for hours looking
at pictures of those fine carvings out of stone. Rocks that contained an
entire world. Swans, flowers, villagers going about their daily chores.
Delicate, miniature universes imbedded in stone.

When I told Charlie that I wanted to name her Jade, he said, "Why
don't you call her Sunset or Aurora? Give her a real California New
Age name." I'd told him for years I really liked the name. Except that
now all her friends called her Jaded. She got a kick out of the grimaces
I made when a friend called and asked, "Is Jaded there?"

"Well, did you have any *fun?*"

"Yes and no," I said thoughtfully. Jade rolled her eyes as we
munched our sandwiches. The sea crashed below. White spray blew
up against the rocks. "It was interesting," I told her. "It was nice to see
everyone."

"Mom," Jade leaned over, squeezing my hand, "aren't you ever
excited about anything? Doesn't anything get you going?"

"Yes, dear, you do." I patted her cheek and she dropped my
hand, determining me to be a hopeless case. With a sigh she handed
me the keys to the car. "You drive," she said, and she slept the rest of
the way home.

———————

When I pulled up in front of the house, gawkers lined the driveway. There were ten or twenty cars. More than I've seen in a long time. "What're they doing here?" I asked her.

"I'm not sure," Jade said, "they've been staked out for days."

The house I live in was built by the poet Francis Cantwell Eagger on a plot of land where nothing would grow. A farmer sold it to him dirt cheap and Eagger spent half a century building his house. When he died, I bought it from his son, who had many debts of his father's to pay off. He told me I was doing him a favor, taking that wreck off his hands.

Of course it needed work, which it still does, but I couldn't believe my luck. To buy a poet's house, built stone by stone, at the edge of the sea. The son said he hated that house—resented it deeply—because when his father wasn't writing, he was piling stones. That is what his childhood was, he told me as he handed over the keys, a pile of rocks.

How was I to know that Eagger would get famous again? That some small press in Minnesota would reissue all of his books in special editions and pilgrims—true believers in his words—would come and stand on the road and stare at me and my children and the house for hours at a time. Still, I had been here over a decade and, despite the oglers and devotees, the constant knocks at the door from readers who want to see the vistas that inspired such poems as "Coastal Views" and "Water at My Window," I have never wanted to leave.

In my living room I have the complete works of Francis Cantwell Eagger. The books have nature titles like *Along the Rocky Shore* and *Rock Climbing in Yosemite*. Sometimes I take down the volumes and read verses such as "The sea pounds the shore/shattering my dreams/like the morning alarm/I wake, unsure of where I am/or ever have been."

It wasn't clear to me why his work was having such a resurgence but Jade told me it was because he wrote about darkness and mortality. I argued that every poet writes about that, but Jade said there was a drunken edge to his. Sometimes he wrote about drinking and Jade, who was contemplating writing a book about the poet (she wanted to call it *Living on the Edge with Francis Cantwell Eagger*), said he drank himself to death in our breakfast nook.

One of the gawkers—a young man who wore jeans and a tweed jacket and a pair of wire-rimmed glasses—who was standing dangerously close to the house (I had warned them that I'd get a court order to keep them off our property) approached me. "It's an anniversary," he said. "Eagger's centennial; he's a hundred years old this month." I'd seen this young man before, as he strode beside me, trying to take my bag with his fleshy palm and convince me to let him inside.

Sweat ran along the side of his brow and he looked as if he had just begun to shave. "Please, Mrs. Winterstone," he said, "couldn't I just see the views from the inside? It's for my doctoral dissertation."

"We'll have to charge admission," I said to Jade, shaking my head as I made my way to the house.

"Mom, why don't we let them in?" Jade pleaded. "They just want to look. Then they'll go away."

"Because it's my house," I said, grabbing my bag from the young man and heading toward the door.

When I walked in, I found everything much the same as I'd left it. Even the coffee mug I'd left as a little test for my children was still in the sink. Ted was sitting, bare chested, listening to ska music in the living room. When he rose and hugged me, I could feel the ring through his right nipple. Every time I saw this ring I cringed. When he was a baby, I used to rub that nipple to soothe him back to sleep. Now someone had pierced it with a staple gun. When he turned his back, I tried not to look at the wing tattooed on his shoulder blade either, the one he said proved he was an angel.

Though he had promised he wouldn't maim his lips, his nose, or his tongue, the rest of his body was off limits to me. Things could be worse, I told myself; he could have purple hair in spikes the way his friend Chuck had. On the other hand, Ted could have a job, as could

Jade, since they were both, at least for the summer, out of school. In Ted's case, I believed he was permanently out. They could help me make ends meet, which appeared to be the constant struggle for which I was placed on the planet Earth. But they preferred to be home, hang out at the beach, cruise the highway.

It wasn't that they hadn't tried to get summer jobs. Jade, a politics major at Berkeley, had landed one for a time at a fish-and-chips place near Santa Cruz, but then she told me jokingly one day that she had other fish to fry and had been home ever since. Before I left, I saw a copy of *What Color Is Your Parachute?* lying around, and the makings of a résumé, so I was hopeful. Ted, who for a short time had worked at a bungee-jumping tower where he'd put a halter around young girls and shout, "One, two, three, bungee," had larger ambitions (film, TV), and his father—his dear father—kept promising to set him up for a big one soon, but I had been married to his father and so I knew what I could and could not expect from that man.

"Hey, Mom," he said, picking up my bag. "Did you have a good time?"

"It was all right." A girl with beautiful cheekbones and green streaks through her hair sat on the couch. "This is Cherri."

Cherri smiled but made no effort to rise. She gave me a little wave, though. "Pleased to meet you, Mrs. Winterstone," she said, her tongue ring clicking against her teeth. She spoke in a voice so soft that I felt like a judge asking her how did she plead. When I took my things to my room, I had a feeling they'd been sleeping in my bed. A little while later when I came out, Cherri was gone and no mention of her was made, as if she hadn't even been there.

That night as the gawkers drove off and Ted and Jade sat in front of the TV, watching various evening specials, I rinsed out the coffee mug and other dishes that had been left in the sink. After the dishes were washed, dried, and put away, I wasn't sure what to do with myself. I thought I could go into the den, read, pay bills, but the television was too loud.

I made myself a cup of mint tea and settled into the breakfast nook with my mail. The breakfast nook has been my preferred place to sit since I bought the house. From here I can gaze down at some pine trees, and then at the drop into the Pacific. It's a pretty sheer drop and when the kids were small, I worried a lot about them falling off that cliff.

Now I sat in the breakfast nook, listening to the surf. Canned laughter came from the living room as I sifted through the pile of mail, bills that awaited me, the note from the insurance appraiser concerning the slippage on the northeast corner that needed to be shored up. I calculated how much this would cost and how long this would be my house. Month to month I was having trouble making ends meet and Charlie was already hinting, now that the kids were technically out of school, that his support would end soon.

Not that I lived off my ex, though I had gotten some things that I felt were owed me. I had seen him through two professional schools by working odd jobs. I'd raised our kids more or less without him so I'd felt some help was due to me, but now the kids were older and I knew that the time was coming soon when I'd have to find the way to really support myself. I couldn't do it just by handling seasonal rentals and time-shares.

I looked at the kids sitting there, the remote between them. When the phone rang, they both jumped. I picked up the phone and heard voices already speaking. A man said, "I just don't know what it is. I don't know what I should do."

"Well, maybe you should tell her," the woman replied. "I think that's always best." The voice of the woman was slightly familiar to me. I wanted her to talk more so I could place it.

The man paused, taking this in, then said, "Well, I know it's best. It's just that there's so much I still like about her. . . ."

"Like what?"

"Hello," I shouted into the phone, "excuse me. You're on my line." I shouted two or three times, but they couldn't hear me so I hung up.

The kids stared at me from the couch, both waiting to see if the call was for them. They had that eager, slightly sad look of pets thinking they might be fed. "It's a crossed line," I said and they settled back down.

Though Jade was basically just veging, Ted wasn't actually watching TV. He was studying it. His eyes stared into the tube and, if I didn't know better, I'd say he looked like a supplicant before an altar.

Of course, Ted, like just about everyone else we knew, wanted to be in the movies. It's the new immortality, he liked to explain to me; it used to be heaven, now it's celluloid. He was a good-looking boy and he believed he'd get his break. Or at least he believed his father would introduce him to the right people. Charlie made commercials and directed reenactments, so I wasn't sure who the right people would be that he knew. But, of course, once Charlie had his own dreams, so I wasn't too hard on him, except where my kids were concerned.

The phone rang again and this time the kids got it. I could hear them talking to Charlie in the somnambulant way they had when the TV was on between them. "Sure, Dad. Uh huh, Dad." Monosyllabic sentences.

"Mom, it's Dad," Jade called from the living room so I picked up the phone.

"Hi, there," Charlie said, his voice perky. "I had the hardest time getting through. Line was busy forever."

"That's funny," I said, "no one was on." But then I thought about that crossed line problem we were having. "Oh," I said, making a mental note, "I better call the phone company. I think there's a problem with my line."

"So how was your trip?" I chatted about the reunion and he chatted back. He had stuff to discuss with me. A trip he was thinking about taking with the kids. His concern, which I shared, that they weren't working. Then I heard someone calling him in the background, the woman he lived with, Luci, whom I'd never laid eyes on, and before I could ask for money, we were off the phone.

Basically Charlie and I had always been friends. When I met him in an art history class at Berkeley twenty-some years ago, I'd liked him right away. I liked his big bear body and his green eyes. He laughed about all kinds of things. We'd only known each other a few weeks when we drove up to Alaska—a long, tedious drive of landscapes moving past us. Yet I loved the sensation of just being beside him for miles and miles of road.

Charlie was writing a paper on outsider art. He drove around the country in search of the primitive, the folksy. We found people with giant bugs made out of wire on their lawns, others who'd turned their yards into a series of pulleys, homemade amusement parks. One man had a spaceship in his yard, the lights of which had caused the air force to make several impromptu inspections of his property.

Charlie loved this stuff and he could talk to anyone: a gas station attendant, a survivalist out in the woods, or some guy with a lot of money who wanted to make a movie. He had planned on writing a book about all of this, but got sidetracked with the costs of raising a family and the desire for money, which moved him into more commercial ventures. He'd had a fair amount of financial success setting up multimedia trade shows. His biggest success, though, had been in reenactments. For various centennials he'd done Washington crossing the Delaware, the arrival of Coronado into Santa Fe, the California gold rush.

In that trip up to Alaska we stayed in cabins that had what we called "outs" with no houses. We showered in ice water until we learned we could bathe at public showers in local Laundromats. In the morning we found bear scat around our cabin. Charlie thought all this was great. He made love to me three times a day and when we were finished, he cradled my face in his hands and told me how much he loved me.

It usually took me a moment after I spoke with Charlie to catch my breath, as if I'd been punched hard in the gut. When I married Charlie, there had seemed to be something that stood between us. I wish it hadn't been that way, but it had. For months after we separated, I thought about what he'd said. How I never gave anything away. I remembered when I was a kid there was a toothpaste that had this active ingredient, Gardol. In commercials on TV Gardol was an invisible shield. When it came down over your teeth, Mr. Tooth Decay, a hideous black creature with nasty jaws, couldn't get through.

For a long time I imagined Gardol protecting me as Mr. Tooth Decay—or whatever else I needed protection from—fought to get through. I imagined invisible shields everywhere and at some point it became clear to me that I couldn't shake them. I kept thinking somebody would come along and fight his way past, but he or she never had. I was always sorry after I talked to Charlie that he hadn't been the one.

I went to the door of the living room and called, "Hey, Teddy, Jade. Why don't we order a pizza? Or I'll make a noodle casserole. Would you guys like that?"

"No thanks, Mom," Ted shouted back. "Not hungry."

"Me either," Jade piped in. I poked around in the fridge, found some leftover casserole, which I dug into with a fork. When I was their age, I had things I wanted to do with my life. Now, night after night, they sat watching *Seinfeld* or listening to Loose Screw. Recently Jade had been saying she wanted to go to massage therapy school. Before that, she talked about being a flight attendant.

I gazed at the bills for a new roof, mortgage, car payments, the appraiser, setting aside the ones that would have to wait a month or so. There was also the set of keys I kept to all the houses I was responsible for. These were houses of fairly wealthy people who were away half the year, but wanted the income from a rental to cover their costs while they were in the Bahamas or back East. Maybe I *should* charge admission to my house, I thought. It seemed like a sensible thing to do.

I had been thinking about opening the bed-and-breakfast in earnest. In fact, ever since my little start-up company, Mind Your Own Business, failed, it'd been about the only thing I could think of. Mind Your Own Business was a company for people who wanted to start their own at-home small businesses, and the idea was that my company would get them set up. I had a partner—a friend from San Francisco—and we offered office design, computer setup and programming, file management, marketing surveys, mailing lists—whatever a client needed. The problem was most people in start-ups didn't have the money for my services. We lasted a year. I still thought it was a good idea.

But for now, turning the house into a bed-and-breakfast seemed the way to resolve everything. Though the house was small—just three bedrooms—it had two baths and I could convert the garage into a separate apartment, which would be good for families. I could even turn the den, which had a breathtaking view of the sea, into a small room. This would give me five spaces to rent out. I would be able to keep my house, which everyone wanted to see anyway. Lots of historic houses (like Lizzie Borden's, Ted reminded me when I brought up this idea) were being turned into B-and-Bs. It would pay for bills and provide a decent tax write-off. I could have guests whenever I wanted, but I wouldn't have to all the time.

Besides, I liked the idea of people from Stuttgart or Bogotá stopping for a night on their way down the coast. I could offer walking tours of this craggy shoreline, share my knowledge of marine life. Or provide the devotees of Eagger with a night within the walls of their beloved poet's home. I'd serve them cranberry scones with whipped butter and cream in ceramic jugs and gourmet coffee in the morning, and slip after-dinner mints onto their pillows at night as they sipped cinnamon tea downstairs by the fire.

And when they left, they would hand me their business cards or write their names in the leather-bound guestbook and tell me to look them up when next I was on the Continent or traveling through the Andes. I'd call it the Eagger House Bed and Breakfast, and I could envision the brochure. A picture taken out at sea, another of the view from the breakfast nook. A perfect place for a monastic rest.

If my father had been alive, he would have told me that the house was a fairly crazy place to live. I could only insure it for fire and theft. I had flood from above but not from below, which meant if it rained I was okay, but if a river of mud flowed down from the hills, I wasn't. I'd tried to get an act-of-God rider but my insurance agent, John

Martelli, said the house was going to roll off the cliff one day and I'd be left with zilch. There was no premium I could afford for that. I had to say he probably had a point.

I knew a little about what natural disasters could do because I traveled with my father to the floodplain and saw catastrophe up close. We traversed a town in a canoe. The cornfields were lakes. Cows waded up to their knees in muddy water as if they were the water buffalo of Thailand. A bed, still made, drifted by. A house stood without walls as a river flowing through it carried its pots and pans away. Trophies, photo albums, a wedding dress flowed past us in the debris.

My father had shaken his head. "Hold on to what's yours, Squirrel," he told me that day. "You never know when it will be taken away."

8

I was Daddy's girl. Everyone said it. All their friends. The Rosenmans, the Lauters. Whenever they came over, they said, She's Daddy's girl, all right. And I was. I clung to his chair when company was over, and when he let me, until I got too big, I'd sit in his lap. It was a firm, muscular lap with bony knees and I could sit there for hours, just rocking on his knees. When he left on Monday morning, I was always there to wave good-bye. And when he drove back in on Thursday after school, I was always there to greet him. "Where's my little Squirrel," he'd call, waving as he pulled in the drive.

When he got home, he liked to put a record on. He enjoyed old jazz like the Jimmy Dorsey Orchestra or show tunes. Once he put on *South Pacific*. When "Some Enchanted Evening" came on, he tried to get my mother to dance. "Come on, Lily," he said, waltzing into the kitchen with an invisible woman. "Dance with me." He caught her in his arms and tried to spin her into the living room, but she batted him away.

"Victor, I've got dinner on." She wiped her hands on her apron.

My mother always had a million things to do—clothes to hang up, newspapers to throw out, meals to prepare. "Now let me be."

Though my father was used to this, he pretended to pout, then turned to me and made a deep bow. "May I have this dance?" he said. He scooped me up and we waltzed, dipping with each glide, singing, my father gazing with pretend infatuation into my eyes.

When the school year ended and summer came, my father took me and Jeb back to the floodplain. I knew he wouldn't go without me. When Art saw we were leaving, he howled again, but our father told him he still wasn't old enough. He'd just turned seven. It was too long a drive for a seven-year-old. You had to be ten. "Next year, Squirt," he said.

My father rolled down the window to say good-bye. "Now, please call if you're going to stay away longer," our mother said.

"Don't worry." He kissed her on the lips. Art shrieked as we pulled away and I put my hand to the glass, gave him a little wave. As our mother held Art back, she gave us a little wave like a windshield wiper, back and forth.

Once he couldn't see them in the rearview mirror, our father clicked the radio on high and began to sing along. I hadn't heard his voice loud and booming like that in almost a year. He knew new songs now. "Pretty pretty pretty pretty Peggy Sue, oh Peggy, my Peggy Sue . . ." Dumb lyrics, but he followed along.

This year I knew the road. It was old hat, an expression Lily liked to use. Old hat. I anticipated the flatness, the yellow land, the smell of pigs and fertilizer. It was less amusing when Jeb and I had to hold our noses. We were too big for road games. That was old hat as well.

The flood was less spectacular. No floating cows, no bedroom sets. Jeb didn't try to fool me that he was going to dive in. Instead he seemed to pay more attention to some giggling girls in shorts by a picnic table. He tried to act cool and pretended he didn't know me.

We stayed in a motel but my father had called ahead this time. We had a reservation. When we arrived, the desk clerk said, "Good afternoon, Mr. Winterstone," even before my father said his name. I missed "acancy." I wanted to go back to that place where the clerk with the bloodshot eyes who smelled of smoke looked startled when we walked in the door. I wanted to surprise him again.

But here we were expected. My father had reserved two rooms. Adjoining rooms, they were called. "One for you, Tess. This year you get your own room." I didn't want my own room. I didn't know what to do in it. It had a connecting door and for most of the evening we kept the door open, moving freely between our rooms. My father wanted to read and rest, so Jeb and I watched television in my room. Then my father called Jeb when it was bedtime. My father gave me a hug, a peck on the cheek, then closed the door between our two rooms.

With the door closed I sat up in the big bed with the scratchy sheets (that was the only thing that was the same). I thought about opening the door, but I didn't. Almost all night I stared at it. I put my ear to it from time to time so I could hear them breathing on the other side.

Every night when he wasn't on the road, my father came and tucked me in. He sat at the edge of the bed, told me a story, sang me a song. Usually it was the Whiffenpoof song about how we're poor little lambs who've gone astray. I sang it to my kids when they were small. But not long after that trip to the floodplain, when I turned ten, everything changed.

He stopped walking into my room without knocking, and after a while he just gave me a peck on the cheek before I went to bed. I tried to get used to being alone in my room. I busied myself with rearranging my stuff on the shelves ("It looks like a museum in here," Lily always said when she came in my room) or trying to read, but basically I was waiting for him to tuck me in. My room had pink wallpaper shaped in squares. If I was tired, lying on my side, the wallpaper seemed to move in strips like film through a projector, like when you're sitting on the window of a train, watching the world go by.

I had two beds. I slept in the one near the window and my stuffed animals slept in the other, unless I had a sleepover, and then the stuffed animals got moved to the shelves. Mostly I used the extra bed for my clothes, which I tossed there on a daily basis and didn't hang up until my mother shouted at me to hang them up, which I did about once a week. There were often big piles of clothes because, God forbid, we wouldn't be caught dead wearing the same thing two days in a row.

I lay there one night watching the wallpaper move, thinking I'd heard footsteps. My father, having had a change of heart, coming to tuck me in. I couldn't seem to get used to it. The silence, the lack of footsteps coming toward my door. Four nights a week my father was on the road, but the other nights, the ones when he was home, I waited for that sound.

For hours I waited. The wallpaper moved miles and miles; dragons, maps, years passed before my eyes. But he didn't come. I tiptoed into their room hoping he'd change his mind. My father was sitting in the chaise longue, reading. My mother sat in bed with the TV on. I asked him if he wouldn't come and tuck me in.

"Why not, Victor?" my mother said. "She's still a little girl."

"No, she's not," my father said with a laugh as he gave me a peck on the cheek. "She's in the double digits now." Then he gently swatted my backside. "Off to bed now."

My mother got up and took me by the hand. "I'll tuck you in, dear," she said.

She brought me down the hall to my room, waited until I slipped under the covers. She kissed my forehead, smoothed my covers, and said good night. But it wasn't the same thing.

I wasn't sure why this double digits was such a magical threshold I didn't even remember passing, except we had a party just like every year (ten girls, swimming, box lunches with fried chicken). I wasn't even sure when my father stopped coming into my room without knocking and sitting at the side of my bed, telling me a story he'd made up while he was on the road driving around selling insurance—about a raccoon who lived in a hollow log or a snowflake that didn't want to fall to earth and leave its family behind. Or real stories about someone he might have met or a tornado he saw twirling in the horizon against the sky. It happened slowly, so I hadn't noticed it at first, but once that swimming party was over, I don't remember my father coming into my room at night again.

Some nights when my father was on the road, I woke up from disaster dreams—the earth splitting, a swirling wind carrying me away. A huge black wave rising above my head. I woke from these dreams breathless, my hands clawing at the air. I'd never had these dreams when he was home, tucking me in. Only when he was away. But now I seemed to have them all the time.

There was one dream I had over and over again. I am sitting in the yard playing when the sky turns yellow. I do not notice the color, but I notice the silence. There is no sound of wind. Everything is still. Two hands reach down and grab me just as the tornado whirls by.

9

John Martelli had his office at the Salinas Mall and he insured me for car, home, life, and theft. Somehow Charlie managed to keep me on his medical plan, but John took care of all my other insurance needs. His office was in a strip mall, beside a Starbucks and a Staples. He brokered for Allstate, but he also put together packages for difficult-to-insure clients such as myself.

I drove over there and parked next to John's car, a beige Volvo with a license plate that reads URCOVERD. John smiled as I walked in. The Beach Boys played on the Musak. "Hey, Tess, how you doing?"

His braided ponytail swung behind his back as he got up to greet me. His office smelled of deli sandwiches and coffee. John's hand was moist as he shook mine, squeezing the knuckles together until I felt the bones crunch. Behind him on the wall a framed imitation Whitman sampler read, "You Can't Be Too Careful."

"What can I do for you?" John Martelli had a big smile that never put me exactly at ease. He made you feel as if he were pulling one over on you and probably he was and I always thought he should be selling cars, not insurance.

He motioned for me to sit across from him. "I understand, John, that I have a slippage problem that needs to be taken care of."

"Yep." He nodded as if he didn't quite remember, shuffling through papers on his desk. "Just one moment now." Punching something into his screen he came up with what I believed was my policy. "Your foundation needs some basic maintenance, you've got to do some shoring . . . I'm afraid it's going to cost you."

I nodded, taking this in. I had just enough money to get me through each month, give or take. If Charlie withdrew his support of the kids, then I wouldn't have enough. I saw no way that I'd be able to repair the foundation of my house without a sizable loan, and I couldn't see who would give that to me. "Well, I've been thinking about turning my house into a bed-and-breakfast, so I was wondering what other improvements I needed to make."

"Good tax write-off," John put in, tapping a pencil on his teeth. But he was already shaking his head. "No can do. You need everything—all kinds of liability, earthquake, mud, brushfire. Who's going to give you brushfire?" John leaned back in his chair, hands over his head. "The premium will cost as much as the house. Can't get you into the Fair Plan now. I don't think there's any way you can get the inclusions you need." He began explaining something about rate adequacy, if this was worth x and that was worth y. I started to feel a surge of something I hadn't felt in a while. I didn't want to be told what I could not do.

"John, my father was in the insurance business." I'd never raised the specter of my father with John before, but now seemed like as good a time as any. "He used to say there are only solutions, never problems."

"Well, times have changed." John raised his arms, that grin on his face. His ponytail bobbed behind him. "He's not in the business anymore, is he?"

"No, John, he's dead." John paled, telling me he was sorry. "But if he were alive," I said as I walked out the door, "he'd find a way to help me."

My father's death seemed to be one more way he slid in and out of our lives, one more sleight of hand he'd perfected. His decline was barely noticeable and he was still a relatively young man, in his mid-sixties, when he died a decade ago. He had the usual complaints, especially about his legs. They refused to do what he wanted them to do, like put his foot on the gas or walk eighteen holes.

He collapsed on the golf course one Saturday, but then got up and insisted on driving himself home. My mother had tried to get him to the hospital, but he said he was all right. When I asked him that night on the phone how he was, he said, "I'm fine. I played the best golf game of my life." Hours later he died in his sleep.

There was a storm at sea that night, the kind of bad weather I'd once associated with my father, and I hadn't been sleeping all that well. Waves pounded the shore and I was lying there, listening, when the phone rang. My mother was calm, almost composed when she told me. "He died happy," she said.

They had met just after the war at a friend's wedding at the Blackstone Hotel in downtown Chicago. The way he liked to tell it, my father said to his brother, "Who is that girl?" She was a Russian Jew, as was my father, but with freckles and a turned-up nose. Nothing about her reminded him of the oily smells and grim corridors he was trying to escape from. On their first date they took off their shoes and waded through Buckingham Fountain. My father thought this was a girl he could have a good time with, and for a few years he did.

I flew in with the kids. Charlie, who had liked my father, joined us. Jeb and his family only stayed for the day, which enraged my brother Art. My father's funeral was well attended. I was surprised at how many people he knew, how many people told me he had helped them along the way. They had enjoyed his magic tricks and his boisterous laugh.

When I turned to look at who was there, I saw Clarice Blair, Margaret's mother, standing in the back of the funeral chapel. She was dressed in a short black dress, the kind she often wore, and a hat with a veil. I thought to myself, What is she doing here? But my mother, to her credit, went over and shook Clarice Blair's hand.

10

Prairie Vista Automotive was located across from Santini's Liquor, where Margaret and her mother lived. Every few weeks I went with my father to take the car into the shop. The Schoenfields had a part-interest in the repair shop, as they did in Santini's Liquor and in the other shabby buildings along the strip—the electronics store and the deli. In fact Cy Schoenfield had an interest in half of Prairie Vista. He'd had made a lot of money during his football years and as my father said, he put his money where it counted. In bricks and mortar.

The car often didn't need repairs when we went there, but still my father liked to go. He liked to schmooze with the boys at the garage. And the car was his livelihood after all, so he had to have it just so. Once in a while he had a fender bender or a scratch where the metal was revealed. Sometimes you couldn't even see the scratch, but it seemed as if he always had to go to that garage and have something done to that car. He told me a body can rust and you don't even know it.

It was our outing, those Saturdays. "Come on, Squirrel," he'd say, "let's get the car checked." I liked to go with him not only because it was something we did together, but also because once in a while I'd get a glimpse of Nick. I went out of my way to look nice, putting on a matching short set. Afterward my father and I stopped at Lindsey's Delicatessen for a corned beef sandwich and a black cow.

At about ten on Saturdays we drove down to the northside of town, then crossed the tracks to Prairie Vista. I waited outside because the smell of fumes—paint, oil, and grease—was so strong. Inside the repair shop was a dark world of mechanical parts, hubcaps, fenders, tires, rusted exhaust pipes, mufflers. I'd only go inside if Nick was there, learning the business from the ground up. If he saw me, he'd give me a wave. "Hey, Tessie," he'd call, smiling from beneath the hood of a car.

I went and stood beside him, peering with one of the mechanics at the twisted guts of the car. He leaned over me, pointing. "That's a spark plug and that's a distributor . . ." His greasy hands tugged at wires. There was a bang on the hood of the car and Cy Schoenfield, who liked to make the rounds on Saturdays and survey his domain, stood there, laughing. "Always flirting, aren't you, son? No wonder you don't get anything done." He pretended to close the hood of the car on his son's head. "Tessie, where's your old man?"

"He's in the front, Mr. Schoenfield," I said and watched Mr. S. wobble on his bad knees. My father and Mr. S. slapped hands. They talked sports, wondering if Winonah would take State and how the Cubs would do, and business until the work on my father's car was done.

The entrance to the repair shop was a narrow passage where your car got lifted up and carried in or where you just drove carefully through the thin opening into that dark circle surrounded by broken parts. It was a grease-stained world of men with blackened hands and faces who stank of fumes and could never light a match for fear of going up in smoke. When the fumes got bad, my father came outside and stood with me.

One day, when Nick was not there working on an engine, I went and stood outside with my father, waiting for a dent to be battered out of the car. My father was smoking a cigarette when Margaret Blair and her mother suddenly appeared across the street. Mrs. Blair wore tight skirts and had a cackle laugh not unlike Margaret's. But there was something buoyant and puffy about her that made me think of pointless things like cotton candy or yo-yos.

They were dressed up as if they were coming from somewhere. They both wore navy cloth coats, though Mrs. Blair's looked a little frayed, and gloves. Mrs. Blair had a red scarf around her neck which looked pretty with her dark hair and red lips. Margaret saw me first. "Tessie," she called, waving frantically, "Tessie," which only my best friends called me at the time.

I watched them coming toward us and my father tossed his cigarette into the gutter. Mrs. Blair's heels clicked on the sidewalk and I thought her navy skirt was too short and tight for a woman her age, just like our laundress, Elena, said. She had long sleek legs and a big friendly smile. She had clips in the side of her hair and shiny beige stockings with a seam up the back. They stopped and said hello. "So you're Tess," Mrs. Blair said. "I've heard so much about you." As she held out her hand to me, I could smell her perfume and her lipstick looked thick and red.

My father smiled, patting me on the head. "Who's this, Tessie?"

"It's Margaret Blair and her mother." I mumbled an introduction.

"How do you do, Mr. Winterstone," Margaret said in a sweet, syrupy voice I'd never heard her use before. She gave my father a big grin and he reached across and patted her on the head too.

Then Mrs. Blair extended her hand to my father and said, "Clarice Blair." I'd never seen him shake a woman's hand before, but she extended hers and he took it. When she smiled, you could see her teeth.

"Well, it's very nice to meet you," my father said.

"It's nice to meet you too," Clarice Blair replied, "and I'm so happy to finally meet Tess." Mrs. Blair paused, then gazed up at the sky. "You know, it's so beautiful this fall. Don't you agree, Mr. Winterstone? I think this is the most beautiful fall I've ever seen."

"Please call me Victor. This is your first fall here, isn't it?" Mrs. Blair nodded. "Well, every fall is beautiful in Winonah."

"You're right," she said, "I'm sure you're right about that." Then she laughed a big hearty laugh, and my father stared at her as if he'd never seen a woman laugh before. There was an awkward moment after that and no one knew what to say so it was good-bye and see you in school. Mrs. Blair called, "You should come over and play some time, Tess," and then she caught Margaret by the hand and walked away.

My father followed them with his eyes as they walked toward Santini's Liquor, where Mrs. Blair discretely slipped her key into the side door. The glass in the pane was broken and the stairs were dirty gray. Mrs. Blair glanced back at us once, smiled an embarrassed smile, then the two of them disappeared up the stairs. "Now, who did you say that was again?" my father asked after they were gone.

"Oh, Margaret. She's just the new girl. She lives with her mother above that store."

My father nodded, looking up, clicking his tongue. "Tough place to live," he said. With my eyes I followed his gaze to the window above the store. It was a grimy building with paint chipping from the front. The fumes from the repair shop reached over there.

"Nobody likes her," I added, as if this would somehow matter to my father.

"Why is that?"

I couldn't exactly think of a reason. "We just don't. She's stuck up and nosy."

"Oh, really?" My father nodded again. "Well, you should be generous to people, especially if they don't have all the advantages you've had. You don't know what her circumstances are."

Mr. S. came out just then and he stood with my father, shaking his head. He seemed to loom over us. He was so big and square and wobbly at the same time. He gazed in the direction of Santini's Liquor, as if he'd known what we were talking about. "They're tenants of mine," Mr. S. said. "My boys can't get much work done when she's around."

"I can imagine," my father replied, making a clucking sound with his tongue.

Afterward on our Saturdays my father went outside while the car was being looked at. He stood with me—the two of us gazing up at the windows with their drawn shades. Sometimes we heard the music from a violin. Once in a while we'd catch a glimpse of someone— even now I can't say who—drawing the curtain back, looking down at us.

11

I stopped at Starbucks for a tall iced skim "even keel" (half decaf, half regular) latte, then the post office. I'd received a notice that there was a package for me. There's always a long line at the post office. A woman ahead of me wanted the new rock-and-roll stamps, which the postmaster didn't have. A man had to report a lost registered package. At last the postmaster took my yellow slip and handed me a small, brown package. It was from Winonah and I had no idea what it was. Opening it on a side counter, I found a blue and white blanket with all the historic sites of Winonah woven into the fabric—the Winonah Wildcats, the train station, one of our Frank Lloyd Wright houses, the old Everett cabin. It was quaint, I thought, wondering what I'd do with it.

The blanket reminded me that I hadn't dropped off the film I'd taken at the reunion. I drove over to Photofax One-Hour Developing, where I left the film, said I'd be back, then sped over to the real estate office, where Shana had several calls for me to handle. "So how was the reunion?"

"You know, thirty years later . . ."

She ran her hand through her hair, which she'd let go gray (I dye mine the same color it was—auburn—when I was a girl, though Jade is always on my case to go natural).

"Time marches on," Shana said, staring into her computer screen. In her sleeveless dress I could see the scar that coursed up her crooked right arm. Shana and I have been friends since we both moved here and basically raised our kids together.

She was a grade-school teacher when I met her. She loved being in the classroom, but one morning during homeroom a little girl got up to ask her a question and Shana rose to answer it. Just then there was a loud, cracking sound, and Shana fell against the blackboard. Shana looked down at her arm and saw blood flowing from her elbow, fragments of white bone shining through.

A half mile away some hunters, having target practice in the hills, had shot a bullet against a rock. It ricocheted down the hills, through the classroom window, through the desk of the little girl who had risen to ask Shana a question, and entered Shana's elbow, finishing its trajectory into the blackboard, which splintered in two. The mother of the little girl, weeping, had called it a miracle, but Shana would never straighten her arm again. She'd never been able to go back into the classroom, either, though she'd tried for years, and finally she'd gotten her real estate broker's license.

Once while she was trying to win her lawsuit against the hunters, I sat with her in the courthouse waiting room and she said to me, "I used to believe that everyone made his or her own destiny. Now I just believe in fate."

"What's the difference?" I asked her.

"Big one," she said. "I know this man. He was walking down a street in Seattle. He had his whole life planned out. He was on his way to law school, engaged to a girl he'd known since college. They even had a house picked out on some island in Puget Sound. Then, suddenly, as he's walking down the street, a steel beam from a construction crew falls off a roof and lands right at his feet, just at the tip of his toes. Another half an inch and he would have been a dead man."

"So," I said.

"So he broke up with the girl, forgot about the house and law school. He's a rancher in Wyoming, married an Indian he met out there. He forgot about his so-called destiny and decided to just do whatever the hell he wanted."

That's what Shana told me she did. Never went back into the classroom; changed her life. She told me that now she preferred this line of work. She liked showing people in and out of houses where they might live, homes they might buy. She liked having the keys to so many homes, this entry into strangers' lives. She even hinted that she sometimes prowled in rooms, dug into drawers.

I must admit that I had come to enjoy it as well, since a year earlier her business was doing so well that she asked me to take over seasonal rentals and time-shares. I enjoyed the jingle of keys in my pocket, the access it provided. Though I can't say I did any prowling, I peered farther into a closet than I needed to, opened drawers I might just as well have left shut. But the fact is, such searches always disappointed. I never found the secrets, the hints of hidden lives I wanted to believe were there, and in recent months I'd stopped looking. Mostly things are what they are; that's the lesson having keys in my pocket taught me.

Now Shana gave me a few rentals to check out, make sure they were in good order before we took clients there.

"Okay, I'll do that, then I have some film to pick up and errands to do. Let's say I get back here at around three?"

Shana said that was all right with her and she handed me the lists of apartments to check on.

"Shana, can I ask you something?"

"Sure."

"You know, your house, it sits out over the ocean, right?"

"Yep, median tide is right under our living room."

"Well, is it insured?"

"Sort of. Under the Fair Plan. But the truth is, if it got washed out to sea, I'd never recover its value."

"That's what I thought," I said, giving Shana a little nod as I headed out the door and she waved back with her crooked arm.

My first stop was the seashell house, which was done entirely in seashell decor. Seashell pillows, cowrie shell artwork, abalone lamps, scallop curtains. It rented well to retirees who may or may not have discovered the porno the wife (the only interesting thing I'd ever uncovered in one of those houses) kept under her clam-shaped dressing table. It was spotless, as always, when I arrived, and I made a quick walk-through, rubbing my fingers along the mantel to see if we needed to send in the Polish cleaning crew.

I stopped at the tchotchke apartment which had knickknacks everywhere that could not be touched. It was the kind of place I loved; if I'd let my nature for collecting things run wild, I'd have lived in a house like that, with a million ceramic dogs and glass goats. Cruise-ship memorabilia was everywhere. An alleged life preserver from the *Titanic,* a crystal goblet from the *QE2.* On one shelf was a collection of cereal-box prizes. The people who lived here were control freaks and I had to be sure that every bear and cat was in its exact place. The husband had handed me a grid when I got this account, showing me where everything should go. Once, just to see if they noticed, I messed things up a bit—put some ceramic poodles where the *QE2* goblet was. They noticed right away.

My last stop was the Mitchell place. The Mitchells put away all their cotton sheets and terry-cloth towels and had polyester for the renters and slipcovers on everything. I didn't know why anyone rented that one, and almost everyone who did went out and bought their own linen. Invariably the renters complained.

Everything was in tiptop shape, ready for the new season. I called Shana to report in and told her I'd be back the next day to take care of some paperwork. On my way home I stopped for groceries at the food co-op, where Ted and I each put in three hours a month and got great prices on organic produce, and finally at Photofax for the film from the reunion I'd dropped off a few hours before. When I got into the photo place, I fumbled through my wallet but couldn't find my ticket.

"I'm sorry," I told the man behind the counter, who knew me since Photofax did all our film, "I can't find my ticket. It must be in my car. It's Winterstone."

He poked around in his box of film that had just been processed and handed me a thick envelope, thicker than I thought it would be. Then I drove home with the trunk full of groceries and the film.

When I pulled up in front of my house, the young man who had planted himself there a few days before was back. This time he had a notebook and pen in his hand as if he were waiting for his teacher. I shook my head when I saw him, but there was something rather sweet in his thin, sandy hair, his cheerless face.

He was probably close to Ted's age, but he looked so much like a boy as he stood there in his glasses and a red sweater, chinos and All-Star Converse monochrome sneakers. I couldn't help feeling he was trying to make a good impression.

I gave him a dirty look as I pulled up, but he rushed over to my car. "Mrs. Winterstone, please, may I speak with you?"

I got out, threw open the trunk, and he stared at the bags of groceries. "I've been away for a while." I stood back and stared at him. "What is your name?"

"I'm Bruno. Bruno Mercedes. I have a letter here that Francis Eagger wrote to my father. They carried on quite a correspondence over a number of years, yet they never met. My father, he was a minister, and he and Mr. Eagger exchanged letters about religion. You know, Mr. Eagger was a deeply religious man, as well as a nature poet."

"No, I didn't know that." So why did he drink himself to death in our kitchen? I wanted to ask Bruno Mercedes. Instead, as I scooped up the film and the blanket, I said, "Bruno, would you help me carry my groceries inside?"

I may as well have been asking him to carry pieces of the cross, the Holy Grail. Bruno reached into my trunk, clasping a brown bag of raw vegetables and rice cakes, another of cereals and paper products. These were not heavy bags, but the boy shook under their weight.

He followed me like a disciple toward the house. He knew, and I knew, that I wasn't asking him to carry these because I couldn't carry them myself. I was asking him to do this so I could invite him inside without actually asking him to come in. I wanted to know what it would be like to have someone like Bruno Mercedes, a devotee, a believer, and a potential boarder, inside my house. Or the former house of Francis Eagger.

With a hushed silence Bruno entered the living room. I heard him sigh and then he said, as if he would fall over, "Where should I put these?"

"In the kitchen," I said, pointing the way.

I paused in the den to toss the blanket over the chair near the hearth, then followed behind as Bruno made his way into the kitchen, where he put the bags down on the counter and then took a deep breath. "Can I see the rest of the house?"

I led him first down the narrow corridor into Jade's room, which faced the woods. It was a simple room and she'd hardly changed a thing since she was a girl. She still had dolls on the top shelf, a collection of shells, Sierra Club calendars, flip tops that she'd been stringing together since she was about five years old. A doll collection nailed to the wall. A large mural on the opposite wall she had painted in shades of gray and brown that had something to do with U.S. intervention in Central America. Little wizards holding crystal balls sat on her desk. A stained-glass rainbow hung from a string, casting rainbows around the room.

When Bruno nodded solemnly, we moved into my room, which was small, with just a double bed and dresser, but it looked out to the sea. There were no pictures on the wall, no photos on the dresser. There weren't even books on the bedstand. It was odd, seeing my room with a stranger standing beside me, and I thought how stoical and barren it looked, as if the person who lived here had moved away years ago.

We paused before Ted's door and the words inscribed on it, "Clato Verato Nictoo," which I gazed at each time I stopped by the door. Bruno paused, hesitating with me as well. He read the words carefully, then nodded. "Do you know what they mean?" I asked him.

"Not exactly," he said, "but I know what they come from."

"You do? What?"

"They are the instructions that needed to be repeated in *The Day the Earth Stood Still*. Clato Verato Nictoo is what you need to tell the robot to keep it from destroying the earth."

"Oh, and what happens?"

Bruno shrugged. "I don't remember, but I think no one tells this to the robot and the earth gets destroyed."

"So this wards off destruction?" Bruno nodded as we entered Ted's room. I hesitated to show him the room, which had a view of the mountains and was papered wall to wall—those precious stone walls that Francis Eagger had built—with James Dean, Bogart, grunge-rock groups (Loose Screw, Nervous Breakdown Number III). His father procured these posters for him—it was the one perk, as far as I could tell, that came from having Charlie as his father. On his dresser was a Kurt Cobain shrine. His bookshelves were lined with *Vampires of the Masquerade* books and assorted other volumes of horror. But the view into the hills was spectacular and it was not lost on Bruno.

In the living room Bruno's hands touched the cold stone walls. He ran his fingers over the exposed wooden beams. At the bookshelf he examined the feathers, pine cones, and shells, giving me a querulous look. "I collect things," I said. "It's a childhood habit."

When we completed the brief tour, Bruno followed me back into the kitchen. "Mrs. Winterstone, I can't thank you enough. I can't tell you what it means to me to see this view—this vista—where he wrote 'The gods rage against me and I can do no more but hope and be humbled by what crashes below, against this fragile shore.' "

"So, Mr. Eagger was a religious man?" I said, curious now to know more about him.

"Yes, he believed, well, not in organized religion, but he believed in a certain power. The power that made this landscape."

"I'm a realist, Mr. Mercedes. I believe that oxygen and various elements and our relation to the sun . . ."

Bruno Mercedes sat down in the breakfast nook and stared out to sea. "It doesn't matter what you believe, Mrs. Winterstone. It's what you feel. What you feel sitting right here. People spend too much time thinking about what they think. Francis Eagger invites us to feel. I like the feel of this place, just like I like the feel of walking on pine needles and looking at a great painting and hearing a piece of music I haven't heard before or seeing a rainbow or having a friend ask me for help. It means there's something bigger than me out there in this world. And yet I can still be a part of it. I can embrace it and it can embrace me. Do you understand what I am saying?"

I looked at this young man with thin, sandy hair and glasses, sitting in my breakfast nook. There was something slightly sad and lost about him. "Yes, I do understand."

"This place should be a temple. A sanctuary."

"It is my sanctuary, Mr. Mercedes."

"Please call me Bruno."

"Well, then, call me Tess."

He nodded. "Mrs. Winterstone . . . Tess, if I could just spend a little time absorbing this place, taking this in. You see, my dissertation is on the religious inspiration in his poems and I believe that the correspondence he carried on with my father—"

"Your father knew him?"

Bruno hesitated, as if he had gone farther than he intended. "Not exactly, but my father was a minister and they wrote letters over two decades. . . . It is a long story, but my parents and I did not speak for many years. We had, well, a falling-out. Eagger had a similar falling-out with his parents, only his lasted a lifetime."

"And yours?"

"In a sense Francis Eagger brought us back together. I became interested in him and then my father shared these letters with me. That was the beginning of our reconciliation." Bruno coughed, looking away. He didn't seem to want to tell me any of this, but had felt he had to. He sensed perhaps that it was his way into my house. I felt badly, as if somehow I had forced him.

"Bruno, make yourself at home. I'll just unpack the groceries, do a few things." I watched him as he sat in the breakfast nook, staring out to sea. Then he opened the small notebook he had brought with him and began taking notes, leafing through a tattered book of the collected poems he pulled from his knapsack. I put away groceries, tossed out dead lettuce. Bruno seemed content looking at the views, touching the stone walls, so I opened the package of photographs from the reunion.

There seemed to be more pictures than I remembered taking and as I opened it, I saw why. The first picture was of the side of a building. The second of an empty room. The third of a table and chair in that room. There was a picture of a refrigerator, a stove, a toilet. Then a suitcase in the room. There was a picture of a cot, more chairs. Chinese food on the table. Plates.

Then people began appearing slowly in the pictures. First one person—a college-age girl with straight, sandy hair—sat at the table, then another. A mother appeared, a father. They were fairly ordinary-looking with brown hair, dark eyes. More people entered the frame. An older woman wore braces. A man had his hair combed across a bald spot.

These were pictures of a family I'd never seen before. Older people, younger people gathering around laughing, eating. Toasting, glasses raised. These were pictures that could matter only to those whom they concerned—and clearly they were not mine. Since I had not had my ticket when I went to get my pictures and had just given the clerk my name, I reasoned that there must be another family named Winterstone who lived in the area. And they had recorded every moment of their move into a rather shabby, not very interesting apartment.

Quickly I put the photos away. When I had to return to work, I looked at Bruno, still sitting there in the breakfast nook. "Bruno," I said, "I have to go now, but if you would like to come here from time to time, if it will somehow help you to write your dissertation by sitting there, then please feel free." Even as I invited him, I wondered what I was doing. What had gotten into me, letting this boy into my house?

"Oh, Mrs. Winterstone . . . Tess, I can't tell you how much it helps. To experience what he experienced. To be here in his home. Listen to this unfinished poem. It is called 'Indigenous to Growing Up' and we only have fragments of it: 'Beneath one dark, soft covering of pine, the hunchback tree stands, its arms sloping like old-fashioned leaves . . . In spring when it rained we lay beneath those branches; touching the places where it curved.' Do you have any idea where that hunchback tree might be?"

"I'm afraid I don't. Bruno, this is fascinating. It really is very interesting, but I'm afraid I have to go back to work." In truth he was making me uncomfortable and I was annoyed that I had been given those photographs that belonged to someone else. I was anxious to leave. I was afraid that I'd already opened the door too much for him and that he would be here all the time.

I walked with him outside, taking a deep breath. Checking to make sure I had the keys to the seashell house because I had a couple who were very keen on seeing it, I waved good-bye to Bruno. "Come back soon," I said, fearing he would.

"I will," he said. "I definitely will."

On my way to the appointment I stopped at the photo store, where I explained to the clerk what had happened. He was grateful that I had returned because, he said, the other Winterstones had been looking for their film. They were very upset, he told me, that he had given someone else their film.

Now he gave me my pictures of the reunion, none of which came out very well. I leafed through them, but most were very dark and everyone had red eyes like rabbits when you catch them in your headlights late at night. In one I saw a person who was clearly Margaret, waving from the back of the crowd.

12

For months after he stopped coming into my room, I still stayed up at night, waiting for my father to tuck me in. I'd sit up, listening for the 9:47 to go through. It was the last train I'd hear before I had to go to sleep. But even after I heard its mournful whistle disappearing in the night, it was still difficult for me to sleep.

One night when it was raining, I heard the train whistle, but I stayed awake, listening to the rain on the roof outside my window. It sounded like small animals running across the shingles. I could hear the TV on in my parents' room and I thought of asking someone to tuck me in. Instead I lay awake, a Nancy Drew mystery open in my lap.

Then it seemed as if the storm had picked up. I heard what sounded like hail at my window. Maybe the storm had turned ugly, though I was pretty sure it couldn't be hail because it was April and it never hailed in April, except once that I could recall, and then Illinois was declared a disaster area because the hail did so much damage, keeping my father busy with claims for the next six months.

I was drifting off with the book open, when the sound of something fiercer than hail woke me. I was past believing in monsters trying to get in, but something was being hurled against my window. Opening the window, I gazed down below. The breeze blew hard. The branches of the maples beat against the side of the house. But in fact it was pebbles, stones from our driveway that were making the sound. I could barely make out a hand waving at me in the rain. "Tess," a voice called. "Come outside. It's me, Margaret."

I could just make her out down there in a wet T-shirt, hair drip-ping wet. "What are you doing?" I shouted, for even I knew that it was crazy for a ten-year-old girl who lived on the other side of the tracks to be at my house at this hour in bad weather.

"Come down," she called. "Slide down the drainpipe."

It had never occurred to me that I could do this, and now it came as a kind of revelation. My bedroom was just above the eaves to the kitchen, and in fact it wasn't much of a drop. But I refused. "Go home," I told her. "You'll get sick."

"Come down," she called again. She was spinning in circles on the lawn, her head tilted back, drinking in the rain. I tore the jumbo rollers out of my hair and took off my pajamas and put on a pair of shorts and a T-shirt. Then I slid down the drainpipe. I was stunned at how easy it was to slip out and escape from my life. Though up until then I hadn't felt the need to.

"Look," she said, holding out her arms. She began to spin again, her ponytail swinging around. She was laughing, head back, mouth open, the rain pouring off her face. I spun with her. I tilted my head back in the wind and the rain and just like Margaret, I spun. It was more fun than I imagined it would be.

Then she stopped suddenly. Taking my hand, she put it on my chest so I could feel my heart throb. "Feel that," she said. "When I was very little," she said, "my father told me I had a time bomb in my chest. He said I had to be careful or it would explode. For years I was afraid to run."

Weird girl. I thought that this was a funny thing for a father to tell his daughter. "Why would he tell you that?" I asked.

"Oh," she dropped my hand, "he always told me strange things like that. You know, my real name isn't even Blair."

"It isn't?" I asked, incredulous.

"No, it's De la Concha. Margarita de la Concha. My father is Spanish. Margaret of the Shell; that's my name. Beautiful, isn't it?" She tossed back her head of shimmering black hair, threw her hand over her head, and gave a little "olé." Then she laughed so that her white teeth shone. She made them clatter together like castanets. "Beautiful?"

I nodded, laughing with her, and we did a little flamenco dance in the driving rain. "Yes," I told her, "it is a beautiful name." And I thought it was. Certainly better than Theadora Antonia Winterstone.

We snuck onto the screened-in porch and I brought down some old beach towels that we hardly ever used so my mother wouldn't notice if they weren't in the linen closet. Margaret and I huddled in the towels. I suddenly felt bad that I hadn't invited her to my birthday party but my dad said I could only have ten kids, and of course the first ten I invited were the gang, so that was that. But now I thought for the first time that Margaret was nice. Strange, but nice. Though I didn't really want to, I found myself liking her.

Margaret said she was hungry so I went and got us something to eat. I tiptoed through the kitchen, carefully opening cabinets, and returned with Cokes, a bag of chips, some cookies. When I returned with the food, I found her cold, shivering, really, her teeth chattering away and her lips turning blue. So I went back inside and grabbed a blanket off my bed and my Chicago Cubs T-shirt. She wrapped herself in the blanket and dried her wet hair with one of the towels. Water flew off her head. Even in the dark her eyes were so white and black. As she peeled off her wet shirt, I saw that her breasts were small and dark. She slipped the Cubs shirt quickly over her head.

My mother hadn't taken the plastic covers off the summer furniture yet. As we sat on top of the plastic, our bare legs stuck to the covers and made farting noises when we moved. This sent us into such paroxysms of laughter we had to stuff the towel into our mouths so that my parents didn't hear us.

"This is a nice house," Margaret said after a while, looking around. "We used to live in a nice house, even nicer than this."

I was a little hurt by her saying she lived in a nicer house than we did and part of me didn't quite believe her, but I didn't think she'd make something up after we'd spun around in the rain and all. "Oh, really," I said. "Where?"

"In Wisconsin. It was a big white house by a lake like the one the Schoenfields live in. My father, he's a very successful businessman. He runs a valve factory."

"Valves?"

"Oh, yes, you know, pipes. They regulate the flow of things."

From science I knew that the heart had valves, but I couldn't quite envision manufacturing them. Still, it sounded plausible that Margaret had a father who did this for a living and did it well. "Your parents are divorced?"

Margaret ignored my question. "We've just hit a bad patch," she said. I remember her saying "bad patch" because it didn't sound like something a girl our age would say. In fact, nothing she said struck me as something a girl our age would say, and something about her seemed as if she were already grown up. "I'll live in a nice house again," she said. "You'll see. I'll live in a big white house by the lake." She said this in a way that made me think she would.

"Yes, Margaret," I said, "I believe you will."

"We're so much alike," Margaret said. "Let's be real friends. Friends for life." She said it in an insistent way that made me uneasy, as if I had no choice. "Here," she said, "You can have my locket." It was a small gold heart on a chain, the kind you can buy at Woolworth's for a few dollars. She slipped it off her neck and onto mine.

Then she asked if she could have something of mine, a keepsake, as if we were sealing a pact. "I won't keep it," she said. "Just let me have it for a little while." I offered her my Chicago Cubs T-shirt, which she was already wearing, but that wasn't a keepsake, she told me. "A keepsake is something you always want to keep with you."

I thought about this for a while, then offered her the scarlet rabbit's foot Jeb had given me the Christmas before. I took it with me everywhere—piano recitals, exams, football games. "Okay," I told her, "you can have this, but you have to promise to give it back." We made a thumb-touch-pinky-twist swear.

That night as we sat huddled on my porch, I felt good about giving her something that mattered to me. After we made our little exchange, I said I was getting sleepy and Margaret said she'd get going.

"Going where? How're you going to get home?" I wanted to wake my father to give her a ride, but she grew adamant.

"Oh, no," she said, "I know the way. It doesn't take that long."

"But it's at least two miles and it's raining." I thought of how far she had to go. Past the police station, the library, through the downtown, along Sheridan Road, under the railroad trestle, then into Prairie Vista. Maybe an hour on foot.

"No," she said, firmly, "I'll be fine."

The porch door banged and she disappeared into the night. I could only see her shadow receding as she walked down our driveway and vanished in the rain.

13

Fisherman's Wharf is my least favorite place to meet someone in San Francisco. I can't stand all the ticky-tacky shops selling T-shirts and caramel corn and the left-hand shop that sells all kinds of scissors and stuff for people who are left-handed. I can't stand the sea lions that live on the docks and have been turned into a tourist attraction.

I've been having this fight for years with the people at the wharf, who claim they don't feed the sea lions to make them stay, but how do you explain a few hundred sea lions hanging out right there on the docks? So when Nick Schoenfield called to say he was in town for business and asked me to meet him at Fisherman's Wharf at such-and-such a time the following Tuesday, I wanted to say no, but then I thought, Tourists, what do they know?

He said to meet him at that seafood restaurant that overlooks the bay and serves dishes like lobster Newburg. Nick was already sitting at a table by the window when I arrived and he waved at me as I came in. He wore an open shirt and jacket and had a breezy way about him I'd always liked. When he stood up to greet me, he was large, looming.

"Tessie," he said, opening his arms. Bending down, he gave me a hug. Then he laughed his big laugh as if my arrival came as a complete surprise. Nick was the kind of person you'd ask to open a jar or unlock a door because he made it seem as if he could do anything. Solve any problem you might have. He was such an easy-going person that he appeared to be almost shallow, as if he couldn't feel very much for very long. But I'd never thought that was the case. Though I'd heard his life had not been an easy one with his father and now his difficult wife, he seemed like someone capable of happiness.

"I'm glad you could meet me."

"Oh, I wanted to. It was no problem," I said, easing my way into the booth. In fact it was a long ride and I'd never been fond of the Wharf, but I didn't want him to know. On the piers sea lions honked. The waiter spilled water on the table as he filled our glasses. Nonchalantly Nick dabbed at it with his napkin.

"I love it here," Nick said. "You're lucky, living at the edge of America." He took a deep breath as if he couldn't get enough air. "I get landlocked back home." I found this a strange comment coming from him since he lived in his father's old house at the end of Laurel with a giant picture window that took in the entire lake.

"My house is on the ocean," I told him. "It's not much to look at, though I bought it from a famous poet's son. You'll have to come see it sometime."

He nodded, taking this all in. "I'm always interested in the sons of famous people," he quipped. "What's the poet's name?"

"Francis Cantwell Eagger," I told him as our drinks arrived.

"Well, I'll have to look for his work if you live in his house. I would like to see where you live," he said, "but not this trip."

"Oh, I didn't mean on this trip."

"Another time." He gazed out across the bay. "I think I'll be coming out here from time to time."

"Well, when you are, you should drive down. We can walk on the beach."

He picked up the oversize menu, which was so large I could no longer see his face. "I'd like that. If this deal goes through, I might be here quite a bit more." His voice came from the other side of his menu. When he couldn't see me, he put it down. He explained that he was trying to create a broader base for Schoenfield Enterprises and was talking with some local people about real estate speculation. He wanted to develop some resort property in Hawaii or the South Pacific.

I reminded him that I knew a little about the real estate business. "I rent time-shares."

"Well, maybe you'll help us. If we ever get this off the ground, it will be very big. I'm trying to interest some money people." He paused as if he'd forgotten something. "I never quite imagined you in real estate, Tessie. I always thought of you as going into nursing or some medical field."

He didn't seem to want to talk further about his business venture and looked away from me as he changed the subject. "Oh, really? Why is that? I can't see myself as a nurse," I said.

"I've always thought of you in the helping professions."

"I'm surprised you've thought of me at all."

"Well, I have." He stared at me with those steely-blue eyes, then glanced down at his menu. "What do you recommend?"

"Seafood. The mahimahi should be good."

As we waited for our drinks, we gazed across at the Golden Gate Bridge. I've loved that bridge since the first time I saw it. It gives me a fleeting sense of endless possibility. "You couldn't ask for a nicer view," Nick said. Our drinks arrived and we sat, looking out at the bridge, and Nick kept saying how it was the gateway to America and what a great bridge it was.

"There was this story in the paper the other day about a guy who left a note in his car that said 'I drove all the way from Iowa to jump off the Golden Gate Bridge.' But they found his car parked on the

Oakland Bridge. The guy didn't even know which bridge to jump off of. Can you imagine?" I told Nick, laughing. "He couldn't even get it right when he killed himself."

Nick started laughing too, but then he stopped. He shook his head as if this had happened to someone he knew. "Poor guy," Nick said. "That's a sad story."

I had the mahimahi with a baked potato and Nick ate a pasta with mixed seafood. He was quiet as he ate, asking me questions about my children. He showed me a picture of Danielle, a somber child with dark circles under her eyes. "She's a pistol," he said, though I didn't see it.

I told him I thought my kids had suffered from the divorce. "They're rather aimless. I worry about them."

"It's probably a phase. Didn't we all grow out of it?"

It was still early after dinner and Nick suggested we walk around. He had never been to San Francisco before and asked if I would give him the grand tour. We wandered up the hill toward Coit Tower, then down into North Beach. From there up through Chinatown and into Union Square where his hotel was. It was a nice leisurely walk to take on an October evening when it wasn't too chilly. I enjoyed pointing out the sights.

When we stopped back in his hotel, he invited me in for a drink. He didn't want to sit at the bar and suggested I join him in his room. It was a standard plaid hotel room with a king-size bed. In the bathroom he had a shaving kit, but nothing was hung up in the closet. It didn't seem as if he'd be staying very long. On the bedstand were a pile of magazines, newspapers, a paperback thriller.

"I like mysteries," Nick said, seeing me glance at the bedstand. "What'll it be?" He opened the minibar. I requested a brandy, which he poured, and we sat down at a small table with two chairs. "So, Tess," he said, "what's it like, living right by the sea? Do you get up feeling great every day?"

"You have the lake."

"It's not the same thing. Salt water, the wild seas."

I told him that in the morning I liked to run up in the hills, then down to the coast. That from my kitchen window I looked out on to the ocean. That sometimes I rescued wildlife stranded on the shore. He leaned forward with his hands folded across his knees as if he really wanted to hear what I had to say. I was beginning to talk more about my children and my divorce, about my stone house and how I wanted to turn it into a bed-and-breakfast, when the phone rang. Nick made a face and for a moment I thought he wasn't going to answer. He let it ring a few times, but then he got up and went to it. He walked stiffly, as if he'd suddenly become an old man or someone expecting bad news.

When he picked it up, I had a sense of what was going on at the other end. He had a deep, husky voice on the phone, different from when he talked to me. I heard him saying things like yes, of course I'm here, no, I'm alone. Don't be silly. Yes, I saw her, but now she's gone home. The kinds of things you say when you are trying to calm somebody down and are lying to her at the same time. His hand tightened around the receiver and his shoulders and back, which faced me, seemed firmly set, as if he were carved out of stone.

I knew it was Margaret and that she was in a flap. It didn't surprise me that they were having a difficult time. I was never quite sure how it was that Margaret Blair had come to marry Nick Schoenfield. They had dated briefly in high school, but it had never amounted to much. After high school, they had married other people, then divorced. Both moved back to Winonah from wherever they had gone. Vicky said they met again over a beer at Paradise.

The Schoenfields were more "our kind" of people—that's what my mother would have said. Prominent Jews with money and maybe some links to organized crime, though no one mentioned those. If I'd stayed in Winonah the way the rest of my friends had, I probably would have married someone like Nick. It was no secret in Winonah that Mr. S. was disappointed over Nick's marriage to Margaret Blair and that he had never quite forgiven his son for marrying her.

The conversation took a long time and I sipped my brandy slowly. It is always strange to be on one end of a conversation, but I could imagine what was being said on the other side. Nick kept saying, "No, that's not true. No, I didn't do that. You know I wouldn't." I had to drive home so I put the brandy aside, not wanting it to go to my head. Finally Nick put the receiver down and with a big sigh looked up at me. "I guess you know who that was."

"I guess I do," I said.

"Well, it just hasn't been easy. She's pretty impossible, you know."

"Actually, I don't know. I mean, I remember how she was when we were girls, but I don't know how she is now."

"You can't imagine. Sometimes she goes into the city and doesn't tell us where she's going. Oh, she's always home by bedtime, but it still drives Danielle crazy. She's nice, then she blows up for no reason. It's as if she doesn't care about me at all, then suddenly she has to have me." Nick shrugged. "I'm going to leave her. I haven't told her yet, but I'm not staying. It's like living with a time bomb."

I was surprised to hear that. It sent a chill through me because I remembered when Margaret told me she had a time bomb in her chest. I was also surprised that Nick would confide so much in me since we didn't know each other well and hadn't seen each other for many years. "But you've been together a long time."

"She's never really loved me," he said. "I loved her, but she never loved me. She just wanted things. That's what's been the worst of it for me, loving someone who doesn't love me."

"I'm sure she loved you."

"No, she didn't. She can't. She loves our daughter. That's the only person she loves. Even then, I wonder. There's a part of her that's just not here."

I nodded, wondering why he had married her in the first place. "There was always something strange about her, Nick."

"Yes, maybe that's what I liked about her." He said thoughtfully, "She was unpredictable, but she made things interesting. That counts for something, doesn't it?"

"It does," I agreed. I said I needed to head back and he walked me down to the lobby. "It was good to see you, Tess." He kissed me on the cheek. "You haven't changed." As I turned to leave, he pulled me to him. I wanted to burrow into his chest and stay there, but just as quickly as he held me, he let me go. "Drive safely," he said, helping me into my car.

As I drove, the highway twisted and turned before my eyes and I had trouble following the road. I'd driven this road a million times and now it was as if I'd never driven it before. But that happens to me sometimes. I'm somewhere I know very well and all of a sudden it's as if I'd never been there before.

When I got home, I went straight to bed. In the morning I went for a long run up in the hills. When I started out I was fine, but once I got up into the wilderness area I started to feel as if I wasn't alone. I felt as if there was something trailing me. Many times my children have begged me not to run up here without a buddy, but then, what's the point of going with a buddy if you want to be by yourself?

As I ran, I kept turning around, expecting to see something barreling down on me, but I never did. Still, I couldn't help but feel that there was something out there and it was watching me.

14

In the dog days of summer, when we could think of little else to do, Vicky and I formed the Firefighters of America. I'm not sure what it was about fires—the heat, the possibility of being trapped with no way out—but it seemed we wanted to stop them. Not that we had ever really seen a fire, except once when Lindsey's Delicatessen burned down, or had ever been in danger of a fire, but we spent hours thinking about how to prevent them and put them out.

We did some research at the fire department and learned that a "dead man's room" is a room with only one exit. We liked the way the firefighters smelled like burning leaves. We made a list of all the kinds of fires we wanted to put a stop to—fires made by foolish children playing with matches, by careless mothers who left hot oil on the stove, by too many plugs in one outlet. Brushfires started when a cigarette was tossed from a moving car or when lightning struck the ground in the woods. Wildfires. We wanted to put a stop to all of these.

We made little badges out of cardboard with FOA carefully inscribed. Small, contained flames leapt into the air on our badges. We colored them orange with a blue glow at the base. We wanted them to be just so, just right. I had no idea how we would protect anyone, but still we made up these little badges.

Then we went from door to door, canvassing the neighborhood. We rang doorbells, and the neighbors who knew us were very nice. I thought that this was what it must be like for my father as he traveled from town to town, talking to people about the disasters they could avert just by signing their names. The neighbors who opened their doors to us listened politely to what we had to say, accepted what we had to offer. We asked for small donations for being members of Fire-fighters of America. The most we ever got from anyone was a quarter and we bought candy with it.

After a few days we had done my neighborhood and hers and weeks of the summer still stretched before us. We thought about expanding, casting a wider net. We followed the road along the railroad tracks, stopping here and there. We cut over to the other side. In some of these houses people didn't come to the door.

People spoke with accents. Dark men, unshaven in T-shirts, answered the door. These men smelled of cigarettes and hair oil and something sour we couldn't quite place. In the background we could see broken furniture, sofas with their stuffing coming out. Often these doors were slammed in our faces.

We knew the houses along the railroad tracks weren't where we should be. It was different here, and we felt as if we had wandered into a foreign country, past the safe boundaries of our own. Old women sat not far from the doors as if they were expecting someone, but not us, to arrive. Strong cooking smells came from behind these doors—greasy meats, sauces, dead animals. Once or twice we passed Prairie Vista Automotive and, looking up, saw where Margaret lived.

"What do you think it's like up there?" Vicky asked.

I thought of Mrs. Blair in her short skirts, her heels clicking on the asphalt, and my father watching her laugh. "I know what it's like," I told her. "The woman who irons my father's shirts has been up there." It was a lie, but I thought of those Saturdays when my father and I stood peering up at the apartment above Santini's Liquor. I concocted dingy rooms that stank of onions and smoke, gray sheets, linoleum floors. I invented walls that were gray, red-striped wallpaper pulling away from them. In her spare time Margaret would peel it back some more. She had found trains in her room, boats in her mother's. The rest of the house was trees.

I found myself making up entire scenarios, full of misery and intrigue. Her mother tells her to stop peeling back the wallpaper. She says there's lead in it or something, and she says she's ruining the walls, but Margaret can't seem to stop wanting to see what's on the other side.

Clarice Blair cleans the place all the time. She gets on her knees and scrubs the floor. She scrubs the cabinets and the counters as if company is going to walk in at any moment, but they never do. Nobody ever goes there. Still, her mother never stops her scrubbing, then she yells at Margaret because she doesn't do anything to help. Margaret is a bastard, but Clarice has never told her. Clarice isn't even sure who the real father is.

Sometimes on purpose Margaret leaves dishes in the sink. She doesn't make her bed. Just to anger her mother. Or she'll make it, but not fluff the pillow just right. She does this just to drive her mother wild. Margaret is ashamed of who she is and where she lives. She doesn't want her friends to hear her mother speak with her cackly laugh or see her put on her uniform to go to work. When Clarice Blair goes to work for Dr. Reiss, the dentist in town, she dresses all in white—white stockings, white shoes, a white uniform.

Clarice Blair should not wear white, or yellow, or any of the pale colors. She should wear blue brocade, red taffeta. She should be presented at balls. Instead she lives with her daughter above a store. She never complains, though her daughter does. Still, this is a woman who once lived in a house surrounded by lilac trees and played the violin on a stage. Now she dresses in white and keeps a doctor's appointment book. She is paying for her many mistakes.

Vicky listened to all of this, aghast and enraptured as I described for her the strange and tragic life of Margaret Blair. "Elena told you all that?"

I was proud that Vicky had believed my fib. "That and more."

Vicky nodded. "Well, it makes perfect sense."

"I'm sworn to secrecy, so please don't tell anyone."

Vicky crossed her heart and hoped to die, promising she wouldn't tell a soul.

That was the summer when the alewives died. They died by the millions. Their stinking carcasses covered the beaches and carpeted the sea for half a mile or more. The stench made its way up from the waterfront and the bluffs to the houses, such as ours, that were blocks away. No one knew why the fish died, but we knew that we could not go down to the beach that summer.

Day after day Vicky and I canvassed the neighborhood, trying to interest people in the Firefighters of America. Our search took us farther and farther from home, deeper into Prairie Vista than we'd ever been. We had more doors slammed in our faces, people shouting at us to go away.

After days of discouragement, Vicky wanted to ring Margaret's door. What's the worst that could happen? Vicky said. I hesitated, knew that all I'd told Vicky was lies, but then it seemed to me that perhaps I hadn't lied. That probably things were much as I'd envisioned them. It was a hot July day and the air stank of garbage and dead fish and the fumes from the repair shop across the way as we rang the buzzer at Margaret Blair's door.

Standing on the hot asphalt we waited a few moments and then I said to Vicky, "See, no one's home. Let's go." We were starting to walk away when someone buzzed us in. We entered a dingy vestibule and Margaret called down to us, "Up here." We climbed a flight of stairs and there at the landing was Margaret, nicely dressed in blue Bermuda shorts and a matching top and smiling as if she had been expecting us all along.

To our surprise the rooms were cheery. The walls were painted bright colors—rose and aquamarine; there was no grayness. No peeling wallpaper. The apartment smelled of soap and potpourri—nothing of what I'd imagined. No bacon-and-eggs smell. Vicky gave me a "I thought you said . . ." look and I shrugged back at her "I guess Elena got it wrong."

"It's so nice to see you girls," Mrs. Blair said, an apron around her waist, a wide smile on her face. Her jet-black hair pulled back, red lipstick on as if she had someplace to go. She invited us to sit at the table and poured for us tall, cold glasses of lemonade. She placed a plate of cookies in front of us, cut into the shapes of diamonds and stars, so buttery they melted in your mouth. It was hot but a fan blew and we felt cool and comfortable inside.

"Margaret, give them the grand tour," Mrs. Blair said with her hearty laugh, so we got to see the rest of the apartment, which was four more rooms. Her mother's room was all white with big pillows on the four poster bed. The bed had a canopy and I'd never seen one before and Margaret let us sit under it for a few minutes. Then she showed us the living room, where there were pictures of horses chasing foxes on the wall, and the bathroom that had pink, fluffy towels. I asked if I could wash my hands so that I could touch one and it was very soft. When I asked Elena if she could make our towels that soft, she told me to shut up and mind my own business.

In Margaret's room the shelves were filled with blue-eyed dolls wearing lacy dresses. Stuffed bears and rabbits and dogs covered her bed. We played with Margaret's dolls and she introduced us to each one and they had names like Deirdre and Gruswalda. Strange, foreign names. Margaret wanted to know about the Firefighters of America and we explained to her what we'd learned about putting out fires. How you never throw water on a grease fire. How if a person is burning, throw a blanket on top. We told her about the "dead man's room" and she seemed very interested in this.

"You mean there's no way out."

"There's only one way out, but if there's a fire, then there's no way out."

"No way out," Margaret said, running her hands up and down her arms as if she had the shivers. "Explain it to me again."

Vicky and I sighed, thinking she was dumb. "You're trapped," I told her.

"Oh, I get it now." After that, Margaret said she wanted to volunteer for Firefighters of America. She wanted to help us the next time we went house to house. We said sure, though Vicky and I soon lost interest in our organization and never went house to house again.

We played until it was dark, when Clarice offered to drive us home. Margaret came along for the ride and she told her mother exactly where to turn. She knew the way to our houses as if she had been there dozens of times, not once or twice.

When she dropped me off, Clarice commented on how beautiful our houses were. "You live in a very pretty house," she said, holding my arm with her long red nails. "Oh, it must be so lovely to live here." As I opened the door, she said, "Say hello to your nice father for me." Then she begged me to come back again. She said it so many times that I found myself racing to the door.

15

Spices filled the air. Cardamom, cinnamon, cilantro. Jade was testing me to see if I could name them. She was cooking something, some kind of stew. "You have to try it, Mom," she said. I took sips, dipped into the savory broth. It was spicy, hot. Jade had become a vegan, announcing she wouldn't eat anything that moved. Nothing with arms or legs.

When Jade wasn't home, I sneaked ham sandwiches, cheese, but lately, since Ted now spent most of his time with Cherri up the coast, this cooking filled the house. Now my daughter brought these savory smells. "So I saw him again," Jade said as she stirred the pot. She said it slowly so I wouldn't think she was crazy.

"You saw whom again?"

She nodded slowly. "You know, the old sea captain. On the cliffs the night you were in town. He was holding his compass."

I wanted to take Jade into my arms, hold back the tide of her fears. Two or three times she had seen this old captain walking the bluff past our house. I'd always attributed this to Jade's wild imagination and to the fact that she's never liked to be alone.

Yet I had a sense, since I'd returned from Winonah, that things weren't quite as they'd been before. I am still, though not to the extent that I was as a girl, an orderly person with an archival sense of where things belong. So it surprised me when I found small objects out of place. A slip of paper was missing from a drawer, shoes were not on their shelves. I found sweaters draped over chairs. There was a scent of perfume. Once in the shower, I felt hands coursing my body. Hands that knew where they were going. For an instant, I couldn't catch my breath.

Jade served me her vegetable stew, which she poured over curried rice. I was taking my first bites as she warmed her hands over her food, said a prayer. She had explained to me something about how she was transferring the energy from the food into her body and how she was thanking the vegetables for sharing themselves with her, but I didn't quite understand it. "This is delicious," I told her, and it was.

"Thanks, Mom. I want to be healthy. I want to eat better food."

"Well, that's a good idea." We ate in silence for a while. "So do you have plans for this weekend?" I asked her.

"Maybe," she said, her head bowed over her steaming rice, "not sure."

"I was thinking we could do something. Drive up to San Francisco. You could see Dad."

She shrugged. "I don't know . . . Weren't you just in San Francisco the other day? Didn't you see one of your old pals?"

"Yes, I saw a man named Nick Schoenfield. His father was a famous quarterback."

"That's nice. You gonna see him again?"

"Maybe. When he comes back to town." I found that I wanted to talk about Nick and our time together, but I didn't think she'd understand. Could I tell her about his bad marriage? About the hopes he'd once had of being a great athlete like his father? Jade would find these things quaint, like old pictures she discovered in dusty frames that were charming but not quite relevant to her.

After dinner Jade took her dishes to the sink. "You cooked; I'll clean up," I told her, so without a protest, she left them there and headed to her room. After a little while I got up and rinsed them, washed the pots. Wiped the counters clean. Then I went and sat in the living room, thinking I'd read for a while.

The den felt chilly. A draft seemed to be coming from the stone fireplace. In some of the rooms of the house—the ones where the light never gets in and the walls are always dank—I kept blankets on the backs of chairs. The blanket from Winonah's centennial was one of these.

I didn't, in fact, like to sit in the den that much, even though, along with the kitchen, it has the best coastal views, because the chill never leaves these walls. There is a dankness to certain rooms and at times I have kept one or two locked. Still there is always a draft and the wind around the house is a relentless howl.

Wrapping the Winonah centennial blanket around me, I sat in the den, sipping my tea. On the coffee table was a volume of Francis Eagger's poems and I leafed through it until I came upon the poem Bruno had liked, entitled "Old Hat." I remembered how that was a favorite expression of Lily's. I read a few lines: "sleepers swathed in gauze; a young girl dashing naked through city streets; wild swans attack children who feed them, engulfing them in their wings. These are just bad dreams."

These lines surprised me. Once my brothers and I were attacked while feeding wild swans. They swooped down on us, battering us with their wings until our parents chased them away. And just recently I'd had a dream of me chasing Jade, who was running naked down a city street. It was as if the poet had read my own dreams, written them there.

I was shivering so I wrapped myself tightly into "Home of the Winonah Wildcats." The train station and Winonah Summer Festival graced my lap. Trying to get warm, I felt restless now and wished Jade would come and bother me. My visit with Nick was on my mind. Our talk over dinner, a sadness that seeped into his blue-gray eyes. I felt uneasy as I thought about Margaret. It seemed she was drinking too much and her marriage was on the rocks. She's not my problem, I told myself. She never was. Other things were my problem—like how I was going to make ends meet.

Money seemed tight and there were bills I had to put aside. I thought of calling Jeb and asking for a loan, but Jeb has a way of making me feel I have mismanaged my life and so I don't like to ask him for anything unless I have to. In the end he always tells me—as does Charlie—to sell my house, which is now actually worth something. It does no good to argue with either of them that this is my home. Instead of calling him, I sat curled up, making income and expense lists on pads of yellow paper. The sea pounded below my house in a way that was almost frightening and made me think about the reunion and what it had been like being back home. How it had felt, parking my car on the beach, being there once more. I felt a funny kind of longing that I can't quite remember ever feeling before though I'm sure I felt it a million times when there was someone I wanted. I sat there, thinking I missed something I didn't even know mattered.

The house felt lonely and cold with Jade in her room with the door shut, listening to music. There was no one I could talk to. I decided to call Shana and see if she'd meet me for dinner the next night. But when I picked up the phone, I heard the voices on the line. The same voices I'd heard a few weeks before. This time the woman, whose voice was still familiar to me, had a problem. A fight with her husband, who was jealous over her friendship with another man. "Excuse me," I said. I tried to shout at them that they were on my line, but once again they could not hear me.

"Well, does he have a reason to be jealous?"

"Oh, I don't know."

"Well, if there's no reason, then what's the point?"

Because the voice was familiar, I continued to listen as they went on to share a recipe for Moroccan chicken, which required lime pickle, purchased from a spice store in Saratoga. Then the conversation went back to some difficulty the woman was having.

As I listened, I suddenly placed the voice. It was my nearest neighbor, Betsy Bernhart, a person I hardly knew, except that she sometimes got my mail and now, it seemed, I got her phone calls. Once I had to return her cat to her and once or twice she'd complained when the kids played their music too loud. But now I listened as she told him that things hadn't been too good lately. That she had been having second thoughts about her childless marriage. "Don't let appearances fool you," she said to the man.

"Really," the man said, "I didn't know."

When I hung up, I decided that the next time I saw Betsy, I'd have to tell her that our wires were crossed. It was not long afterward that the phone rang again and I decided that if it was another crossed line I'd have to go and discuss the problem with her now.

Instead I heard a man's voice on the other end. "Can you talk?" Nick said.

I was surprised at how glad I was to hear his voice. "Yes, I can talk." I curled up with my legs under me, the blanket across my lap. His voice sounded distraught and far away.

"Listen," he said, "I know you don't live here anymore, but you did. You know what it's like. I can't really talk to anyone, but I thought I could talk to you. I felt as if you understood my situation the other night."

There was something warm and comforting in Nick's voice. We could be friends; we could be there for one another. Yet at the same time it seemed as if I were sinking into a dark hole, a place I wasn't sure I wanted to be. A strange, slightly scary place. I didn't know what I had or hadn't understood. "I'm not sure I can be helpful."

"Tessie, you know Margaret. You were once friends."

"I don't know if we were ever really friends."

"But you know things about her." He sighed. "I wish you were here. I wish we could sit and talk. I have so much I want to tell you. If we could sit across from one another and talk all night long, I think you'd understand."

Holding the phone tightly against my ear, I nodded. "Yes," I said, "I think we could tell each other lots of things."

"I'm going to leave her. She lies to me all the time. She's a drunk. We aren't a couple anymore. We haven't been for a long time. She threatens me with all kinds of things. . . ." He sounded very tired. "If it weren't for Danielle—"

"She threatens you?"

"Oh, she says she'll kill herself. Or she'll take Danielle away from me. But that's mainly when she's drunk."

"You have to do what you think is best."

"Best for me or best for everyone?"

I hesitated, not because I didn't want to answer, but because I suddenly thought about my neighbor, Betsy, and the crossed line. I wondered if she could overhear this conversation the way I could overhear hers. And what would she be making of it?

"I like you, Tessie. I feel as if we can be friends."

"We are friends," I said.

"Yes," he said, "we already are. But I want to know about you. I don't want to just talk about me. I want to learn about you. . . . Listen, can I call you from time to time? When I want company . . ."

His voice wasn't as bold, as sure of itself, as it had been. There was a slight tremor, a shaky edge that I hadn't heard before. I'd never thought of Nick as being weak when it came to emotions. He always struck me as a person who had the upper hand. But now he sounded almost afraid.

Wrapping the blanket more tightly around my legs, I found myself reassuring him. "Of course you can."

"That's great, thanks." He sounded relieved. "I'd really like to know you're out there if I need you. Look," he said, "I've got to go. I'll call you soon." Then he hung up quickly, as if someone had just walked in the room.

16

"We really should have them over, don't you think?" Lily said, running her hands through her hair. I was sitting at the dining room table, doing my homework while Lily perused some cookbooks. She entertained more than she used to, poring over recipes when our father was on the road. Sometimes she tried her recipes out on us, but mostly they were for guests. On counters lay open *The Joy of Cooking, The Secrets of the Italian Kitchen*. She made *canard l'orange* and *steak au poivre*. "At first I didn't want to, but now I just think we should."

"Have who over?" Victor replied, a Cincinnati—half beer, half cream soda—in his hand, standing in the kitchen doorway.

"You know," Lily went on, not really looking up at him, "the new family, the new people. The mother who lives with that girl over the liquor store. In Tess's class, the one she walks to school with now and then."

"I'm not sure which girl that is," Victor said.

"Oh, yes, you do, you know the people. I feel sorry for that girl. There's something about her. Something so sad. They are nice, actually. The mother—she has an odd name, Clarice—she works for Dr. Reiss. I've spoken with her from time to time when I call for appointments. She has the nicest things to say about Tessie. I think they're just, well, poor. Down on their luck."

Victor pondered this while Lily made her case. "Oh, yes, I met her, didn't I, Tessie? A few weeks ago. The mother and girl who live across from the repair shop."

"I don't think they live there anymore," I said, looking up from my homework. "They've moved to one of those houses just past the railroad trestle."

"Well, that's good," Lily said. "I'm sure it's better over there."

"And the father?" Victor asked. "Has anybody met him?"

Lily shrugged. "There doesn't seem to be a father."

"Margaret talks about him all the time, but I've never seen him," I offered.

"Well, I think we should invite the mother." Lily flipped through her cookbooks, scribbling down future menus.

"So then, yes, why not. Have them over." My father disappeared back into the kitchen with his Cincinnati.

"Don't you think we should have something small, something simple?"

"Sure," my father called, "whatever suits you." But something always came up and Lily never quite got around to making the phone call, inviting them over. She thought about it, the way my mother thought about everything, mulling it over, thinking it through, weighing the pros and cons, then forgot about the idea for a long, long time.

We lived a block or so from the railroad tracks on the south side of town. During the day when I wandered around, I liked to walk along the tracks, where I found the crushed remains of birds and squirrels. Once I found a cat cut right in two.

As soon as I crossed under the trestle, I found myself in the part of town where the houses were small and gray with front porches with broken screens, tricycles on the front lawns, laundry hung out to dry in the warmer months. The Skid Row of Winonah, my father called it.

There were smells I couldn't quite recognize but they left an oily taste in my mouth and there were garbage cans you could see, not hidden in a big bin like ours were. I don't even remember my parents ever taking out the garbage, though of course they must have, but here you could see it in cans that lined the sides of the houses, sometimes spilling over the tops. Often I saw men in uniforms coming in and out of these houses and they weren't coming to fix things, but actually lived here.

It was to this row of gray houses with battered front porches that Clarice Blair settled with Margaret a year or so after she'd arrived in Winonah. She'd taken a job as a receptionist for Dr. Reiss, a dentist who worked out west near Crestwood, and I guess she'd done well enough to move. It wasn't the house on the lake that Margaret said she'd once lived in, but it wasn't over Santini's Liquor Store either.

You could tell that Clarice had tried to fix the place up because the porch screens were repaired and she'd painted the house white. Though there wasn't any trash on her lawn and she had even planted a few pink and white flowers out front, there was plenty of trash on the lawns around hers so it seemed a little pointless. She'd tried to make the house look pretty, but it still looked shabby like the others around it, as if it were going to fall down.

Whenever Clarice or Margaret saw me walking by, they invited me inside. It seemed as if I couldn't walk down this road without being seen by one of them. I had a feeling after a while that they were waiting for me. Usually Margaret came onto the porch to greet me, then asked me to come inside and play.

The house was small and smelled like cats, but Mrs. Blair had tried to make it cozy. Pictures of dogs and flowers hung on the walls. There were toys in corners and a few potted plants by the windows and one plant I liked very much, with long, purplish-green tentacles, that hung in the kitchen and Mrs. Blair told me was called a Wandering

Jew, which I thought was a strange name for a plant. "Just like you, Tessie," Mrs. Blair said, "always wandering around."

Whenever I stopped by, or whenever they spotted me walking and called me in, Clarice Blair always gave us milk and a plate of cookies and then Margaret would ask me to go upstairs into her room. Margaret's room was done up nicely with pink bedspreads and white curtains. But Margaret never wanted to just sit in the sun and gossip about the boys the way the rest of the gang did. Margaret had elaborate scenes she liked to act out. Pioneer sisters was one of her favorites. I was a sick sister who had to be nursed back to health and only Margaret could do this, pressing poultices to my head. She liked to save me more than she liked having me save her. She wanted me to do dramatic things that went against my nature—stagger into the room, collapse breathlessly upon the bed so she could rush to my side and lament. Once real tears coursed down her cheeks, which I thought was taking the game too far.

When we played pioneer sisters, she had calico skirts and bonnets we had to put on. Or satin and tulle skirts if we were princesses. When we were princesses, we were sentenced to the Tower and only Margaret knew how we'd escape. These games were complete with informants, guards, and go-betweens, often played by Margaret as well, and we played them as if they were not games at all, but something very real.

Before I left, Clarice Blair always made a point of telling me how much she appreciated that I was friends with Margaret; how much that meant to her. She said that Margaret hadn't had an easy time because they had moved around so much and that sometimes little girls misunderstood her. I was ashamed when Clarice Blair said these things to me and I hoped when I left the house that none of the gang would ever know I went there.

To get from my house to Margaret's you had to walk a block or two, then pass under the railroad trestle. It was just a viaduct. The trestle itself led to a big turnabout where engines could be turned around. Before Margaret came to Winonah, I never walked on the trestle because it was a bridge and if a train were coming, there was nowhere to go. Some of the boys—the bad boys who hung out at the Idiot's Circle, that small circle of grass at the train station where boys with nothing better to do sat and smoked and drank beer after school—raced the trains across the trestle, but no girls did. My brother Jeb came home with stories about boys who almost didn't make it, boys who'd had to make a dive for the bushes. The most I ever did was put a nickel on the tracks and see how flat it came out after the train rode over it.

But Margaret, once she'd moved from Santini's to the house near the trestle, always dared us to go with her to play there. She taunted us. She stood in the middle of the trestle, waving her arms. "What is it with you guys? You so scared?" We got tired of her taunting and agreed to go along.

The first few times we crossed the railroad trestle, we dashed across. But Margaret stood in the middle, arms akimbo, laughing her high-pitched laugh. She stood there, her black hair blowing in the breeze, her olive skin looking so sleek and smooth, and you almost had the feeling that she could stop a locomotive if one came barreling down on her.

In October we had a burst of Indian summer and the knowledge that the warmth and freshness in the air were the last hint of summer we'd have before winter set in. We wanted to take the long way home, to meander through the ravines one last time before they were filled with ice and snow. I was the only one who knew the routes the way Margaret did and together we ambled through the ravines, soaking our shoes, but we didn't care. The air was warm and the sunlight shone through the maples that had already turned gold. Scanning the ground, we searched for arrowheads but found none.

We walked until we came to Lincoln, past the library, the police station, under the trestle to where the old turnabout was. We lingered here, tossing stones, and when we looked up, we heard Margaret calling to us. "Last one across the railroad bridge gets a free milk shake." That was always the dare, not to be the first, but the last.

Because I lived so close to the tracks, I knew the times of the trains. I could recite them in my sleep. The 8:05, the 9:32, the 10:27, and so on. I was used to the bell ringing, the gates going down. "The four twenty-four is due," I said, but Margaret laughed and raced up the grassy embankment to the trestle. We scrambled on with her and then started to run. But in the middle we paused because Margaret had some nickels and pennies she wanted to place on the tracks. She was meticulously lining up her coins when I heard the train whistle.

"Run, Tessie," Vicky, who was already across the railroad bridge, shouted. "Tessie, run!"

Behind me the 4:24 was barreling down. I ran as fast as I've ever run before or since. The train seemed to be gaining on me and I heard its whistle blow as if it were right inside my head. I ran perhaps only twenty yards or so before I dove for the bushes, breathless, my heart pounding.

Even as the train approached the trestle, its horn blaring, I heard that sharp, staccato laughter. That *ta-ta-ta,* almost like an opera singer during a mad scene. "Oh, Tessie," Margaret shouted from the middle of the railroad bridge, "you looked so funny and you had it beat by a mile."

When we turned, we saw Margaret standing there, arms outstretched, black hair waving in the breeze. Her eyes were shut tight and she seemed to be taking enormous pleasure in the moment. I shouted to her, "Margaret, run, *run!*"

When it already seemed too late, as if all were lost, she began to run. She dashed across the bridge and just as the train seemed about to run over her, its whistle blaring, she dove for the bushes. She lay there, still, and we thought she was unconscious or even dead. Blood trickled from scratches along the side of her face. Other cuts bled on her hands where she'd landed in the briars.

"Oh, my God," said Samantha Crawford, who was always a little afraid. "What're we going to do?"

"She's fine," I said, "she's just faking it." I shook and shook her, but she didn't move.

"We should go get help," Vicky said.

"I'll go," Lori Martin, with her take-charge attitude, said. Just as Lori dashed off, Margaret opened her eyes and laughed that high-pitched laugh. "Fooled you, didn't I?" she said, laughing as blood trickled down her cheek.

"It's not funny," I told her. "We thought you were hurt."

"Oh, Tessie," Margaret said, "you take things too seriously."

One night, just a few days later, Margaret came to my window and tossed pebbles until I came down. I was still angry with her for the trick she'd pulled on the tracks and I told her so. "I'm sorry, Tessie. It's just that you guys seemed so scared."

We sat down together on the grass and she picked a blade, made a whistle of it between her teeth. I plucked a blade and tried to whistle through it, but I couldn't get that high, piercing sound Margaret got with hers.

In the distance we heard the 8:35 rushing through, announcing my bedtime. "Have you ever had this sensation?" Margaret asked me. "You are sitting in a train in the station and the train next to you starts to move. You think you're the one who's moving when, in fact, you're standing still."

I told her I couldn't remember ever having had that sensation.

"Well, when you have it," she said, getting up to leave, "you'll know."

Those were the last warm days of fall and then winter was upon us. It seemed an especially hard winter that year. The snow drifts were six feet high and we had to wade through them to school. I stayed inside more than I wanted and found it confining, as did my brothers. So we were relieved in January when there was a thaw. An unusual warm spell, you could never predict. The temperature rose and the snow melted. Big soggy pools of it. There was mud on the lawns. Puddles to jump in, splash through. For days we frolicked. Went to school in our shirtsleeves with just windbreakers on. We played ball, skipped, and the air had the green freshness of spring, as if the flowers would pop out of the ground, and the woods behind our house were carpeted in jack-in-the-pulpits.

Then one night it began to rain. We were asleep so we hardly noticed the rain or the temperature falling. It dropped steadily in the night so that before dawn a freezing rain was falling and by morning it was a glazed-over world. Everything white and shiny, slippery to the touch.

The power lines were down. There was no heat. Our father built a fire in the fireplace in the middle of the day, and we toasted wieners, marshmallows, whatever could be toasted over the flame. We huddled by the fire while my father thought about what we should do because it was all slick outside and nowhere to go.

When I pressed my face to the glass, my steamy breath made little snowflakes, and when I wiped it away, there she was. Skating on our lawn, up and down our driveway. "Look at that," our father said.

I wiped the glass, pressed my face closer, and saw for myself. Margaret was skating across our lawn in long, even glides. When she saw us at the window, she beckoned for me to join her. "Well," my father said, laughing, "you've got to go out there."

At first I was reluctant, but then I put my skates on. Together we skated up and down on the lawn, then on the streets, my parents gazing at us through the frosty glass.

In the spring of that year when the air was fresh and there was a hint of leaves and grass—you could already feel things starting to grow—my mother told me that we were having company for dinner. She didn't say who, except that it was a surprise. She told me I should go upstairs and get cleaned up. Since we often had company for dinner on the weekends when my father was home, I wasn't particularly curious, though I always wanted to know what we were eating.

Soon the house was filled with the bustle of preparations. We had "help"—a grumpy older woman named Emma who came in a white uniform when there were parties—and my mother told her exactly what to do. My mother fluttered through the kitchen, her hands flying as she chopped something. She could whip up just about anything in half a second. She made creamed spinach I can still taste, buttery and smooth. She fried fish with almonds and brown butter so it came out so crunchy you'd never know it was fish. It wasn't like other houses, where you got meatloaf every night of the week. People loved to come to our house.

When I asked who was coming, Lily looked distracted. My mother always seemed to have a million things to do, but if people were coming over, she never stopped until the party was over. The freckles on her nose glistened with sweat as she pushed a strand of hair, which I noticed for the first time was turning gray, off her face. Her hands arched over whatever she was chopping. Nobody, she said, just a few friends.

I didn't bother asking how "nobody" could be friends, but I was surprised when I found Clarice Blair sitting in our living room with a cocktail napkin on her lap. She wore dark stockings and a short black cocktail dress. She had this funny hat on with a veil that looked ridiculous to me, as if she were coming to a funeral, not a dinner party. Her dress was straight and tight and she had difficulty keeping her legs together. She had great legs, legs Margaret would eventually inherit, and she kept swishing them back in forth in a single motion.

We had other people over as well—a golf partner of my father's and Mr. and Mrs. McKenzie from next door, who was blind as a bat, and Mr. and Mrs. Lerner, whose daughter was known for doing things with boys after basketball games, though these parents obviously didn't have a clue. While I was passing out a tray (my mother made me do stuff like this) with little cheese puffs, I heard Mr. Lerner say to Mr. McKenzie, "I can't tell you how many friends we have who don't even know they need an oil change." This was hardly my mother's A list of friends, not that she exactly had an A list, but my mother was a good hostess and she treated everybody, even the man who mowed the lawn, like equals, no matter what she thought about them or said behind their backs.

There were many stories circulating about Clarice Blair. Everyone wondered who she was and where she'd come from. It had never made sense that a white woman with a child would come to town and live above Santini's. People hinted that there'd never been any husband. I'd heard mothers talking over coffee: She acted like a lady, but she didn't live like one. Some said she was running away. That she was a tramp. I'd heard women say that they should be careful with someone like that in town.

But as my father sat next to her, playing host, I saw a thin, small woman with an oversized laugh who put Hershey's Kisses in her daughter's lunch and gave me fresh-baked cookies and cold milk when I walked by her rented house. She had eyes like someone asking a judge for mercy. You couldn't help but feel sorry for her and I guess my mother did since she had invited her.

My father could be a very good host, offering people drinks, making sure they had cheese puffs and cucumber sandwiches on their hors d'oeuvre plate. "Clarice, would you like another martini?" he asked. "Clarice, more cheese and crackers?" He passed her a tray. He made small talk with her about the kids and school and those kinds of safe things adults talk about when they don't know what else to talk about. "Oh, yes," I heard him say, "you really can't be too careful these days."

Careful about what? I wondered as I watched Mrs. Blair cross and uncross her legs awkwardly as she tried to maneuver a little hors d'oeuvre plate and a drink. My father was talking to her about his work. About the disasters he'd seen. When the tornado chased him down the road; the river that carried an entire living room set, one piece at a time, downstream. At each disaster she put her hand over her mouth and said, "Oh, and then what happened," over and over, still balancing her martini and plate on her lap.

My father went into great detail with each story as Clarice Blair listened intently, her eyes round as saucers. Then he paused and now he seemed to be watching her carefully, as if he expected her to top-ple over at any minute. From time to time she crossed and uncrossed her legs. Even from the other side of the room I could hear the sound of her silk stockings scraping together, a slick, whooshing sound like hockey skates turning on ice.

Later that night I sat on a chair in front of the mirror in my room. In the other room I heard my parents arguing through the walls. More and more common an occurrence, it seemed. My mother shouted something about how he had talked to that woman all night, telling her his lies.

I wasn't exactly listening as I tried crossing my legs the way she had, knees and shins tight together. First to the left, then to the right. Like a pendulum I moved my legs back and forth. Then I parted my legs and saw how dark it was. How you could hardly see what was inside.

17

Christmas is about the worst time to be in Illinois if you don't like winter. I actually do like winter, but I have a fear of being snow-bound, trapped. A fear that I can't get out. But shortly after Thanks-giving my mother had declared that she didn't have long to live and asked me to come home. "This will be my last Christmas," she said. Of course, it wasn't, but since she hadn't asked me to come from Cal-ifornia in a while and she often came to see me and the kids, I agreed to fly home.

Besides, Nick had been calling me almost every night and I thought this might be a good excuse to see him. I'd found myself wait-ing up for his late-night calls. I imagined him slipping out of bed, tip-toeing down to the kitchen in bare feet to the phone. He whispered into it when I picked up. I loved the way he said my name, with that silibant "s," the way people once said his father's. "Tessie," I'd hear.

Some nights if I couldn't sleep, I'd wrap myself up in an armchair in my Winonah centennial blanket, hoping the phone would ring. Some nights it did; some nights it didn't. When it didn't, I was surprised at how disappointed I felt.

Often our conversations revolved around him, around his marriage to Margaret. How she drank too much and seemed indifferent to everyone except Danielle. How it was hardly a real marriage anymore, though once it had been. But slowly the conversations began to turn to me. He wanted to know more and more about me so I spoke of my marriage, never quite able to pinpoint what had gone wrong. I told him that there seemed to be something that stood between me and the world.

I pondered these conversations as the plane flew. Though it was the holidays, perhaps I'd get a chance to see Nick while I was in town. From the window of the plane I looked down upon those long flat stretches; the green farmland; the wheat from what were probably now cooperative farms blowing in the wind, but that from above still looked like the wheat of the prairie I had always known. Even as I flew above the floodplain in winter, the Mississippi was swollen, its banks flooded, pockets of the river looking more like small lakes. Land laid to waste.

I have seen what water and wind and disaster can do. When I was a girl, I had to get away. I could not bear the open expanses. Everything was flat. I had a feeling even then that anything could happen. There was nothing to stop the water, the wind. It could all be swept away.

For a few days I slept on my mother's hideaway sofa and helped her with things around the apartment. I wanted to call Nick but resisted the urge. He knew where to find me. He knew I was at my mother's and where she lived. But still I found myself thinking about him, wondering if he was shopping for holiday gifts, if he would get something for me.

The first morning my mother and I ate cottage cheese and crackers and she talked about her will and who was getting what. In the last five years or so she always talked about her will and who was getting what, and it hadn't changed all that much. But it made her feel better to go over everything with me again.

As she was discussing her will, I kept waiting for the phone to ring. It did from time to time. Always a friend of hers. That evening I picked up the phone and called Nick. A child answered. It was the first time I'd heard Danielle's voice and she sounded older than her years. I hung up quickly.

My second day there my mother handed me a book of Santa Claus stickers, the kind you put on gifts, and she told me to put one on whatever possessions I wanted when she was gone. My mother sat watching CNN as I wandered through her apartment with my box of stickers. I paused at her silver, a pewter plate I'd always admired, a painting done by someone who was briefly famous in Chicago. I glanced at these objects, but I did not put a sticker on them.

My mother was slowly unencumbering herself of her belongings, she told me, shouting above CNN. "Art's gonna come and take whatever you don't want," she called. Silver trays, porcelain pitchers, antique tables. I could see them all in Art's collectibles shop on Walton. I moved from room to room.

I paused before a photograph on the wall of me and my brothers and my father and Lily. We are standing in front of a tepee and an Indian chief in full feather is doing a little dance. Jeb has a tomahawk in his hand, Art wears a silly grin, always the clown. I'm a bit crumpled, my long stringy hair falling in my face. But we are all smiling, mugging for the camera.

We are dressed like pioneers. Art and Jeb and I have on coonskin caps, my father is in a buckskin jacket, and my mother in a long skirt. I don't remember the trip we took to the Dells, where this picture was taken, except for one night.

We were sitting in a circle of bleachers around a campfire and the

Indians were dancing. I did not know that this was for tourists; I thought it was for me. They were dancing and as they danced they dropped colored sand onto the ground. Blue and red and green, and they made designs on the ground—a lake, an eagle, a cornstalk, the sun.

The music of the drums grew loud and the Indians moved in their moccasins, heads thrown back, and the colored sand was being tossed to the ground. An intricate pattern was emerging and I saw it illuminated by the light of the fire. Perhaps I was tired. I was cold and a chill ran through me. During the dancing, my mother reached for my father's hand. She touched him gently, but he pulled away. In the glistening light of the fire, tears formed in her eyes.

I took out a Santa Claus sticker and put it on this picture. It was the only object in her apartment that I put a sticker on.

18

Every Monday as soon as our father's car disappeared under the railroad trestle, Lily took over the house. She spread out into all the rooms. She slept wherever she wanted. Some nights we'd find her on the couch or on the chaise in front of the TV. Other nights she'd appear in one of our rooms, the cover pulled up to her chin, snoring slightly.

It frightened me to find my mother in my room as if she were a ghost, as if she were already dead, all white with the sheet up to her chin, but then I heard her breathing, and I knew that it was one of those nights when my mother roamed. In her own way it seemed as if she ached for him. Yet she seemed to do better when he wasn't around.

It was as if in his absence she had to fill a void. What was it about water—how it seeks its own level? How it displaces whatever has filled the space within. That's what she would do. Lily would expand, fill up the house. Some wives, when their husbands go away, fold up like a flower when the sun leaves the sky. I was this way with Charlie. But not Lily. She opened. She beamed and expanded. Projects suddenly presented themselves. Came out of the closets, where she'd tucked them. There were quilts to be sewn, family albums to fill. Bulbs she'd been saving suddenly got planted. Letters were written. Books she wanted to read piled up at her bedside.

And then on Thursday she started to pull it all in, put it away, as if the photo album or the quilt or the letters on her desk were some big dark secret, something she had to hide. Back in the closet they'd go. And then she cleaned up the house and did all the chores she'd been avoiding doing before Victor got home.

Then just as suddenly as he'd left, he'd be home—Victor Winterstone, the deli man, cutter of chubs, fine slicer of cheeses, full of stories from the road. No one could layer a corned beef sandwich like he could. He made us his favorite drinks—black cows, 7-Up floats. Then he would pour himself a Cincinnati.

We sat around the table and he'd say, "I want to hear everything. Everything you did all week." He listened to every word. Grades, friends, points we scored, what we lost. He wanted to hear it all. Then we begged him to tell us the things he saw. A house turned around in a tornado so that its front door was now its back. A cat, clawing the water, being carried downstream. Disasters, lives in disarray, those were the stories my father brought with him from his weekly trips on the road.

When our father came home, he was gentle at first. Subdued. He had the weary look of the traveler about him and on that first night he'd sleep a dozen hours. Never mind the chores, the home repairs that had to be done. He looked at Lily as if they'd just been introduced and it was beginning all over again.

Indeed, their children got to witness their parents' courtship begin all over again every Thursday. They locked their door on Thursday night and we could only imagine what might be taking place behind that closed door.

And then by Friday night they would forget they had just met. The shouting started from upstairs and downstairs. He called for his boys, his girl, his best girl, his Button, his Squirrel, his little men, and Lily, oh, Lily, never bothering to walk the flight or two to find us, but shouting for us just the same. His big, amplified voice carried through the house, past closed doors, and headed out toward the lake, out to the prairie, the plains, rattling through the Midwest, his voice like a sonic boom, bursting the limits. "Okay, guys, I'm home," he'd shout, and we'd make a pretend grab for the crystal.

Lily heard, but acted as if she hadn't. Hands over her ears, she walked around complaining of the noise, the disarray our father brought with him when he returned from the road. Soon our father grew subdued. It only took a day or two before Victor Winterstone became an intruder in his own home.

Every Monday like clockwork our father left and every Thursday, though sometimes it stretched itself into Friday, he returned. Those trips with him to the floodplain stopped, but we still begged our father to let us go. Art especially wouldn't let up because Art had never gone. To Art the cow floating on its back, the cars resting in trees were just stories we'd made up, something we lorded over him.

We asked in the summer on our vacations, "Can't we go, Dad?" and he'd say, "Come on, aren't you kids getting a little big for that sort of thing?" We'd kick and punch him in the arm, but the truth was we loved to go to those truck stops and eat pancakes stacked with butter and maple syrup. We loved the motel rooms with the TVs. I longed for "acancy" again.

But the trips dropped away and after a while we grew accustomed in the summer to the melancholy feel on the Monday mornings of our father's departures, the quiet that came over the house when he was gone, and the excitement that grew as the day approached when he came home.

We grew so accustomed to the way he eased himself in and out of our lives that after a while we didn't notice. After a while it seemed as if he hadn't really gone anywhere at all.

But obviously he had. The roof sprang leaks, paint peeled on the walls. He spent what little time he had at home fixing things, but still he seemed to leave earlier each week and come home later. Sometimes he didn't make it home on Thursdays at all. The Thursday night rituals, the platters of deli food, Victor and Lily acting as if they'd just met, none of this seemed to be happening anymore.

Though I can't say that I noticed. I was a busy girl. I was gone all the time to baton twirling and basketball, to student council and school paper. I had so many activities I couldn't think straight. On my wall there was a chart: "Where I Have to Be and When," it was called, and just about every box was filled in.

And Jeb. He was running wild, hanging out at the Idiot's Circle by the train station with the other bums. I'd see him smoking cigarettes, and he'd give me curt little waves. "You're going to get in trouble," I'd yell at him, but what did he care.

Jeb got straight A's. He never cracked a book. "How do you do it?" I'd shout at him in the evenings.

"I just listen and learn," he'd say, mocking me.

Lily walked around, cursing. Shouting at me to go get Jeb and bring him home. She'd say her children were running wild, all except Art, who still cried on Monday morning when our father left. Even though he was older we still had to pry his fingers off the car.

One Friday afternoon when my father returned, Lily gave him the silent treatment. Walking around in a huff, slamming doors. Then she stomped upstairs and he followed her. I heard them fighting in their bedroom. This was becoming a more common occurrence, but still I stopped to listen. Just like Jeb said. Listen and learn. I heard the voices rising.

"Why do you even bother?" Lily shouted. "Why do you even bother coming back here at all?"

"Because this is where I live," he shouted back.

"No, you don't. You're hardly ever here," she yelled at him. "We never see you. You don't really live here at all."

One night I woke to find my mother standing at the foot of my bed. She wore a white gown and at first I thought she was a ghost. She was weeping. It was a silent weeping, but I saw the tears that streaked her face. I closed my eyes and pretended to sleep.

19

Paradise was decorated for Christmas. Dozens of little angels were suspended everywhere. Colored lights were strung from one end of the room to the other. Stockings hung off the draft beer levers. Vicky was sitting at the bar, nursing a bottle of amber. I'd called her the day after Christmas and said I wanted to drive up. Jimmy and the kids were skiing in Wisconsin. She was glad for the company.

She looked a little older, as if she needed a vacation. Even she would admit how strange it was that she worked in a travel agency but never went anywhere. Vicky gave me a big hug as I looked around the place. "Forget it," she said, "he's not here."

Chills ran up and down my arm. I hadn't told her I'd been in touch with Nick. I wondered if somehow she knew. "Who's not here?"

"Oh, you know, Patrick. Seriously, did anything happen the night of the reunion? I'm dying to know."

"Things that slow around here?" I didn't want to talk about Patrick. I had other things I wanted to talk to her about. But I sensed that it was perhaps best not to talk about Nick. That it wasn't the right time to tell anyone, especially not in Winonah. It wasn't that I didn't trust Vicky. I didn't trust the town. It had a way of finding out what you didn't want it to know.

I ordered a rum and Coke and Vicky kept giving me the eye. "Okay," I said, "nothing happened."

"Nothing? You didn't make plans to see one another again?"

"Not at all. He walked me to my car. That was it."

"Oh, brother." She was still laughing when Patrick walked in. He didn't see us at first as he said hello to his bartender, to the cashier. The music was Del Shannon's "Runaway," and he turned it up as he walked by the stereo. He was going over the receipts, humming to himself, when he looked our way. Then he sauntered over in his jeans and flannel shirt. "You must be moving back."

"My mother's been sick," I said. "She asked me to come home for the holidays."

"I'm sorry to hear that." He looked genuinely concerned. He also looked tired and his bad eye started to wander.

"How've you been?"

"Oh, hanging in there." He laughed, slipping into the booth beside me. We chatted for a little while with his arm dangling across the back of my seat. Then he said he'd love to get caught up. "I don't want to intrude on your girls' time. I've got some things to take care of. Come back tomorrow and I'll take you someplace nice." He spoke to me, not to Vicky.

"I've gotta be back at my mom's tomorrow night."

"Well," he patted my arm, "next time then."

"Next time," I said.

When Patrick left, I was suddenly hungry so we ordered a pizza. I wanted a vegetarian but she wanted pepperoni and anchovies so we split the difference and got an anchovy and broccoli, which wasn't very good. "You know, I like that guy," Vicky said after Patrick disappeared somewhere back in the kitchen. "I don't know why, I just do."

"Well, I like him too."

"So how is life really treating you?" Vicky asked over another beer.

"Actually, it's not the easiest time for me. The kids can't seem to leave home and I want to get on with my life. I'm having trouble making ends meet and keep thinking about getting a real estate broker's license. What I really want to do is turn my place into a B-and-B."

"Good tax write-off."

"That's what everyone says, but I can't seem to get the insurance I need. I actually like the idea of people coming to stay. I love where I live. I don't want to have to move. We aren't getting any younger, you know—"

"You're telling me."

Vicky paused, staring at her hands. She turned them to the right and left in front of her. They were beautiful, with long, white, slim fingers, and she could hold them gracefully in front of her like a dancer. She had wanted to model her whole body, but only her hands had had any success. "You know, I used to be able to make real money with these hands. But it's not the same now. Ten years ago I did Pampers. Now I expect I'll be getting calls for Depends. I used to do Flintstone's aspirin. Last week I did Geritol. The producers are getting younger. They call me a 'tweenie,' somewhere between old and young. They look at me and say, 'Can we float her over a table? Can she stay awake for a two A.M. shoot?' In a few years, I'll just be doing the travel agency stuff. I don't mind it, but it's not what I think I was put on the planet to do. You know, we could get into something together. Start our own travel business or something. Specialize in spiritual journeys, some New Age thing that will make us rich. I've been looking to start my own business. You've always got the ideas, Tessie."

I tried to imagine what it would be like to go into business with Vicky and decided it wouldn't be so good. I loved to see her once or twice a year, talk about old times over a glass of wine. But a business was just something I knew I couldn't do. "Well, let's think about it." Resting her hands on the table, Vicky gave me a nod as if to say, sure, we'd think about it. Then she pulled them into her lap.

We had one more beer between us and I was pretty far gone by then. When we asked for our bill, we were told it had been taken care of, and we both started saying how nice that was of Patrick, how he shouldn't have. Then we staggered arm in arm across the parking lot. It was a freezing winter's night and the cold air stung our faces. When I breathed, my nostrils burned. We gazed up at the proliferation of stars. I'd forgotten how clear nights in Winonah can be. "Are you okay?" I asked. "Are you sure you can drive?"

"Oh, I can drive. . . . Can you?"

"If you stick to a straight line, I think I can follow you."

Vicky drove and somehow I stayed behind her on the way back to her house. Snowbanks were piled high along the road. My car slid a few times. I'd never been to her house before, but it was down Hazel, about a half a mile from the lake.

The room she put me in smelled fresh and clean, though the bedspread was some kind of polyester. The sheets were a little scratchy but, thinking how it was the first night I'd slept in Winonah since I'd left for college, I fell asleep as soon as my head hit the pillow.

20

Many nights I woke to the sound of pebbles tossed against my window. I tried to ignore it, but it would go on for a long time. When I opened the blinds, there she was. I didn't know how she got out, how she slipped away from her house. But she did. She motioned for me and I slid down the drainpipe and we huddled on my porch, eating Eskimo Pies and giggling over boys. I liked Patrick and Margaret was starting to hint—as many girls did—that she liked my brother Jeb.

Even I liked Jeb then. He had pale blue eyes, dark black curls, and he played basketball well. I thought Jeb liked her as well because sometimes he'd ask me why I didn't bring Margaret over on Saturdays to hang out.

She started following me home after school during the day. I didn't want her to, but she just seemed to appear on my corner, near my house, and what choice did I have but to ask her in?

Now she was below my window again, tossing pebbles. I slid down the drainpipe and she asked where my mother kept her sewing kit and I told her downstairs in the basement. We went down there and dug around until we found it. Then Margaret plucked a needle from the tomato-shaped pincushion. "Here," she said, "this is what we need."

"What are we going to do with that?"

"We're going to be blood sisters."

I didn't know if I wanted to exchange blood with her, but Margaret told me we should. "We're closer than you think; we're already like sisters, you know." I told her I didn't know. "Anyway, neither of us has a sister; now we'll be sisters for life." I didn't want to. I didn't want the feeling of Margaret sticking something into my flesh. I didn't want her to inflict pain on me.

But she reached for my hand, holding it tight. Slowly she opened my fingers. She massaged one finger, forcing the blood up to the tip as if she'd done this before. I pulled my hand away, but she grabbed it back.

"Don't do it," I said. "It's going to hurt."

"No, it won't. I'll do it very quickly."

"You won't and it *will* hurt."

"If I hurt you, you can stab me with the needle."

"Why would I want to do that?"

"You can do whatever you want."

"I don't want to do anything; I just don't want it to hurt."

"Look, let me see your hand." She unfolded my fingers once again, rubbed my hand with her finger, and then before I could pull away, she sank the needle in. It was quick and just a prick. Then my blood oozed.

"Okay, now you do me."

She opened her hand, which I saw was fraught with many lines jutting this way and that. I glanced at my palm and saw it was cut only by a few lines, clear highways. But hers was like some incomprehensible street map of an old European city, a city with twists and turns and secret alleyways you get lost in if you walk down, and years later when I traveled to some of those cities and saw their maps, I thought how they reminded me of Margaret's hands. "Do it," she said, staring at her finger.

I tried to sink the needle in, but I was surprised at the resistant flesh. I tried again and with a pop the needle sunk. Margaret jumped a little, bit her lip. The feeling of it going in made me cringe.

Then we pressed our fingers together, smeared blood to blood. And our blood became one. "Now we are friends for life," Margaret said, pressing her finger to mine. "From now on," she said, "when you cut yourself, I will bleed."

My stomach felt queasy and I thought I might retch. Out of all the friends I had, I wasn't sure that I wanted to be her friend for life. I didn't want to make this pact with her. I didn't even like her that much, but now she'd done this and I had joined in; she'd made us one.

Then she said she had to get going; she needed to head home. We went upstairs and Margaret walked outside. It was a warm, spring evening and I decided I'd walk her part way, until we came to the trestle. "Well, here we are, the great divide," Margaret said.

I knew what she meant, but I didn't say anything. Then Margaret turned to me as she was leaving. "You know, my father, he's going to come and get me soon. He wrote me just the other day and he was going to send for me in the next few weeks or so. I'm old enough to choose which parent I want to live with and I'd like to get away from my mom."

"She seems like a nice mother," I said, thinking how Clarice Blair seemed to try so hard.

"She drove him away. It was her fault," she said under her breath, as if speaking to herself. I was surprised by the bitterness in her voice.

"Well, it must be hard for her, being alone and all."

"Oh, she's not that alone. Anyway, it won't be that much longer. I'll be gone before summer's through."

I was slightly hurt that she said this. I didn't even want to be blood sisters with her and now I was and she said she was leaving. She must have read my thoughts because she tapped me on the chest. "My blood goes through you and yours goes through me. So even when I do go away, you'll be with me forever. From now on if I cut myself," Margaret said, "you'll bleed."

Shouldn't this be the other way around? I thought to myself. If *you* cut yourself—but no, she said it this way. *If I cut myself,* you'll *bleed.*

Margaret walked toward the trestle. She waved good-bye in long, arching waves. When she disappeared under the dark shadows, I turned and headed home.

21

When I woke in the morning, it was late and Vicky was gone. It took me a while before I could move my head and then the rest of me to get out of bed, so I'm not sure how long I lay there before I got up. Vicky had left me a pot of coffee, fresh-squeezed juice, and a jar of aspirin. She'd also written a note, saying she'd had to head off to work at the travel agency; she'd see me later in the day, and I should make myself at home.

Sitting in her kitchen, I sipped the juice. I ran my hand across her Formica tabletop, her pristine kitchen. A framed photo of her husband and kids was on the countertop, and on the icebox was a magnetic things-to-do pad, but other than that there wasn't the smallest trace of clutter, a crumb anywhere, and it made me sad to think of how I couldn't keep order in my own home, where Jade and Ted left their dishes in the sink, their sweatshirts draped across chairs.

I could envision the unpaid bills that lay tucked between newspapers and mail-order catalogs, the laundry that never quite got folded. The den I'd never gotten around to fixing up. But Vicky had somehow mastered her domestic tasks. Even her dog, Liberty, a big blond mutt she'd picked up at Orphans of the Storm, seemed somehow to eat neatly out of his bowl.

I was famished and made myself a breakfast of bacon and eggs, buttered toast, and more coffee. I ate slowly, looking out the window as I sat at her kitchen table. A blue jay and a few winter sparrows fluttered at the bird feeder. I took my time, savoring every bite of breakfast. It seemed as if this was how I started my day every day. When I was done, I let Liberty lick the yolk off my plate. Then I washed my dishes, the frying pan, cleaned every crumb off the kitchen counter. Next I took a long hot shower, using her lavender soap, her herbal shampoos.

I settled down to read some magazines—they were all lying in a big basket—after breakfast and the dog sat at my feet, staring at me. Every time I made a move, he followed me—upstairs, downstairs, into the bathroom.

I tried to read an article about a toxic-waste site near Crestwood, but the dog kept looking at me, reminding me that here I was back in Winonah with nothing to do. "Do you want to go out, boy, is that it?" Liberty leaped to his feet and began racing back and forth from my chair to the door. I wondered if he'd need a leash or if he'd just follow. I searched for the leash and couldn't find it. The dog was jumping circles in the air so I decided to let him follow me.

It was a freezing-cold morning, as cold as it was hot when I'd first come home last August. The weather of my childhood was a study in contrasts and extremes, and it was perhaps the one thing I'd missed since I had been living in California, the seasonal change. Out there I know it is winter when the fog settles in. Mud, earthquake, drought. Those have become the seasons of my adult years.

I wasn't sure which way I wanted to walk. At first I thought I'd stick to the road and just follow the houses, and Liberty trotted along, tail drooping. The wind was frigid off the lake and I decided I wanted to see Lake Michigan, to see if there were ice floes. I cut down Mulberry and over to the lake where the Indian trails were. The trails were old blazed paths. You could follow them through Winonah, then dip into the ravines and wind up just about anywhere. The spirit of Winonah was said to wander these ravines. The Potawatomi gave Winonah its name. Winonah was a princess ravished four times by a manitou god named Ae-pungishimook and she gave birth to four sons. Through her mating with a god, Winonah acquired fertility and long life. When I told Jade about the spirit of Winonah, she chortled, "So you come from a place named after a date-raped single mother with a lot on her plate."

There wasn't much trace of the Indians—except for the trails that wound their way down to the lake and the trees that they had bent and tied to mark those trails—because the Potawatomi were nomadic and lived in moveable lodges. It was less that they were wiped out than that they seemed to have just moved on, though some of their descendants live on a reservation in the Dells.

The wind was fierce off the lake and already I felt the cold seep into my lips, my cheeks. The dog walked with his head cast down, fighting the freezing wind. As we approached the first ravine, I thought we could get away from the wind if we climbed down into them. I often did this as a child, navigated my way home along the ravines. They wended their way through the town like trenches dug out at a time of war, cut by glaciers during the last Ice Age, and the Potawatomi used them for traveling. Gazing down, the ravine didn't seem that deep and its bottom was covered with snow. Liberty looked at me warily as I slipped down the embankment.

It was steeper than I recalled and I was surprised at how far down I went. The embankment was icy and slick and I lost my footing once or twice on my way down and slid partway on my rear. The dog refused to follow me, standing on the lip of the ravine, howling. He looked small up there, pathetic in his howls, and I had to call to him several times before he'd come. Then he just rested on his paws and slid down.

The bottom was icy with a layer of crusty snow, but at least we were shielded from the wind. In some places the snow had melted and I could see frozen leaves beneath the ice. It hadn't snowed in a while or else the bottom of the ravines would have had thicker snow. I was a little disappointed to be walking on ice, though perhaps it would be easier on my feet.

I hadn't been down in one of the ravines since I was a girl, when I liked to roam them on my way home, sometimes with a friend or two, but mostly alone. The ravines contained all the mysteries of the place to me. I loved the way they turned and wound their way into one another, and there seemed to be a million ways to go when you wandered in them, but no right way, exactly, and no way to get lost. They weren't that deep so you could always climb out, but they were deep enough so nobody could see you when you were inside. In this sense they were the perfect place to hide.

Sometimes in the spring, water ran heavily through them and I'd clomp along in boots, sloshing through mud. Though they have never overflowed, it is dangerous to go into the ravines when there is the rush of melting snow. But during the winter and fall they were dry, except for the piles of wet leaves or snow that collected, and I could make my way along them as if they were canyons.

As a girl, I'd found things down there. Arrowheads, or so I liked to believe of the polished stones I uncovered in the sandy slopes of the ravines beneath the underpasses, and bits of shard, which more likely than not were from broken beer bottles that boys flung down from their cars as they crossed the bridges on Saturday night. I pretended I was a pioneer girl or an Indian scout until I'd hear my father calling me to come home.

It didn't seem to matter which way we went so I let Liberty decide. He turned right and I followed him, taking the turns of the ravines. The air was fresh, but also freezing. My fingers and nose were already numb. Liberty lifted his leg by a pure white bank of snow. A yellow stream like a snake sizzled into the snow, leaving a yellow stain. I had to pee as well. I'd had too much coffee, but I couldn't bring myself to pee there. I kept going, my bladder aching.

I followed their twists and turns until we came to a small bridge with a culvert running under it. There were names graffitied to the walls of the bridge. There was also a condom and a crack vial. I never saw these when I was a girl and was wondering if it was a good idea to be down here when I heard the crunch of my boot on the ice. As soon as I stepped on the thin ice, my boot went through. It hadn't occurred to me that where the water flowed out of the culvert under the bridge, the ice might not hold. Cold water surged around my shoes as I stumbled past the soft spot, and the chill of the icy water seeped into my boots.

Liberty followed quickly behind me and he too stumbled into the shallow pool of freezing water. He yelped and jumped off to the side, licking his paws. Already my wet feet were starting to freeze. The dog whimpered and I decided we should climb out at the next place where the ravine was shallow. We walked on a little ways but in fact the ravine bed seemed to be deepening and I suspected we had turned northeast and were heading back along the lake. I remembered as a girl how this was the deepest part of the ravine, the part where the glaciers came off the lake.

Now the dog began to cry in earnest and my toes were turning numb. I tried to wiggle them in my boots, but they were stiff and aching. I figured I had about half an hour to get them warm before I was in trouble. Hadn't I grown up here? Didn't I know what the freezing cold and wetness could do? I was like a caged animal that had lost its instinct for the wild. I felt foolish and mad as I decided to climb out wherever we were, go to a nearby house, and call Vicky to come and get us.

The embankment was a sheet of ice. Icy and slick. It would be almost impossible for us to climb out. We wandered the ravine a little further until we came to a part where there was a clump of trees. I tried to claw my way up, holding on to the trunks of the saplings, and I got up a little ways before I realized that Liberty couldn't make it. He sat in the depth of the ravines, trying to scramble after me but slipping back down. I called to him, "Come on, boy, come on," two or three times but he just slipped back, howling at the bottom.

Somehow I would have to drag or carry the dog. I wasn't sure how I was going to do this since he must have weighed fifty or sixty pounds, but I knew that's what I had to do. Unless I left him there and went for help. But what if he wandered off and got lost? Or froze to death? I decided not to leave the dog but figure out a way to pull him out.

I slid back down the embankment and walked on a bit farther. Here the ravine evened out and I could see the tops of some houses. I knew we must be near the lake now and I thought I could hear its waves crashing against the icy shore. There were some clumps of trees I could hold on to. Once more I tried to coax the dog up the embankment, but he just sat back on his haunches and whimpered. Now I scooped my right arm beneath him. I would have to hold him in one arm as I pulled myself up the embankment with the other.

With my first step I slid back and the dog tumbled into the hard, crusty snow. I took off my gloves and found I could get a better grip, though my hands were freezing and already the tips of my fingers were turning white. Stuffing my gloves into my pockets, I reached for the dog again.

He was trembling now, shaking from head to toe and looked at me with pleading eyes. "I am so stupid," I told him, "bringing us down here." To think I had taken such a wrong turn, hadn't planned for this eventuality. Had forgotten the rules of this place that I'd known by heart as a girl.

Before my hands froze, I had to get us up that embankment. I looked for an easier place to climb and found one slightly ahead under another little bridge. It was less steep beneath the bridge and also there was some exposed ground. Sandy patches where I could get my footing. I called the dog to me, but he wouldn't come. Then reluctantly he limped over, the pads of his feet half frozen now.

"Come on, boy, give me a hand." Again I scooped him up and felt him trembling in my arms, a soft whimpering coming from his throat. "Not a very tough guy, are you?" I said. I used my free hand to brace me as I clawed my way up, first grabbing a branch, then digging into a patch of exposed earth. The dog started to shake harder, then struggle in my arms, and I almost lost my balance, slipping back down, but I scrambled, digging my heels in, pulling myself with my free hand wherever there was a branch or a sapling trunk.

The top was the most slippery because ice had formed a solid lip there that jutted out slightly and made it difficult to get over. As I felt along the ice, I knew that I would need two hands to get over the top. Bracing myself just below this icy lip, I tried to scoop the dog into both my hands and heave him over the edge. My feet slipped and I couldn't get any leverage.

Now I held him against my knees and shoved him up the side. He cried, then disappeared over the edge. A moment later he came back and peered down at me, a worried look in his eyes. "Stand back," I told him. I got as close as I could to the lip, then reached across it as far as I could and, finally, I hoisted myself over the top.

When we came up, I looked around. I knew I had to get to a house nearby and ask for help. At first I was disoriented, unsure of where the ravines had taken me, but as I looked around, I knew exactly where I was. I was on Laurel, and if I turned right it would take me to the bluffs and down to the lake.

That's where the Schoenfield house was. At the end of this street was where Nick and Margaret lived. Now I knew where I was going. I'd been going there all along.

22

"Let's have a sleepover," *Margaret* said. "Let's camp out in the woods." Some of the gang were hanging out in my playroom. The rec room was an idea of my father's; he built it himself with his own two hands. Grace Cousins, who had bad breath and never stopped talking, was there and so was Maureen Hetherford, whose hair would turn stark white when she divorced her first husband years from now. Vicky sat at the bar, sipping a Coke.

Lori Martin said, "That's a great idea." Lori was already set to organize things. "Let's go home, get sleeping bags. What about food?"

"Camp in the woods?" Grace Cousins, who was always chicken, said. "No way."

But the rest of us liked the idea. The best place to camp, and we

knew it, was the small woodsy area behind my house. The rest of the
Winonah woods were far from houses, but there were still a few acres
behind my house, a small forest that sloped toward the bluffs. In the
middle of it was a small clearing. It was close enough to my house that
we could come back in if we got hungry or cold. Or scared.

Everybody called home, checked with her parents. My father said,
"Whatever makes you happy, Tess." Lily told me to air out the sleeping bags because they'd been lying in a cold basement all winter long.
Grace Cousins didn't bother to check with hers because she wouldn't
be caught dead sleeping out of doors, and Vicky called Samantha
Crawford because she was so nice and everyone liked her. It was a
warm afternoon of early June and we agreed to meet back at my
house at six o'clock.

With my father I went to the store. We bought hot dogs, potato
chips, soda, marshmallows, graham crackers, Hershey bars for
s'mores. My father said he'd help us build a small campfire, but we'd
have to put it out before we went to sleep. I knew how to put out a
fire—you kicked dirt on it; that's what you did. We could roast our
hot dogs and marshmallows over it.

On the way into the woods we collected roasting sticks. I put a
box of matches in my pocket and my father came with us, leading the
way. In the clearing, with a small spade he brought, he dug a ditch.
He'd brought some charcoal and he put it on the bottom. Then we
piled on twigs and leaves. Some of us went and looked for logs. When
my father had the fire going, he was ready to leave. I wanted him to
leave so I could be with my friends. It was embarrassing that he was
here at all. "Is there anything else you girls will need?" he asked and
we told him no, but I saw in his eyes there was something uncertain,
like a little bit of fear. He didn't want to leave us here.

"Well, if there is, just come back to the house. All right, Tess? If
you girls need anything, you come home."

My father wandered off, clomping back the few hundred yards
through the woods. His head was bent as if he was sad and thought

he'd never see me again. Quickly we spread out our sleeping bags, everyone fighting for her space. Samantha wanted to be near Lori, but I wanted to be near Vicky and Lori did too. Nobody wanted to be near Margaret but somehow she wound up with her sleeping bag on one side of me. I made a face at Vicky, who shrugged, then moved her bag to the other side of mine.

With our roasting sticks we sat on logs and roasted hot dogs, marshmallows. We made s'mores with chocolate and graham crackers. We sat until it was dark, eating and telling jokes about boys. Everyone said who they liked and who they thought liked them. Then Lori Martin said, "Let's share secrets!" And Maureen, who always went along with Lori said, "Yes, let's share secrets."

We squealed and said we didn't want to, but Lori said it would be fun and we'd all get closer. We'd be better friends after that. Samantha Crawford told that she had borrowed some of her sister's clothes and worn them without telling her, which hardly seemed like a secret at all, especially since the Crawfords owned the only clothing store in town and Samantha was always loaning everybody her clothes anyway. Then Lori, who we'd always thought of as being the good citizen, told us that she'd stolen money from her mother's drawer and that seemed like a crime and something that should be kept a secret. It didn't seem like something Lori would do and we were quiet for a while, even after she added that later she confessed and paid her mother back.

Vicky said her mother kept this weird rubber disk in her drawer by her bed and Vicky and Ginger Klein got caught playing catch with it one day. Then Ginger told us that her parents made gross noises in their bed and she listened through the wall.

Margaret said she had one, but hers was such a big secret she couldn't tell, not to any of us, that's how big it was. We begged her, we pleaded, but she said no. Her secret was just that big. I didn't have a secret. I'd never had one and as hard as I tried, I couldn't come up with a single real secret. I couldn't even make one up. This bothered me a great deal that night as we sat around the campfire; that I had nothing I'd been holding on to, nothing I couldn't give away.

We were sitting, pondering our secrets or the lack of them, and suddenly Margaret jumped up and whipped off her shirt. "Let's be Indians," she said. "Let's dance around the fire." She began to whirl in a circle, her feet flying off the ground. With her hand over her mouth she whooped like an Indian. Her breasts were tiny buds, but by the light of the fire they bobbed up and down. In her underwear alone she twirled, her hair catching the light of the fire, its blue blackness like dark water reflecting the moon.

Her frenzied feet tapped as she reached for each of us, grabbing us by the hands. "Come on," she said. "Come on!" She pulled Samantha up and Samantha, who was always shy and cried at the slightest thing, whipped off her T-shirt. Her breasts weren't even formed. They were there flat on her chest, but she danced, pulling up Vicky. Then she reached for me. Now we were all whooping, whirling, bare-chested, circling our fading fire, our voices rising in the light of the moon.

I saw it only when I paused, looking at them. A shape or a shadow lurking in the trees. Now moving among them it was white, but barely. A specter moving among us, slipping in and out among the trees. "Look," I said, pointing, "what's that?" I'd heard about the ghost woman, bearer of Indian braves, whose heart was made of flint. She was there in white, darting, watching us from between the trees. We had disturbed her resting spirit with our brazen and disrespectful dance.

Now I saw the spectral form the ghost of Winonah peering at us from among the trees. "Stop," I told them. Their dancing ceased slowly, one at a time, as they paused and gazed where I was pointing. Suddenly hands went up to cover bare chests. They saw it too—the woman in white, watching us as we stood there frozen, naked, and scared.

Scrambling for our shirts, we dressed. We were screaming, shouting. Then we watched in silence for a moment as the apparition moved between the trees. "It's a person in a sheet," Lori said, but the rest of us trembled. Beside me Margaret cried, "I want my daddy; I want my daddy." There was a strange keen to her cry, a howl almost. I had never heard anything like it before.

"Shush," I told her. "Be quiet," I told them all.

I kicked dirt into the fire, putting it out. We hid our faces in our sleeping bags. When we looked up again, we saw that the spirit—whatever it was—was receding, disappearing in the direction of my house. A few days later Jeb would ask me what all that commotion was in the woods and if we'd slept all right.

Now as we lay in our sleeping bags, Margaret sidled up to me. "Tess," she whispered into my ear, "I can't sleep."

I always got stuck, I thought. I always got stuck with her. "Here," I said, unzipping my bag, "crawl in with me."

We zipped our bags together and I felt her long legs wrapping themselves around me, and her thick, unreal hair tumbling across my shoulders like a blanket.

"I want my daddy," she said again, trembling. Then she sobbed and sobbed. It was an otherworldly sob that came from deep inside of her and its desperation startled me. As she cried I realized that her father hadn't come and taken her away like she'd said he would. I stroked her cheek, told her that everything would be all right. Before I knew it, Margaret was asleep. I felt her warm breath on my neck as I peered into the woods, thinking that the specter would reveal itself again.

Step on a crack, you break your mother's back. Step on a dime, you break your mother's spine. It was that same June, just days later as I wandered through the town, playing the game I knew only too well. I avoided the cracks, fearing what would happen if I stepped on them.

I didn't see the storm clouds as I headed toward the tracks. Stop, Tess, I should have told myself. Don't go there. But I did not stop. I kept going, one foot at a time. I followed the street, across the road, under the trestle. I wanted to climb up on the tracks, go to the turn-about, but charcoal clouds gathered above me. The wind rose, dust devils spun at my heels. A storm had suddenly come upon me. The sky turned black as night and I couldn't see the cracks in the pavement anymore.

Lightning crashed overhead and I was frightened. I could run home, but I'd never make it. But if I dashed under the trestle, up the street, there, just ahead, not five minutes away, was Margaret's house. Not the one over the store but the one she moved into not so far from mine. Just under the trestle on the other side of the tracks. I would be safe there, I told myself. I raced the storm past houses with broken-down porches, automobile parts on the front lawns.

Then I reached the door. It was all like a nursery rhyme to me. *Knock, knock. Who's there? It's me. Tess.* Thunder cracked, lightning sliced through the sky.

Slowly Margaret opened the door. The smile on her face turned to a look of surprise. I heard voices, voices behind her, and one was a woman's laugh and the other the big, noisy laugh of a man. He had a big, boisterous voice that took up the whole room. Margaret stepped aside, making room for me to pass, and I walked in, shaking the rain from my hair.

My father was sitting in the living room. He had one arm draped across the sofa, feet resting on the coffee table as if he lived there. Suddenly he jumped to his feet. "Tessie," he said, "you're all wet. Did you get caught in the storm?" He was up, patting my hair. "Clarice wanted help with her insurance," he said, drying me off with his hand. "But I think we're about finished now, aren't we?"

Clarice nodded her head, smiling at me. "Would you like some cookies, Tess? Would you like a dry shirt?"

I was thinking about what day it was. How it was Thursday afternoon. It was early for him to be in Winonah. My father wasn't due home until suppertime. "Come on, Tessie," he said, putting his arm firmly around my shoulder, "I'll drive you home."

In the car my father tapped his fingers nervously on the wheel. He drove north toward the high school, taking the long way around. We drove in silence until he turned to me with his gray eyes and said, "Lis-

ten, no point mentioning this to your mother. You know how she is."
Actually, I didn't know how she was but then he reached across, patting
me on the arm. "Let's just keep it between you and me, okay, pal?"

"Sure, Dad, no problem."

"That's my Squirrel," he said, landing a fake punch on my jaw. As
we drove home, I felt a sour feeling in my stomach, as if I'd eaten
something that had gone bad. But it didn't bother me as much as it
should have because now I had something the other girls had. I had a
secret too.

23

I'm not sure what I looked like with a half-frozen dog in my arms as I
made my way into the small courtyard and rang the bell. I waited, but
no one came. I thought I would freeze on their doorstep when at last I
heard footsteps coming slowly to the door. The door was opened and
a girl stood there.

She was perhaps nine or ten and she looked as glum as any child I'd
ever seen. She had dark circles under her eyes, as she had in the picture Nick had showed me, and her hair was a stringy mess. At first I
thought she was ill or even disabled, but she spoke in a clear, distinct
voice, a little old for her years. "May I help you?"

"Yes, is your mother home?"

The girl hesitated. Then she shook her head. "No, she went to the
store."

"Well, could I use your bathroom and your phone? We've had a
small accident. The dog is very cold and so am I."

The child hesitated again but it didn't seem as if she was afraid to
let a stranger into the house. I felt more as if I was intruding on her,
imposing on her solitude. As if she was busy with something and
didn't want to be disturbed. But what solitude could a child need at
this age? I had no idea, but I asked once again. "I just have to make a

phone call. We've been trapped in the ravines. And if I could use the bathroom . . ."

Looking somewhat annoyed, she flung the door open. "Do you have a towel? So I can wrap the dog?" The girl left and came back with a red and blue beach towel with a giant bear on it. I took off my boots and my feet burned.

"Okay." I turned to the girl. "My name is Tess. I went to school with your parents and I need to use the phone." She looked at me as if I were from Mars and then pointed to a powder room in the hallway and into the kitchen for the phone. "Are you home alone?" She nodded, then disappeared into the back of the house.

I went into the bathroom first, where I thought I'd burst. It was all pink with a powdery smell, fluffy pink towels just for guests. I could barely get my fingers to work as I unzipped my pants. The toilet seat was cold and the hot stream of urine that seemed to go on forever burned my thighs. Then I ran my hands under hot water for a long time.

When I came out, the girl was nowhere to be seen so I made my way into the kitchen for the phone. The kitchen was messy, dishes piled in the sink, but there was lots of counter space. Shiny copper pots that hung overhead looked as if they'd never been used. I didn't have Vicky's work number with me and tried to remember the name of the travel agency she worked for, but couldn't. There were North Shore Yellow Pages tucked under the phone, so I looked under "Travel." Six were listed in the area. I phoned the first one but Vicky didn't work there. I tried another number and she didn't work there either. I was still shivering, my teeth chattering, and I decided to warm up before I tried again.

I walked in my stocking feet into the sunken living room. The house was a sprawling white ranch with lots of windows and wings jutting off. A small Japanese courtyard opened onto the living room. The large picture window of the living room looked over the lake.

The living room was furnished impeccably in whites and grays, but it was oddly devoid of personal possessions. There were no pictures, no mementos, except for one picture of Nick's father, a football he was about to hurl held in his hand, eyes set dead ahead. Except for that picture, the living room looked as if it were about to be photographed for *Architectural Digest*, not a place where people actually lived.

I couldn't help but think how far Margaret had come from that apartment above Santini's Liquor and that she had accomplished exactly what she'd set out to do. It's true I lived in a house by the sea, but it was on a spit of questionable terrain, badly in need of repairs, and I was barely making ends meet as it was. Part of me was filled with envy. And part of me was filled with surprise. I couldn't imagine how Margaret Blair had come this far.

I was standing in her living room in my stocking feet and Vicky's dog lying on a beach towel in the entranceway when Margaret came walking in. She was dressed in black stretch pants, a bulky red sweater, a small parcel in her arms. Her high black leather boots with stiletto heels clicked on the marble. Thick eyeliner rimmed her eyes. She moved stiffly, like a toy soldier, crossing the room. I wondered if she had been drinking.

She saw me before she was entirely in the door and, dropping her parcel, she ran to me. "Tess, my God, what are you doing here? And whose dog is this?" She looked at Liberty, curled up asleep on the beach towel.

"It's a long story. I had a little accident down in the ravines. Got down but I couldn't get up."

"The ravines? I haven't been down there in years." She gave me a look. "You did?" Her daughter stood in the doorway now and gave a little shrug. "It's okay, Danielle," her mother said. "This is an old friend."

"It's Vicky's dog," I said.

"Oh, Vicky's." Margaret took this all in, trying to understand what I was doing with someone else's dog. Suddenly I felt very tired and my head hurt. I was shivering, my teeth chattering.

"I'm staying with her. We took a walk. Look, I need to call Vicky and tell her where I am. Or maybe you could drive me back there."

Margaret took me by the hand, leading me to a chair in her sunken living room. "Tess, you're frozen. Why don't you have something hot? Or better yet, take a hot bath."

A hot bath did sound tempting, but I thought I should get going. "No, really—"

"Look, I'll call Vicky. You take a bath. I'll let her know you're here and she can pick you up after work." That sounded to me like a reasonable plan, not one to put anyone out, so I agreed. Margaret opened a closet and took out a fluffy white towel, a terry-cloth robe. She led me down to the master bedroom, a huge room with a giant, king-size bed and clothes scattered everywhere. "Oh, such a mess," Margaret said, picking up some dirty socks and looking at them as if she had no idea what to do with them. "The maid comes tomorrow."

"Oh, don't worry about it," I said.

"You did the right thing, coming here," she said.

She led me into a large, white-tiled bathroom that was the size of my kitchen. It was complete with Jacuzzi tub, bidet, glass shower, and heat lamp. Margaret started the tub, which I noticed had a ring around it. I thought Margaret might make an attempt to clean it out, but instead she just poured in a green liquid, made a thick bubbly foam. She sprayed the air with eucalyptus. "Here, you just relax. When you come out, I'll have some tea and something for us to eat. Then Vicky can come and get you."

When Margaret left, I slipped out of my robe and stood for a moment in front of her mirror. I wondered how often Margaret had stood in front of this mirror, admiring herself. Her long, lanky legs, her thick black hair. Now I gazed at my small but taut breasts, my firm thighs, my skin.

How many times had Nick stood in this bathroom watching her soak in this tub? Had they bathed together? Did he rub soap all over her body in here? I didn't want to think of this, not really, as I slipped in. The hot water stung my freezing feet. My body sank in, burning. Sweat broke out on my brow. I lay in the water, my eyes closed, and soaked for a long time in the steamy water. It seemed inevitable, somehow, that I was here.

Perhaps half an hour later I wrapped myself in the robe and made my way to the kitchen, where Margaret sat sipping tea. "All right," she said, "it's all set. Nick's on his way home. He's thrilled you're here. I talked to Vicky and you'll both have dinner with us."

"Oh, we don't want to impose. . . ."

She flicked her hair, waved her hand away. "Oh, please, you're not imposing. We want you to stay. Nick's going to pick up some wine and some food."

"Really, I should get going."

But Margaret waved away my protests. "Please just relax. Have dinner with us."

I thought perhaps she'd offer me something to drink, but she didn't. I sat down in my robe, moving an empty coffee cup out of the way. "Your place is beautiful."

"Oh, we've been lucky."

"This doesn't look like luck to me. It looks like hard work."

Margaret nodded, turning away. "Yes, I suppose it is. Nick's done all right, you know, with his father's business."

"Yes, I can see that he has."

"He's been able to do some development. He's got an idea for a resort somewhere. Fiji or something? I'm not sure. Ask him."

"Yes, I will." I was struck by how much I wanted to ask her. Over all these years I'd never really known. I thought to myself I should confront her. What about my father? I wanted to say. I'd always wanted to ask her, but never had. Was it really true and had she always known? Had she known even before we became blood sisters? Had she'd known but hadn't told? Was that her big secret? The one she'd kept from me all these years?

I was gathering up my nerve to ask her when a car pulled into the driveway. There was a screech of brakes that made Margaret wince. The car door slammed and moments later Nick walked in in a blue parka, arms loaded with groceries. He kicked the door open with his foot and a cold breeze swept into the room. "Tessie," he said, putting the groceries down on the counter, sweeping me up into his arms. "Are you all right? You aren't frostbitten anywhere, are you?"

"Yes, I'm fine. It was a stupid accident." He was examining my fingertips, my nose.

"But why did you go into the ravines? You could have been hurt. People have frozen—"

"Can't you see, Nick?" Margaret said flatly. "She's fine."

"Well, thank God for that." He hugged me and I found myself lost in the down of his parka, the tug of his arms, and the smell of chicken. I had to wrench myself away.

"Here," he said to Margaret, pointing to the bags, "I brought some things." When she opened the refrigerator to put the beer and soda away, I saw that it was almost empty. "Are you warm enough now?"

"I had a bath. Really, this is so embarrassing. . . ." I excused myself, slipped away to get dressed, thinking it odd that there seemed to be no food except for what Nick had brought in.

When I got dressed and returned to the kitchen, Vicky was there. She had arrived just as it started to snow. Not terribly big flakes, just a dusting, but it seemed to be coming harder and faster as the wind picked up off the lake. When she walked in the door, Liberty leaped from the corner where he'd been lying all afternoon and practically into her arms. "My God," she said, stomping in, covered in white snow dust. "Tess, what happened to you?"

"Oh, it was a dumb thing. I took a walk. It was cold, I went into the ravines. Then I couldn't get out."

Nick shook his head. "I'm so glad you're all right."

"I thought you were Miss Out-of-Doors," Vicky said.

"I haven't been in ice for a while."

"How about on ice?" Nick asked, holding up the bourbon.

"Sure," Vicky said. "Tess?"

"Why don't you just stay?" Margaret said, all bubbly now. "Why don't we have a good time? Can't we do that, Nicky? Have a good time. Let's make dinner. What did you bring? It's snowing; you may as well stay for a bite. Nick, you'll get them drinks, won't you?"

Nick was unpacking groceries. He put down the precooked chicken, a head of iceberg lettuce, a pound of spaghetti. "Of course. I've got some spaghetti sauce I made the other day."

"I didn't know you were a cook."

"There's lots you don't know about me," he said with a wink. "You'll be surprised. I'll make you a wonderful meal." Margaret disappeared inside the house, then returned, dressed in a blue silk shirt with black velvet stretch pants, gold earrings. Nick poured a good-sized bourbon for each of us. Large tumblers where the ice clinked. Margaret passed them around and we toasted. "To old friends," she said, taking a sip. "Oh, this is nice." She reached over for Nick, gave his arm a squeeze.

He pulled back, gazing around. "Where's Danielle? Where's my little Danielle?"

"Oh." Margaret took another sip. "In her room, somewhere. She's been a grumpy girl all day."

Nick frowned. "Well, don't you think we should ask her to join us?"

"I thought since we hadn't seen one another—the girls, I mean—in so long, it might be nice, just for once—"

"I know," Nick said with a laugh, "to have an adult evening."

"Well, yes, that's what I was thinking."

In the end Danielle came out of her room, looking sullen as she had when I first laid eyes on her. Obediently she helped her mother set the table. "Can I do anything? Can I give you a hand?" I asked.

"Oh, you can come talk to me," Margaret said. "I want to know everything. Let's get caught up."

I followed her into the kitchen while Vicky sat by the fire that Nick had built, legs up, reading a magazine. "It's so good to have you here."

"You seem to have done quite well for yourselves."

"We've done well enough, but not spectacular. Nothing spectacular, you know."

I looked out toward the window in the living room and saw that the snow was coming down hard. "Look at that," I said.

Nick, who had followed us into the kitchen, peered out toward the lake. The wind was howling around the house and a purple darkness fell around us. "Yes, it does look like a storm."

From the living room, Vicky glanced up as well. "What is it with those weathermen? They never get anything right."

"Maybe we should get going. I don't want to get stuck here."

"From the look of it," Nick said, taking a sip of his bourbon, "you already are. We may as well eat. Then see what's happening."

I was anxious and wanted to get going, but they all made me see that the blizzard was coming down from the north now and there wasn't really anywhere to go. But the thought of being trapped didn't appeal to me. I peered out at the blizzard and found myself wanting to be anywhere else but where I was. I longed for my ramshackle house and wondered what had conspired to bring me here. Margaret looked nervously outside. "It is coming down awfully hard." Then suddenly she seemed excited, as if this were a great adventure we were embarking on. "It won't be so bad."

"Really," I said to Margaret and Nick, "I should get going."

In the living room Vicky was peering out through the curtain at the swirling snow. "You can't see a thing," she said.

"But I just can't—"

"It's much too dangerous to go anywhere on a night like this. We have plenty of room," Margaret said. "I won't hear anything of it. You'll both sleep here. It will be fun. Just like when we were girls." She was still drinking bourbon, though I had switched to white wine.

Nick gave me an odd look, as if he was uncomfortable with this arrangement. I shrugged, mouthed, "Sorry." Then I glanced outside again. There was nothing but whiteness. "It's so strange," Margaret said. "We hardly see you for years, Tessie. Now you seem to be around all the time."

"Just twice," I told her. "I don't think I'll be back again in winter."

"But there's always spring and summer," Margaret said with an almost angry voice now. "So perhaps we will see more of you?" Her words slurred a little.

"Perhaps."

"Well, I'd like that," Nick said. Margaret shot a glance his way.

We sat down and ate the roast chicken, salad with Thousand Island dressing from a jar, green beans, and a side dish of spaghetti with meat sauce, all of which Nick had prepared. It was tasty and Nick served a nice California Chardonnay that made me groggy and homesick. Margaret only had a few pieces of lettuce and a chicken wing on her plate. She didn't eat the wing, but she drank glass after glass of wine.

Danielle again made a brief appearance during which her father coaxed her to eat, but she disappeared soon afterward without saying good-bye to either her mother or her father. Nick shook his head as if to apologize. "Funny kid," he said. "She gets moody. She acts weird when people she doesn't know are around." I found her a strange, reclusive child, and seeing the way Nick watched over her made me think that he did as well.

Afterward we cleaned the kitchen and decided to call it a night. "We should get some rest," Nick said. In the unlikely eventuality that the storm stopped, we'd have to dig ourselves out in the morning.

"Oh, let's stay up and play charades or Scrabble," Margaret said. "Who wants to go to bed now?" Margaret began making charade signs—three words, first word, sounds like.

I yawned. "I guess I'm tired from my adventure in the ravines."

Vicky said she wanted to turn in as well, but Margaret put her foot down. "Nobody wants to have any fun. I don't understand it."

"They do want to have fun; they're just tired," Nick offered.

"Well, we could stay up and talk awhile," Vicky said. We agreed to polish off a bottle of wine in the sunken living room, discussing old times. What had happened to whom, what hadn't happened to so-and-so. Margaret wanted to know who was married to whom, who had children, who was divorced. She wanted to know about people who seemed irrelevant to me, people she hardly knew. Margaret appeared to be oddly out of touch, considering she lived in Winonah. Vicky told her about everyone she asked about. With almost every word we said, Margaret tossed her head back and laughed until it became annoying. Even when Vicky told her about someone who had died, she laughed. When she dropped her glass, it occurred to me that she was drunk.

Suddenly Margaret stood up and went to the window again. The light from the room reflected on the whirling snow. "I hate being trapped," Margaret said. She shuddered as if the wind that was blowing outside had come right into the room. "You know, when there's no way out."

"No one likes that," Nick said.

"You don't have to remind me," Margaret said, snapping at him. Then she turned to us. "What was that room in a house called when there's only one exit?" We looked at her, perplexed. "You remember, when you guys went door to door with the Firefighters of America?"

Vicky and I looked at each other, not quite remembering. Then I did. "It's a dead man's room," I said flatly.

"That's right; that's what this reminds me of. A dead man's room. There's no way out." Margaret kept staring out at the snow, still as a statue, as if she could not move. She let the curtain drop. "I'm tired." She covered her mouth as she yawned.

We agreed we were all tired. Margaret offered Vicky an extra bedroom on the floor where they slept and gave me a small guest room off a wing of the main floor. Then we went to bed.

I couldn't sleep that night as the storm settled in. From somewhere in the house I thought I heard shouting. It seemed as if loud voices had woken me, but perhaps it was the wind. I've never been very good at sleeping in unfamiliar places—I wake at the slightest creak of the walls, the sigh of an unknown bed—but now it was especially hard. The guest room was drafty, and no matter how deeply I huddled under the covers I couldn't get warm. Everywhere around me were noises of rattling, branches flailing about. First the wind seemed to come from the north and then from the west. I could hear Lake Michigan pounding the shore, and the force of its arctic gale sent shivers through me.

From time to time I gazed out the window by my bed and saw the blinding white. I thought how in blizzards like this cows freeze standing up. It brought back all the frigid winters of my youth and I knew that when the storm was over, we could be trapped for days.

I'm not sure what time it was when I got up, threw a robe over my shoulders, and made my way through the house. Besides the wind, the house was oddly quiet as I followed the long corridor that led toward the living room and the kitchen. I was suddenly hungry, though I didn't know what I wanted. Sometimes I wake up in the night with these unspecified needs. Hot fudge sundaes, granola, Stolichnaya.

Tiptoeing down the corridor I passed Danielle's bedroom with the door ajar. Peering in, I saw the child asleep. The light from the hallway illuminated her face, which wore a scowl. I wondered what could make a child look that angry. Her room barely seemed like that of a child. There were a few stuffed animals, a unicorn poster on the wall, but other than that the room seemed barren, not the kid's room overflowing with things I was used to.

I made my way to the kitchen, which was dark, the linoleum cold on my bare feet. Outside the wind howled like a crying child and something in it frightened me. Liberty was asleep in his makeshift bed in the corner and he looked up at me with sleepy eyes, yawned, and went back to sleep.

Though I wasn't comfortable snooping around someone else's kitchen, I wanted to eat something. I opened the refrigerator door. There were a few old pieces of orange cheese, two eggs, some milk. Celery stalks. If we were stuck here in the storm, I wondered how we'd survive.

I poked around in the dark, illuminated only by the whiteness of the snow. Outside the moon peeked through. The storm was breaking up. Liberty got up suddenly and pattered across the kitchen floor. "Well, look who's here." Nick laughed as I jumped, pulling my robe, which was too big, tightly around me.

"I got hungry," I said. "I couldn't sleep."

"Let's find something." He was still dressed in his jeans and sweatshirt and looked as if he hadn't been to bed.

Peering into the refrigerator, he shook his head sadly as if its emptiness reminded him of something he preferred to forget. "Why don't we have a drink instead." He began producing tea bags, honey, cinnamon sticks, and a bottle of bourbon. "I'll make toddies."

"Toddies?" I smiled and then I knew that that was what I wanted. Nick boiled the water, prepared the tea, put in the honey, a splash of bourbon, and capped it with a cinnamon stick. Handing me a mug, I warmed my fingers around it. I sniffed and took a sip. "This is good," I told him.

He nodded. "Just what you need on a night like this."

He sat across the Formica table from me, both of us with steaming cups in our hands. Liberty went back to his bed, satisfied that nothing was amiss. "So," Nick said, "isn't it strange? I've been thinking about you all the time, almost willing you back into my life, and here you are."

"Yes," I said, "here I am. It was just an accident really that I wound up here at all."

"Fate," he said, "Though Margaret doesn't seem to think so. She seems to think you came here on purpose and there's something going on between us."

"I thought I heard angry voices."

"She has a temper. So is there?"

"Is there what?"

"Something going on between us?"

I shook my head. "I don't know." The steam warmed my face. "And I don't think this is the time to talk about it."

He stared down into his cup. "You're right. It probably isn't."

I gazed around, changing the subject. "You've done well for yourself."

He made a face as if none of it mattered. "I haven't done much at all, to tell you the truth."

"But you have this. . . ." I waved my hand around the room.

He grinned bitterly. "I have nothing, in fact. I wanted to go to medical school. Do you remember that?"

I shook my head. "Is that why you thought I'd be a nurse?"

"Maybe. I wanted to make something of my life. Now I'm just running these businesses I inherited, living in this house I inherited. I've accomplished nothing."

"That's not how it appears from the outside. It looks as if you've accomplished a great deal."

"Not what I would have liked." Nick paused to listen to the wind. "You know what I remember about you once? You know what you did? We, me and Jeb, were playing ball and you wanted to play. We were maybe twelve or thirteen. We didn't want you to so we decided to play rough with you. We threw the ball hard into your stomach. You caught it and threw it back just as hard. I aimed one at your head. I know it wasn't very nice, but you caught it. Then you came right up to me, right in front of me. You threw the ball on the ground and walked away. It was like you just wanted to prove you could play with us. You wanted to show us. I always thought you were a pretty tough kid."

"It hurt like hell," I said. He gave me an odd look. "Catching those balls you threw. It hurt."

"But you had guts. I admired that. Will you accept my apology?"

I took a sip of my toddy. "I'll think about it."

Except for the wind swirling outside it was quiet in the house. Everything was still inside and raging outside. We sat in silence for a few moments, listening to the storm. Nick reached over and touched my hand. "Now you're here and I don't know what to do."

"Don't do anything," I said. Then I got up. "I'm going back to bed." Nick rose as well and walked toward me as if he were going to put his mug in the sink. Instead, he stopped right in front of me. "Tess," he said, then, "Tessie . . ."

"Go back to bed," I told him.

He hesitated. Then he gave me a pat on the head as if that was what he'd intended in the first place. "You too. Get some sleep." As he walked to his room, he gave me a backward wave. When he was gone, I went into the living room and watched an eerie purplish light spread across the sky.

24

My secret was growing inside me. I was surprised at how big it grew, at how much room it could occupy. Whenever I saw Margaret or thought about her, I thought about the pact I'd made with my father. It seemed as if it could take up all the space that was not filled with history dates or algebra or phone numbers.

When my mother came into my room and opened my shutters in the morning, I thought, There is something I know but I can't tell you. My mother always wanted the truth. "Don't tell stories," she told me once. "Don't tell fibs."

When she kissed me good night and I smelled her minty breath, I thought, There's something I know that you don't know.

It wasn't that I wanted to tell her. It was that not telling her was getting harder and harder. It wasn't anything, of course. It hardly mattered at all. The previous summer my father had stopped to sell insurance to Clarice on a Thursday afternoon before he headed home. It was nothing more than that, and it only mattered to my father and me. It was the thing we had between us now. That was what I told myself.

He'd never mentioned it again. It was never discussed. My father never said, "You know that thing I asked you not to tell . . ." It was as if he had forgotten about it. As if it was nothing to him. But it weighed on me like when you eat too much dough. I kept thinking that if I talked to him about it, he'd tell me it was all right. I could tell her now. I wanted to ask my father about it. About how long I had to keep this secret to myself. But he was hardly around anymore.

He came home on Friday afternoon, left Monday before we were up. When he was back, he was on the roof, fixing shingles, or playing golf. He hardly noticed that his children were running wild. When Jeb was not downstairs, hanging out in the rec room, he was at the Idiot's Circle. The Idiot's Circle was across from Mrs. Larsen's Stationery Store; Winslow Drugs and Faulkner's Hardware were also across the street from it, and those store owners had complained plenty of times about the kids hanging out there in black leather jackets, smoking cigarettes and doing God knows what else.

There were other rumors about my brother that came back to me, things that the gang whispered to me about. Trouble he got into, the fast crowd he hung out with. And talk about Jeb with girls—fast girls, girls who did things with boys behind trees, girls who boys lined up for. Things I didn't want to think about or imagine my brother doing.

My brother leading two lives. On weekends watching our father put drywall up in the basement, and during the week hanging out at the Idiot's Circle. That's where he spent his high school years, with a duck-ass haircut and tight black jeans, a black jacket, sunglasses, while Lily walked around the house moaning, "I don't know what to do. I don't know what's happened to my little boy."

When our father came home on Friday afternoon, she shouted at him, "The boy needs his father. The kids need their parents. Can't you stay home?"

Sometimes I heard her cry into the phone, "It's not about me. I can manage. It's about the children. Do you really have to keep doing whatever it is you're doing?"

Sometimes Lily went after Jeb, made him come home. Or she sent me, but God help me when I rode up on my bicycle. All those boys laughing so loud, hitting Jeb in the back. "Hey, Jebbie, Miss Goody Two-Shoes says you better come home."

That was the nicest shout I'd get. Miss Goody Two-Shoes. Little Miss Apple Polisher. Miss Straight A's. I was a good student, a straight-A student, because I worked. I studied hard. I worked ferociously, madly. Memorizing everything I could.

But Jeb was the one who knew all the answers. Mr. Smarty Pants, I called him. He knew it all in his head. Right up here, he'd say and point to the old bean. He went to school without a notebook or books, just a pencil tucked behind his ear, and he sat in class and just listened. I didn't know this because people told me. I knew it because I saw him, heading out to school; or when I was on hall patrol (which was a perk for honor roll students), I saw him sitting there, no paper or pencil in front of him, just taking in every word.

After school he hung out at the Idiot's Circle with the other bad boys. Jeb hung out there and got straight A's and all the teachers would remember him. Even as Art came up through high school, they'd say, "Oh, you're Jeb Winterstone's kid brother."

Like our father, my brother was hardly home. No matter what, Lily set a place for him. Sometimes after dinner on a summer night I had to go find my brother.

I didn't know quite how this was, but it seemed to me that my secret had something to do with what was happening to Jeb, though I didn't know how. But in my head I practiced saying what I wanted to say. I'd tell my mother while she was standing in the kitchen that I'd gone over to Margaret Blair's one afternoon because of a storm. My mother would understand this. She knew I was afraid of storms, afraid of what the weather might do. She even understood how this came from a deep-seated fear, from our dinner-table talks of tornados and floods. I would tell her that I'd gone to Margaret's because I was afraid of the storm. She would understand that. And I'd found my father there with his feet resting on the coffee table. And he'd asked me not to tell.

In my head, I rehearsed how I'd tell her, what I'd say. But whenever I saw Lily, ladling soup, testing a roast with a fork, the blood rushing into the pan, I couldn't. I'd see her, bent over, poking a chicken, and I'd want to tell her, but I didn't. I'm not a tattletale. I'm someone you can trust.

———

Baton-twirling practice had begun. We met in the mornings just before eight or on Saturdays at the football field. We worked on our figure eights, our hand-to-hands. We marched in formation. In unison we jumped in the air, released our batons, then caught them, still twirling, before they hit the ground.

One Saturday my mother came to pick me up. I was surprised to see her, but she said I needed new clothes and she wanted to take me shopping. We took the highway because it was the most direct way to get to the shopping center at Old Orchard. "Now let's see," Lily said. "What do you need?"

In the car as we drove we made a list. A pleated skirt with matching sweater, a dress for parties. Some corduroys. We went from store to store and she bought me whatever I wanted. Usually I had to decide between two things, but she said, "Just take whatever you want. Take everything."

I'd never seen her spend so much money at one time. I finally said to her, "Mom, it's all right, I don't need all this stuff."

"Who cares what you need? If you want it, it's yours."

When we finished shopping, we carried all our packages to the coffee shop that was in the shopping center. I ordered a hamburger and a chocolate soda. My mother ordered a Coke and a salad. She smoked a cigarette, which I rarely saw her do. She sat staring across at me, blowing smoke, and I thought she wanted me to tell her something. That this was why she'd brought me here and bought me all these clothes. So I would tell her what I knew. I was gathering up the nerve when I said, "Thanks for the clothes."

"I want you to be beautiful, Tessie," she said. "I want you to have everything you deserve." Tears came to her eyes. She fanned her hand in front of her face and said it was from the smoke. Then she crushed out her cigarette and asked for the check. Gathering up our bundles, we headed for the car and drove back the same way we came.

25

Ted believed in vampires. Not the kind you see in late-night movies or on TV, but real vampires. By day they go to school, hold normal jobs. At night they come out and suck your blood. He used to play Dungeons & Dragons. Now it was Vampires of the Masquerade. He told me it was a cult game, but I saw him leaving the house dressed in a red cape. "Why are you doing this?" I asked him and he shook his head.

"Vy not?"

Lily still spits in the air to keep away the evil eye. I do it from time to time myself. But garlic and crosses? Living on human blood? When I returned from Illinois, Ted informed me he was going to live with Sabe, a woman he had met at Vampires of the Masquerade in a role-playing session. Sabe had black fingernails, a thumbtack through her tongue. When she talked she rolled it around in her mouth and sounded like someone who'd just had a stroke.

I didn't say to him what my mother would have said to me: "Okay, it's your life. I did what I could."

I returned home to find my life in disarray, like the pieces of a jig-saw puzzle scattered on the ground. Pieces were missing and what I had didn't fit together anymore. Jade seemed to be avoiding me whenever I was in the house and Shana had left a message saying that business had slowed and she did not think she'd be needing me much over the next month.

When I arrived, Ted was literally moving, a big carton of CDs in his arms. "Honey," I said, "what are you doing?"

"I'm moving, Mom, I'm going to live with Sabe." In my mind I tried to remember who Sabe was. Blond, green eyes, small? Leggy, dark, tall? Nose ring, didn't get up to greet me from the couch? Then it came to me—black fingernails, pierced tongue. I frowned. I had given up having long talks with Ted about his future. About how smart he was and how he should be going back to school, but suddenly I couldn't bear the thought of my son just walking out the door.

"Ted, sit down; tell me about her."

With an impatient look, he put his box down. "She's a nurse practitioner."

Is she a vampire? I wanted to ask. "Oh, she looked so young."

"Naw, she's older than you think. She has a kid. Sonia is three."

"Oh, and the father, is he in the picture?"

Ted laughed as if this were a very funny joke. "He's definitely not in the picture. Anyway, Mom, I gotta go. We'll have you by for dinner in a week or so. I left her number on the fridge."

He gave me a hug. When I checked the phone number, it was for an area code in Oregon. A pile of mail sat on my desk, all of it, I felt certain, bills, and I had no idea how I was going to pay them. Charlie owed me a little money in back support payments and I had some income still from my father's estate. If I called Jeb, he'd send me whatever I needed, but I didn't like to ask. Night after night I poked the papers on my desk and listened to Jade come in and go out, sometimes hollering to me, "Be back later." Sometimes not. If I asked her what was going on, she said, "What will be will be."

One morning I pinned her down. "Jade, I want you to have dinner with me this evening. Can you be home by seven?" Reluctantly she gave me a nod and was out the door.

I was straightening up that morning when the phone rang. "Tess," a voice said, expecting me to know who he was, "How're you doing? Listen, I've got this idea for you. Isn't that house of yours famous for something—the guy who built it? The way he made it out of coastal stones?"

"Yes, it is." It took a moment for me to realize that I was speaking with John Martelli, my insurance agent.

"Well, I've got an idea for you."

Two hours later John Martelli's car with the URCOVERD license plate pulled into the driveway. From my living room I saw John fling his ponytail back, scoop up some files and head toward my house. I greeted him at the door. "Let's walk around it," he said.

In silence we walked around my stone house. John looked at the foundation. He shook his head at the distance between my house and the Pacific Ocean. "Well, it's going to be a tough one," he told me.

"John, what do you have in mind?"

"How famous is this poet, Tessie?"

I led John into my living room and sat him down in front of the complete works of Francis Cantwell Eagger. At the same time John handed me my new insurance policy with a premium I'd have to sell the house in order to pay. "John, I can't—"

He nodded. "I know, I know. That's what I'm here for. What did your father say? No problems, only solutions? Okay, I'm here with a solution."

He gazed around the stone walls, the ocean view. He opened one of the volumes and read the first few lines of "Coastal Views." "So he's a pretty important guy, I guess. Well, it's a long shot, like I said, but why don't you try to get your house on the National Registry of Historic Houses? Then it becomes like a national treasure. It has to be protected. Like I said, it's a long shot, but I'd give it a try." He handed me a brochure with their number, which was in Washington. "I've done a little research for you."

"Thanks, John," I said. "Can I offer you anything?"

"Well," he said slowly, his brown eyes turning dewy. "Maybe you could have dinner with me sometime."

I hadn't expected him to say that. I imagined that John was in his early thirties, closer to Ted's age than mine. "Well, I'm seeing someone right now," I replied, wondering if I really was.

John got up, slightly embarrassed. He flung his ponytail back again. "You know, sometime . . . in the future."

I thanked him for the brochure and his help. Pebble in the head, I told myself. After I heard the screech of his tires, I decided I needed some fresh air. I headed out along the cliffs, then wandered down to the shore, where I found a peach-colored shell I didn't have and a small animal skull, white and polished bone. I stuck these in my pocket. Then I gazed up at my house, which was going to fall down this cliff if I didn't do something about it. Looking at its stone walls, the way it fit so neatly into the hillside, I knew I wanted to stay here. I never wanted to leave.

When I got back up from the beach, I made a pot of coffee and phoned the National Registry of Historic Houses. The woman who answered seemed to be eating a sandwich as we spoke. She told me they'd need photographs, architectural drawings, documented historic information, and an on-site inspection. She also said that the chances were slim that my house would qualify and, off the record, they had hundreds of requests every week from people who wanted their houses taken off the registry so they could remodel. I said I wasn't planning on remodeling and I wanted it registered. The woman said she'd send me an application and wished me luck.

Then I made a veggie casserole and I put it down in front of Jade when she came home, but she looked like a cornered animal with nowhere to go. "I'm a little lonely around here," I told her. "Maybe we could eat together; just tonight."

"Sure, Mom," she said, but she got a look in her face I'd seen many times before. For a time when Jade was little, she went everywhere with a rock. She didn't want dolls or stuffed animals. She just wanted her rock. Charlie and I used to joke to each other that it was because of her name, but actually she didn't know that jade was a stone until she was older. It had to go everywhere with her—beside her in the car, to the dentist, to visit Charlie's family. If anyone tried to take it away from her, she got the look she had on her face now as she sat down to have dinner with me. Like I was going to take something away from her.

"Honey, we've hardly talked. I've scarcely seen you since I got home. You know, I have things I'd like to tell you about. I'm sure you have things as well." She sighed a deep sigh as she picked her way through brown rice and mushrooms. I reached across and touched her hand. "You can talk to me, you really can."

"Can I? I'm not sure." Her voice was barely audible.

"Yes, please, I want you to," wondering if I did want her to and dreading the worst. "You know, darling, I'm on your side. I'm in your camp."

"Which camp is that?" Her eyes got that cold, ironic look they sometimes had. A look I'd seen in her father's eyes as our marriage unraveled. "Summer, boot, or concentration?"

I smiled. "That's funny," I said. "It really is."

"Maybe I could do stand-up," she said in a way that made me think she was seriously pondering this option.

"Honey." I reached across for her hand. "Why don't you tell me what's wrong?"

Her face darkened. "Well, I'm just confused about some things right now. . . ."

"What are you confused about, dear?"

"Well, there's this person I like—"

"Person," I said.

She looked up at me, glaring. "Woman," she said.

"Okay, woman." The word slipped out of my mouth. I wasn't sure what to say. "Person. It's okay. It doesn't matter. I'm sorry," I blurted, "I didn't know."

"Well, now you know. But it's not what you think. Not really. Not quite. I still like men. Or I think I like them, but I'm also just not sure. I'm experimenting."

"Dear, you have to do whatever makes you happy."

"Do you really believe that?"

"I do. I think that's what you have to do."

Jade looked at me, tears coming to her eyes. "Is that what you did? Have you done what makes you happy?"

"I'm not sure," I said. "I've tried. I haven't always succeeded."

I reached up to touch Jade, who moved away from me now, her face shattered. "Don't touch me," she said, sobs rising in her throat. "I'm confused; I don't know what I want." Her fork clanged against her plate.

"Sweetheart, we don't always know——" but she shook my hand away. Jade, I thought, that soft green stone that is so easy and yet so difficult to carve. All those precious things sculpted there. But now I saw her hard, heavy gaze—stubborn and impenetrable. Why did you walk around carrying a rock? I wanted to ask her.

"Mom, I'm sorry, but I've gotta go. I have to figure this out for myself." She got up from the table and walked out, letting the door slam behind her. I listened to it slam and knew that I wanted someone I could talk to. I wanted Nick to be there. I wished I could call and tell him to come and be with me, but I couldn't. Still, I wanted him with me. It hadn't seemed that clear before.

I finished eating the casserole on my plate. Then I picked up the dishes, scraped the remains back into the casserole dish. I cleaned up the kitchen and put everything away.

26

"You must be this tall to ride the Bobs," the painted face of the clown with the outstretched hand read. For a long time we weren't. We'd stand in line and the ticket taker would shake his head, nudging us away, but then suddenly we were. If we stood on tippy toes and stretched our legs, we were just above the thumb of the clown. That was the go-ahead.

In the summers on Friday nights or whenever we could coax one of our parents—some parent who wasn't drinking or too tired from commuting all week or working late or cavorting or had the lawn to mow or the taxes to figure out or the bills to pay or just wasn't too sick and tired of the kids—to drive us to Riverview, we'd go.

Often my father would be the one. He'd be back from his week of traveling, but right away he'd want to leave again. He'd drive us to Riverview, then wait in the car. He never went to movies or to the swim club or into Riverview. He just sat in the car. As I swam with my friends or watched monsters arrive from outerspace or kissed my first boy, I knew that my father was outside, waiting for me.

On the weekends before I turned sixteen and was old enough to drive, my father drove me everywhere. He drove me ice skating, to piano lessons. He drove me to the movies to see a show, to the circus when it was in town. But he never came inside. He never watched me skate or ride a horse. He never came and watched a show or ate pop-corn at my side. Instead my father sat in the car, as if he were casing the joint. He could easily have been taken for an undercover cop, sip-ping his coffee, glancing at a newspaper but not really reading it.

Of course I pleaded with him. We all did, though Art least of all because he knew. He'd learned from all of us. I pleaded, "Daddy, please come and watch me skate." Or "Come see the show." But he never wanted to. He wanted quick departures, easy escapes.

I never saw a lion act or galloped through a field or kissed a boy without the thought that my father was sitting in the car, waiting for me. Even to this day I still have the sense that someone is out there, in a hurry for me to be done.

My father seemed to enjoy driving the gang to Riverview. It was as if he had to keep moving. Even though he'd just gotten home, he wanted to go out again. He seemed to like driving us to a big parking lot, then smoking cigarettes until we were done.

The girls were always grateful. "Thanks, Mr. Winterstone," Mau-reen would say, then Wendy Young, then Ginger, and then Margaret because somehow she always came along. She seemed to know when we were going and called just as we were leaving. If she didn't call, my father would ask, "Aren't you going to ask Margaret?" Even if we had a full car, we could always squeeze one more in.

So we all scrambled into the back of my mother's car, the station wagon that smelled of wet shoes and groceries and cigarettes. On the Bobs, Margaret and I shared a little car. We stared down the mountainous drops. We squeezed each other's hands. Afterward I was sick, thinking I'd retch, but Margaret looked stoically my way, that reckless look in her eyes. "Let's do the Roter," she said.

But I didn't do the Roter. I'd stood above it and watched as the floor dropped away. I'd seen faces arched in terror, arms and legs trying to crawl to a safe place. Others with their faces stretched back like a mask, arms out, crucified to the wall. I didn't do the Roter; I never had, but I pretended I did. "Oh, that Roter. It's nothing to me," I'd say, knowing that if you're chicken, they'd make fun of you. "That's a boring ride."

"I want to do it," Margaret said. "Do it with me."

"Let's do the Jet."

She started walking away. Although the Roter was not so far from the Bobs, Margaret took a weaving, circuitous route, through the arcades, the first of many circuitous routes she would take me on. She didn't turn around, but I was following. For a moment we lost the others, but Margaret, even as she weaved through the arcades—the Johnny Jump Up and the bean toss and the pie in the face—Margaret knew I was right behind her.

The Roter was a big round tub like a mixing bowl with a column up the middle. We went in through a little door. I was at the base of the bowl. We stood along the sides. Mostly boys rode this ride. One or two girls were wearing skirts, and we knew what was going to happen to them.

Even before it started to turn I felt sick. But I couldn't be sick because if I was, I was chicken. Margaret was across from me and I saw her face as they shut the door. It was a funny, laughing face at first, but then it wasn't. It was a different kind of face, a face like "I have to get out of here." But already the Roter was turning. It turned slowly at first, but I could tell it was picking up speed.

My face was pulled back as if someone had stuck tape on my mouth. My hands were pressed along the sides and now we were spinning. The skirts of the two girls near Margaret went up over their heads and their panties were revealed. They kept trying to push them down. One boy laughed, but then I saw him throw up. Vomit sprayed in the air. Everyone moaned and looked away.

Faster now. The bottom was starting to recede. Drop back. Down, down the floor fell away. It was a law of physics happening here, but which law? Centrifugal force, that was it. We were flung against the sides, pinned to the wall, glued, butterflies impaled. I looked across at Margaret. Her eyes were pressed back into her head, her face was plastered into a smile. Her hair slung around her as if she were Medusa, her arms were spread at her sides. And now the Roter spun faster and across from me Margaret was screaming, a loud cry coming out of her, and I saw her start to curl.

She folded first her arms, then her legs into her body, then turned on her side. All curled up, she started to crawl. Like a baby she moved her arms and legs, crawling as if she were trying to escape. "Don't do it, Margaret," I shouted, "stay still," but she was crawling away, heading toward the top of the ride and then, when she realized she couldn't, she just curled back up again, quivering like a baby, stuck to the wall.

She looked so frightened and small and I almost felt sorry for her. Then the ride slowed down. Skirts dropped, hands were released, Margaret straightened up. Her feet came down, her hands uncurled. The bottom came back and we planted our feet. The ride came to a halt and it was done. We staggered through the little door, down the wooden steps, and out to the arcade.

When we were outside, I put my hand on her shoulder. "Are you all right?"

She swatted my hand away. "Of course I am. Why wouldn't I be?"

Then we headed back to the car where my father waited, sitting as we'd left him. "Did you have a good time?" he said.

"We had a blast," we replied; no matter how sick we felt, our stomachs quivering, or how our hearts had stopped a hundred times, we'd say we had a blast, we'd had a wonderful time. Then my father put a hand on my back and another on Margaret's.

Shoving us gently into the car, he took us home. Margaret sat in front between my father and me. Everyone else rode in back. We had just gotten onto the highway when Margaret clutched my father's hand. "I'm going to be sick," she shouted. Quickly my father pulled over to the shoulder, hopped out, and yanked Margaret from the car. He kept his hand on her back as she vomited on the side of the road. Then gave her his handkerchief to wipe her mouth.

The rest of us made faces, grimaces. "Ugh," we said. When they got back in, my father was gentle with her. He made her sit by the window with the air blowing on her face. We dropped the gang off one by one until we came to Margaret's house. Then my father got out and helped Margaret to her front porch.

In the amber light above the doorway, I saw Clarice, dressed in only a housecoat, holding it at the waist. It was a peach-colored housecoat and the light of the porch seemed to shine through it, giving her an otherworldly glow. I assumed that my father was explaining to Clarice what had happened because I saw her put her hand over the little "O" her mouth shaped, the way it had when she'd first sat in our living room as my father related to her stories of disaster. Then Clarice ruffled Margaret's hair and with a pat pointed her into the house.

I thought my father would leave then, but instead he lingered. He said something and they both laughed. Clarice had that deep, gut cackle, the kind that betrayed her class. Or the lack of it. Then she reached out, touching my father's sleeve as if she were picking a thread off. And he paused the way he did when he was about to say something, then forgot what it was.

27

The Department of Coastal Studies is located in a shack just off Otter Point, a few miles below where we live. I'm on the list for wildlife rescue. The next morning after my dinner with Jade, Joe Pescari, who headed Coastal Studies, phoned to say that four young pilot whales had beached themselves five miles down the coast from my house near Gray Shark Cove, and could I help keep them wet until the tide came in. I put on a bathing suit and tossed my wetsuit into the car and drove down to the Gray Shark Cove.

From the ridge above the beach I could see four black whales, their thick bellies heaving on the sand. They breathed in heavy, asthmatic breaths and a crowd of volunteers had gathered around them, tossing water on their backs. I ran down to the beach, put on my wetsuit, and met Joe, who told me to splash as much water as I could on their backs. In two hours the tide would come in and we could ease them back into the water.

The whales lay passive, breathing. They were young and fairly small, but immobile and helpless where they lay. Their eyes were cloudy gray and their breathing sounded like sighs. With a bucket I heaved water on their backs. Slowly the water began to rise around them and by late afternoon we could begin to ease them off the beach. We pushed them. I got under the blubbery belly of one to get it off the sand.

As the tide flowed in, we guided the whales gently through the shallow waters, careful not to let them turn around and beach themselves again. They flopped, rolling from side to side, as if they could not navigate. We swam with the whales until they got their bearings. Often young mother whales, when they are giving birth, are followed up and down these coasts by older females, no longer of calf-bearing age. The old females swim with the young ones. When it is time for the young females to birth, the old ones shove against their the bellies, midwifing the birth. When the calf is born, the older whale will carry it to the surface until it begins to breathe.

Now we were like midwives to these whales. Coaxing them along. Keeping them on the surface, on a straight course. At last they began to breathe. Water spouted from their blowholes. The whales oriented themselves and when we were a few hundred yards from shore, they headed for open seas. We watched as they swam out past the point, and when we were sure they had gone in the right direction, we swam back to shore. From the shore we watched the whales turn north, heading up the coast, where they would beach themselves again—and die—the next morning.

When I got home, there were disturbing messages from Charlie on the phone. He wanted to know what was going on with Ted. Where he'd moved to. And with Jade. "What are these kids doing with their lives?"

I made myself a cup of tea and called him back, picking up where his messages left off.

"I don't know, Charlie. Ted has moved in with some woman I hardly know. Jade doesn't talk to me. It's too bad you don't live closer. Maybe they need their father more."

"Well, it's too bad you moved away."

"It was within the limits of our agreement."

"It's a fucking two-hour drive."

"I wanted to be down here."

"Jesus, Tess, you just wanted to be away. That's all you've ever wanted. I should've taken out a court order to stop you."

We've been in this one fight on and off for about a dozen years. Charlie decided he wanted joint custody after I bought this house. But it's his guilt that's got him. He doesn't come often to see them. When something goes wrong, he blames it on my living two hours south of the Bay Area.

When we were married, after Charlie and I made love, he used to cradle my face in his hands and say, right into my eyes, "I love you, Tess, I really do." Then I'd go to sleep right there in his arms. And I loved him too, or I wanted him. But there was always something I could never quite get past. This thing that had stood in my way.

A few days later Jade sat in the breakfast nook, writing in her diary. She was bent over, intent. A small satchel, like the overnight bags I used to pack for her when she was going off to camp, lay at her feet.

"Where're you going?" I asked as I walked in. She looked up, running a hand through her short, spiky hair.

She told me that that morning a seagull had landed on her windowsill and it had stayed there half the day. It just sat, looking in at her, its fat body pressed to the glass, as if it were beckoning to her, waiting for her to follow.

Jade puts her faith in miracles, omens. Everything is a sign. It's better than vampires, but still, as her father—a master of the understatement—would say, it's not perfect either. She believes that little signs, omens, will tell you which path to take. She leaves clippings on my desk about Ganesha, the Indian god, half elephant, half man, whose stone statues sip milk. About the anti-Christ coming to take the children of Bogotá away. When a tornado scattered Texas Christian University to the four winds, making atheists of several of the faculty, Jade said it should have made believers of them all.

Her friend Sigrid was in a car accident and when the first rescue worker on the scene fell in love with Sigrid, Jade said it was meant to be. She surrounds herself with crystals and amulets. Some of these she makes herself out of feathers she finds, and seed pods, dried flowers, and coffee beans.

Now she told me that all morning she watched the gull until she knew why it had come. When the gull flapped its wings and soared, Jade knew it meant that she was going away.

"Where are you going?" I asked her, thinking that suddenly I would have a house devoid of children, whereas just weeks ago it had been full. It was the oddest thing about being a mother, but I could still feel this child's mouth at my breast, smell the sweet smell of talc and her milky breath. I wanted to suckle them again, even Ted, though he had struggled against me. He had tried to get everything I had. When he didn't get enough, he had fought and turned away. But Jade had always been peaceful, lying there, content with what came her way. Suddenly I wanted to take her into my arms, tell her she could sleep there.

Now she looked at me as if she had never been close, as if she had never been content just falling asleep in my arms. She had that look like "I have no idea who you are."

"Oh, I don't know," she said coolly. "Maybe L.A. or Chicago."

"Chicago? To visit Grandma?" No, she told me, to volunteer for the Night Ministry bus that drove around after hours, offering prayer to the pimps and drug dealers. "I want to join something," she said to me, "I want to belong somewhere."

But you belong here, I wanted to tell her. You belong with me. Instead I said, "Honey, isn't there volunteer work you can do right here? Surely in San Francisco—"

She said she needed a change and she was leaving that night.

"Tonight?"

"Tonight I'm going to stay with a friend. Look, I waited until you got home to tell you. I could have just left you a note on the kitchen counter."

"Yes, that's true."

"It's just a friend, Mom. Don't be so judgmental."

I didn't think I was being judgmental. I thought I was just being a parent. "Honey, you're almost twenty-one. You can do whatever you want, but—"

"But what?"

"I don't want you to go."

Her face relaxed. She put her pen down. "Thanks, Mom. I understand that and I appreciate your saying it."

"And I can still be concerned about you, can't I? I mean, I am your mother."

She nodded, then put her pencil down. "May I say something?"

"Of course you may."

"You know, Mom, you should get in touch with your sadness."

"My sadness?" My hands fiddled with a piece of paper on the table. "What do you mean, my sadness?"

"There's this big dark cloud hanging over your head. I can see it wherever you go. It really holds you back." Gazing up, I pretended to look for my cloud. "I'm not kidding, Mom," Jade said.

"Just let me know where you're going to be so I can reach you."

"Okay, I'll try and do that." She kissed me good-bye. I realized I had no idea where she was going or when I'd see her again, but it seemed as if this was how she needed it to be. Still, I wanted to reach out and grab her, hold her to me. She was still a child in her own way, a floundering child, and, though this was the hardest part to admit, I didn't want her to go.

When she left, I got into the shower, scrubbing my flesh, my hair, my nails, but I couldn't get rid of the smell of dead fish and the sea. It permeated my hair, my hands. It reminded me of the stench in the air when I drove through Winonah on the night of the reunion. After the shower, I made myself a cup of peppermint tea. Jade was gone and an unfamiliar quiet settled over the house.

I wasn't sure what to do with myself so I decided to fill out the forms that had just arrived from the National Registry of Historic Houses. It was a huge packet, requiring all kinds of documentation and description. I began sifting through what needed to be done. I filled in the description of the house, the date it was built (which stretched over some twenty years), its materials, current owner information, and reasons for wanting it on the historic registry.

I spent perhaps an hour or two going over the materials, to which I would have to attach the deed to the house and other notarized documentation. When I was finished, I read over what I'd done. Everything seemed in good order. But then I noticed the address of the house. I hadn't written Box 406, Pacific Coast Highway. I'd written 137 Myrtle Lane—the address of a house I hadn't lived in for a long time.

28

I knew when it was February because the tapping began. The steady *tap, tap, tap.* Coming from the basement. It was always the same sound, like a woodpecker down there. My father lined up all the tools he needed—the hammers, the chisels, the screwdrivers. From my bedroom I could smell the shellac, the glue. The workbench had been dormant all winter, but now the house was alive with the sounds of hammers and saws.

He was building us a finished basement. Art had his Boy Scout troop now and I had the gang. It seemed kids were always tramping in and out. Though my father had stopped fixing things around the house, he got this idea in his head. Our father decided he needed to finish the basement so that we would have a place to play. A linoleum floor, bathroom, paneling, cabinets, even a bar.

As our father was downstairs, hammering away, Lily, hands pressed across her ears, walked around saying, "Oh, God, I can't stand this. I really can't stand this noise." Lily thought the upstairs playroom was good enough, but my father had his project and this occupied him for the better part of the spring.

But my father didn't seem to notice Lily's annoyance with the sawdust and din. He was downstairs, renovating the basement. It was a decision he'd made during the winter as he'd watched the gang stomp through the house in their wet shoes to the upstairs playroom. One day he said, "I'm going to finish the basement. Then the kids can play there." He drew up some preliminary plans, ordered some supplies. I have no idea how my father knew how to do this, but he did. Some afternoons he let me help him. He showed me how to hold a hammer, how to drive a nail. Straight on, keep your fingers away, hit the head, not your thumb. I held the paneling in place as he nailed it to the wall.

The new basement was to have a laundry room, a recreation room with a Ping-Pong table, a bar, and a TV room. There would be a bathroom off the laundry room. It was a fairly elaborate project, but my father hired no help. It seemed he could do this on his own. Some days he got Jeb and Art to pitch in. "Okay, now, Squirt, hold that board in place."

Art would put his shoulder against the board while our father hammered it in place. Often Lily came downstairs with grilled cheese sandwiches, potato chips, Cokes. She'd comment on our progress.

"Oh, that's going to be very nice." Or "I like the way there'll be storage cabinets in the rec room."

Then she'd go back upstairs. I'm not sure when I noticed, but my parents didn't seem to speak to each other during these brief visits she made into the construction area. My mother moved like a marionette when she came downstairs, as if someone else were pulling the strings.

One afternoon in the summer Margaret asked me over to play. She said Vicky and some of the gang would be over and did I want to come as well? I rode my bike, parked it on her lawn. I noticed that the porch looked painted and spruced up. Clarice Blair must be doing better in the world, I thought. When I walked in, something was different. "You've changed things around here," I said.

Margaret and the gang sat in the living room, eating chips and plates full of M&Ms. The Little Rascals were on. "Oh, just a few touches," Mrs. Blair said. She came around the corner with a plate of cookies that made my mouth water. The living room looked freshly painted and the small den off the living room seemed darker. It had nice wood paneling too.

"Our basement is paneled like this," I said.

And Clarice Blair, putting down the plate, smiled at me. "Yes. I've heard it is."

29

Traffic was heavy on 280 as I drove into the city through patchy fog. I didn't like this kind of weather or this kind of driving. It slowed me down, made me stop and start, think too much. And it was stop and start all the way to Chinatown. Nick had phoned and said he was coming West. He wanted to meet at Fisherman's Wharf again, but I balked. I told him to meet me at my favorite dim sum place.

He was sitting in a booth in the back, wearing a blue workshirt and jeans. He looked disheveled, his hair not quite combed, like someone who's had a bad night. He rose when he saw me, wrapped his arms around me, buried his face in my hair. "I'm so glad to see you," he muttered against my neck.

He smelled of aftershave and a smoky smell that was all his own. "I'm glad to see you too."

He had never had dim sum before so as the trays came by, I began to point at things I thought he might like. Soon our table was filled with shrimp dumplings, rice noodles, spring rolls, mushrooms with pork. Nick ate heaping portions. "This is so good. Can I have more?"

"Just point at what you want."

He pointed at me. "That easy, huh?"

I gave him a scolding look. "Not quite."

"You know how to show a guy a good time."

"Well, I'm glad you think so."

"I do." I sat back, watching him enjoy the dumplings and noddles. "Things haven't been going very well," he said softly.

"I'm sorry. I'm sorry to hear that."

"I've had a terrible time," he said. "My father was right about her."

"Your father?"

"He begged me not to marry her. He said she wasn't 'our kind.' I hated it when he said that. And sometimes I think I hated him. He was so big, so powerful. Everybody knew him. He was famous. I wanted to stand up to him. I think I wanted to do something he didn't want me to do. He was a hard man to stand up to, you know."

"I'm sure he was."

"I made a big mistake when I married her. I was infatuated. I thought she was beautiful. She was a free spirit. And perhaps I knew that it would gall my father. That he wouldn't be able to stand the fact that I'd married a girl of unknown origins whose mother had been our tenant. I don't know what I was thinking . . ."

"We've all made our mistakes." I put my hand across his. "God knows, I've made mine."

"You know," Nick said, "sometimes even now, and he's been dead awhile, I can hear my father say, 'Oh, you missed that easy shot,' or 'There was a hole in the center; you should've run for that.' Do you know what it was it was like all my life to hear my mistakes rattled back at me? It's as if he's still shouting from the sidelines and I'm never sure which way he wants me to go."

"Which way do *you* want to go?" I asked him.

Nick put his hands under my chin, lifting my face toward him. "Ever since we were kids, I've wanted to kiss you."

"You have? Well, maybe that's another mistake," I quipped. Even though it seemed inevitable, I wasn't comfortable with this turn in the conversation. "Anyway, if you've waited this long, you may as well wait a little longer." He gave me a hurt look. "I think we should wait . . . until things are resolved. Settled between the two of you." I was trying to be logical, but the fact was I wanted to kiss him. I hadn't wanted to kiss anybody in a long time, but now I did.

I knew I had to get out of there or I never would. "Look," I told him, "I'd love to see you. When you break up with Margaret, when you really leave her, why don't you give me a call?"

"I'm not going to be married much longer," he said thoughtfully, "and you don't have to live here."

"No," I said, "I don't, but for now I do. And this is my home. My children are here and I don't want to be responsible for breaking up someone else's family."

"You are not responsible," he said with a little laugh. "I absolve you."

We left the restaurant and as we walked down Grant toward Union Square, where I'd left my car, he kissed me. Not a gentle, tentative first kiss, but a hard one, his mouth pressed firmly against mine. I felt the strength of his arms, his tongue moving between my teeth. He kept his arms around me as we wandered back to his hotel. "Come up to my room. Have a drink with me."

In his hotel room, he poured two scotches from the minibar. He put on the radio to the best jazz station in San Francisco. Stretching out on the bed, he listened to the soft horn. I sat across the room until

he said, "Why don't you come and sit here." Then I walked over and he pulled me against his chest.

I wanted to nestle there, to feel safe, but then I felt his mouth hot against my mouth, his tongue working its way between my lips. I was conscious of every moment, each gesture, and at the same time I was swept up in it. For all his bulk, he was gentle as he unbuttoned my blouse, slipped his hands on my breasts. Finally I found myself pulling away. "You know," I said, "I'm really not going to do this."

He sat up, his face flushed. "But what harm would it do?"

I didn't want to leave, but I knew I had to. "I've got to go," I said. "You're still living with her. It's not right."

"Tessie, please . . ."

"It's not just about her; it's about me. I'm already finding myself thinking about you. Wanting you. This isn't what I should be doing. Not now. Not yet. When you leave her, give me a call." Nick lay back, arms folded behind his head. He closed his eyes as if he were going to sleep as I opened the door.

I drove fast along the highway, taking turns faster than I should have. At any moment I could careen off the cliffs or have a head-on, but I still drove fast. I don't know what the rush was. I returned to an empty house. There was no message or note from Jade. There were several messages on the phone machine, including one from Charlie's lawyer, informing me that his client was ending his child support since neither child was in school. This didn't surprise me, but still it was another blow. But my thoughts were far from support payments and bills and how I was going to make ends meet. And then, there were several hang-ups, some of which lasted a long time.

When the phone rang, I was sure it was Nick and I rushed to answer it. "Hello," I said, "who's there?" but no one was. Wondering if it was another crossed wire, I listened for a long time to the breathing at the other end, as if somehow I would be able to recognize it.

In the morning I was awakened by the ringing again and once more no one was there. But this time the person was slower to hang up and I heard the breathing more clearly. "Who is this?" I asked insistently this time. "Is anybody there?"

And then I heard her speak. "Tess, it's me, Margaret. I need to talk to you about Nick."

"What about him?" I asked her.

"It's just that I know he's in San Francisco, but I haven't been able to reach him. He's not staying at the hotel where he said he'd be. Danielle is worried and so am I. I thought he might contact you. Do you know where he might be staying?"

"No, I don't. I haven't seen him." I wasn't sure why I felt the need to lie to her, but I did. Even as I lied, I wondered what Nick had said. Did she know if he'd seen me?

"Well, he was depressed when he left and I'm worried about him."

"He was depressed? Well, I'm sure he's all right."

There was a long pause. "Yes, he probably is. But if you hear from him, would you have him give me a call?"

Later when I phoned Nick at his hotel, he said she knew where he was. He'd spoken to her that afternoon. "She's just trying to trick you," he said.

"But why would she do that? Does she know anything?"

"It doesn't matter," he said. "It's just the way she is."

30

In eighth grade Margaret began to dress like me. It was fall, a bright September day. The first day of school. In just a few weeks Kennedy would be elected president and his Thousand Days would begin. The Cuban missile crisis would follow and Vicky and I would sit, spellbound, clasping hands in my finished basement, listening as the handsome young president told us we might be going to war. Soon I would know that there was a world that was not of my making. That the safety of our homes, the quiet little niches our parents had created, were just that—small corners tucked away from the real world.

But for the moment what mattered most was that I had my books in a bag and a new outfit. A red cardigan, a blue-and-red-plaid pleated skirt. A white shirt with a Peter Pan collar. New saddle shoes. I loved the first day of school. Number 2 pencils, sharpened to a fine point. Pads of paper, erasers, the sound of cracking book spines.

The halls smelled freshly painted, the floor slick and newly polished. Everything about the school and its smells and my new outfit was filled with promise. The gang gathered in the hall. Ginger was lamenting the fact that she got Mr. Green's homeroom and that Lori Martin, Maureen Hetherford, and I were all in Miss Olden's, who was known to be easy. Samantha told Ginger not to worry because she was in Mr. Mitchell's and there wasn't anybody she liked in that homeroom.

We were looking at our class lists, peering into our new books, when I saw Margaret. She too wore a red cardigan, a blue and red pleated skirt. A Peter Pan collar. I put my hand to my mouth, but Margaret smiled at me. I had planned for weeks to wear just what I was wearing. Now Margaret stood in front of me wearing the same thing.

"It's not possible," I shrieked.

Margaret laughed. "I can read your mind, Tess. I can read your mind."

Our teacher, Mrs. Chilford, gave us an assignment: Describe the person you'd most like to be. I wrote about Jackie Kennedy because I wanted to be married to the president and live in the White House. Vicky did Jane Addams and the rest of the girls did Eleanor Roosevelt, though a few did their mothers, not thinking it meant they'd be married to their fathers. A few days after the assignment, Mrs. Chilford stopped me in the hall. "What a nice tribute to you from Margaret, Tessie!"

"What's that, Mrs. Chilford?" I asked.

"Oh, don't you know? For some reason I thought you would.

Margaret said that out of all the people in the world, living or dead, she'd like to be you."

Samantha Crawford invited us to a party in her basement. There'd be Cokes and boys. It was one of our first parties like this, but now that we were thirteen, it would happen more and more. Samantha Crawford had some records. Bill Haley and the Comets, Del Shannon, Frankie Avalon. Motown was just getting going and one of the boys had brought a new record by the Miracles. Then the lights went dim and Johnny Mathis came on. "Funny you're a stranger who's come here; come from another town."

We chose partners and we were dancing. But there weren't enough boys to go around. The girls who were left began pairing up. "So dance with me," Margaret said.

"I will not."

"Dance with me."

She pulled me to her, swept me into her arms. I felt her breath against my ear, her hand on my back as we moved slowly through Samantha Crawford's basement. She pressed her hips into mine. In my ear she sang along, "I'm a stranger myself, dear, small world isn't it. . . ." I was relieved when Chubby Checker came on and we could do the twist.

A few days later we were sitting in Mr. Whitcomb's class. He taught math and was very strict. You had to sit straight in your chair. You had to have your paper and pencil neatly on the top of your desk. You could never be excused. No matter what.

Margaret raised her hand. She had to go to the bathroom. Mr. Whitcomb said he was sorry, but there would be no bathroom privileges. No one was allowed to go before the bell. "But Mr. Whitcomb," Margaret said, her voice pleading, "I really need to go."

"You'll have to wait like a big girl."

Margaret sat there staring straight ahead at him. As Mr. Whitcomb went on at the board about multiplication of fractions, she sat even as the mumbling began and someone pointed. "Look," I heard a voice behind me say. We turned and stared. A small puddle of blood like a crime scene had formed at the base of Margaret's desk. Blood ran down her legs, pooled on the floor. Even as Mr. Whitcomb, a shocked, flushed look to his face, told her she could now be excused, she just sat there, not moving, staring straight ahead.

Of course they wanted her. All the boys. How they wanted her. It didn't matter who they were or what side of the tracks they came from. They whistled when she walked by, they called to her. They touched that long black hair. They dreamed of touching her milky white skin. And the breasts. They didn't dare dream of those, but they did.

When she walked by, there was the smell of lilacs and cigarettes, of something moist and sweaty. They sang after her, "There she was justa walking down the street . . ."

We watched them want her. We watched and pretended we didn't see what it was all about. She was just the new girl, wasn't she? Even though she'd already been living in our midst for four years. She would never make it here. She'd never fit in.

I pretended not to notice the smooth curve of her hips, the shape of her arms. The way she walked, dressed like me. How was it that she was always dressed like me? And then in the summers stripped down, in two-pieces in the backyard. Margaret always called to see who was coming over. Who'd be there. One day we were all sun-bathing in the backyard, all of us in our two-pieces, Cokes in our hands, and when I went inside for a pitcher of something, Jeb came up to me and said, "Squirrel, which one is that one?"

He pointed out back and I squinted in the sun to see. I couldn't quite follow his finger as it pressed itself against the glass. "Who?"

"That one. I've never seen her before."

"Yes, you have. You know who that is."

But my brother looked at me dumbfounded and then I saw a look

I'd never seen in his face before, one I couldn't quite place, but I said to him more gently now, "You've seen her a million times. That's just Margaret. That's Margaret Blair."

One day on my way to tell my brother to come home from the Idiot's Circle, I ran into Margaret. "I have to tell my brother to come home."

Margaret laughed. "Oh, I'll come with you. Let me tag along."

It was summer and we were in shorts. I was wearing powder-blue shorts and Margaret wore black and pink stripes that showed off her long, bronzed legs, her black hair pulled back. We were thirteen years old. Jeb was fifteen. As I approached, all the boys in leather started hooting, calling out names. I said to Jeb, "Mom says you have to come home." I didn't have to describe for him Lily at home, tearing out her hair, slamming doors, muttering to herself about her kids running wild, her kids having gotten away from her.

He gave us a wink. "Sure, Tess," he said, docile as a lamb, "I'll come home." With a great flourish like I once saw Gene Kelly do before he was about to dance, Jeb took Margaret by the arm. "I'll come if you'll come too."

We all went home and down into the rec room, where Jeb put on a Sam Cooke record. I stood against the bar, clapping, tapping out a beat, watching Jeb and Margaret. They danced close during the slow dances. Only when the music was fast would they dance with me.

31

Nick wanted to see where I lived. He called to say he had some time. A meeting he'd been waiting for had been postponed and he could drive down. "I don't think it's a good idea," I said.

"I want to see the objects you have around you."

"Well, it's mostly feathers and shells. Stuff I find on the beach."

"Well, then, I want to see that. The beach, those vistas you told me about," he said. "Tessie, I want to see you." For some reason I imagined he would come out here and we'd still be friends. But there was something inevitable about all this. I couldn't stop it anymore than the driver of a runaway truck on a downhill grade could. We seemed to have been heading here for a long while. I knew it even as I told him, "Yes, I want to see you too."

I planned to have everything ready—table set, house cleaned—before I had to do my volunteer work at the aquarium. I was just finishing cleaning up the kitchen when there was a knock at the door. I was afraid it might be John Martelli. He had taken to stopping by. Once or twice he'd even dropped in. From time to time I thought I'd seen his car driving past my house.

I opened the door hesitantly, and instead I found Bruno Mercedes standing there. He'd come over to interview me about the house and to ask questions once or twice. But this was the first time he'd stopped by uninvited. He stood there, rocking on his heels in his navy slacks and tweed jacket. He had on glasses, which I didn't remember him wearing before. "Mrs. Winterstone . . ."

I gave him a little glare.

"Tess, I was wondering if we could talk."

"I'd love to talk, Bruno. But it's not such a good time." He stood there, looking so sad, almost begging. "Why don't you come in?"

He breathed a sigh of relief as I led him into the kitchen, where I poured both of us a cup of coffee. He took his light and sweet. "Lots of milk and sugar," he said.

I sat down across from him and we both gazed out the breakfast nook window through the grove of pines, the cliffs, to where the earth dropped away. "I've written something," he said. "I was going to mail it to you, but I decided to bring it myself."

He pushed across the table the envelope he carried, and the moisture of his fingers left an imprint. Slowly I opened it. It was a tattered manila envelope with coffee stains and assorted other stains on it, unspeakable things, I imagined. There was a neat title page and perhaps another thirty pages. The title page read: *Water and Rage: The Dark Vision of a Metaphysical Poet—Francis Cantwell Eagger*.

Bruno looked across at me, his eyes filled with anticipation. I turned to the next page, where I saw "This dissertation is for TW, who let me inside" and then the epigraph, which was a quote I remembered from one of the Eagger poems, "Dark winds batter all that I know. A tree crashes down the dunes, leaving a hole with which to view the sky."

"Bruno, is this for me?"

"Just read the preface," he said, his eyes never leaving my face. I felt awkward, as if something was expected of me that I did not have to give. Opening the manuscript, I read,

> *For many years I have tried to penetrate the dark vision of Francis Cantwell Eagger. I have tried to understand his work from what I could piece together of his life. Eagger left no journals, no unfinished poems, and only a few letters, several of which were exchanged with my father.*
>
> *The focal point of his work seemed to be the house where he lived, the one he built with his own two hands. After many months of waiting I was finally granted access to that house and it was only once I was inside that I felt I had found the way into the poet's spirit. Poetry does not arise from nowhere. We all know that the writer draws from what he or she knows. In building those dark, narrow walls of stone, Francis Cantwell Eagger perfected the dark poetic vision for which he is known.*

I turned the page, but that was all he had written. The rest was a bibliography and a list of poems. "Well, it is a very good start, Bruno. Very exciting for you."

"It's as far as I've gotten, but I found this fragment of a poem in a letter. It's a big discovery. I think it's from 'Desire Paths,' a poem he worked on for a long time, but it was never published and is believed lost." Bruno held the page in his hand, his fingers shaking. " 'Along the wind-racked bluffs/we have made our way/to the edge and back again/so many times/That we have made a path, worn down weeds and shrubs.' That's all that was in the letter."

"Well, you've got a good start. I think you should keep going."

"I want to," he said, "I really do, but I just need more. . . ."

I looked at his boyish face, his sandy hair that was already starting to thin, his tweed jacket. I wondered what my life would have been if I'd met a boy like this when I was a girl. "Is there something you want?"

He sat still, gazing off to the rooms of my house. "I was thinking you should turn this place into a museum."

I paused, wondering if I should say what I planned to say next. "Actually, I was thinking of turning it into a bed-and-breakfast."

His eyes widened in disbelief. His face turned pale.

"I need some income. Quite frankly, I'm broke and my alimony and support payments are running out. My plan is to turn the kids' rooms into guest rooms. It will give me a good tax break and provide a little income."

He looked at me, almost angry now. "You aren't serious, are you?"

"I'm very serious."

"The man who lived here was a holy man, almost a saint. . . ."

"Who drank himself to death and whose own son couldn't wait to get rid of this place because it reminded him of his terrible childhood."

"He drank to fill the void."

"We all have a void to fill."

Just then the back door opened and Jade walked in. Or dragged herself in. It had been days since I'd seen her and she looked dejected, miserable. As she ran her fingers through her cropped, purple-streaked hair, my arms ached to take her in. "Jade, darling," I said, my voice trembling, "how are you?"

"I'm okay," she said, though she didn't look or sound okay. She gave me a wave, Bruno a nod, went to the fridge, got out a Diet Coke, and flipped it open. "This is Bruno Mercedes," I said. "He's writing his doctoral dissertation on Francis Eagger."

Leaning on the wooden counter, Jade took a sip of her Coke. "Really?" She looked at him closely. "You used to stand in front of our house."

Bruno blushed a little, gazing down. "Yes, I've been working on his poems for a long time now. But I've just begun—"

" 'Where the sea falls, I fall. Where it rises, I rise . . . ' " my daughter said, looking out the window.

Bruno kept his gaze on her. " 'It is the place I come back to, the one I cannot leave, nor can I dwell in another land. . . . ' "

She looked up at him now, smiling. I hadn't seen a smile on my daughter's face in weeks, maybe months. " 'Coastal Views,' " she said. "That's my favorite poem."

"One of mine too," Bruno said. "It's about finding God."

"Oh." Jade gave him a funny look. "I didn't see it that way. I thought it was about love. But that makes sense. Well." She hit her hand on the Formica counter. "I've got a job." She gave me a look. "Back at the fish and chips. It was nice meeting you."

"It was nice meeting you too." Bruno got up and extended his hand. Jade looked at it as if she didn't know what she was supposed to do. Then she shook it and headed toward her room.

Bruno watched her leave. "Interesting girl."

"Yes, you could say that."

As I walked Bruno to the door, he said to me, "This is what I'd like to ask you. I'd like to come back here every now and then. I'd like to think in this house."

"Of course, Bruno," I told him. "Come back whenever you like."

That afternoon I sat at the edge of the tidal pool at the aquarium, where I volunteer from time to time. I was showing a starfish to a group of schoolchildren from Santa Cruz. They squealed as the starfish writhed, its tentacles sucking against their hands.

32

I wasn't sure whose car it was or where she got it, but in the spring of our junior year, Margaret showed up at my house in a red convertible with a stereo radio. I had no car. Or rather I had no use of a car. My father had taken that privilege away the week after I got my license. I had managed to have two minor accidents in a very short time span, including backing out of the garage into the car of a friend of my father's who'd stopped by to ask my father if he wanted to hit some balls. I knew that the car was there. I mean, I saw it as I backed out, but for some reason I drove smack into its front fender. My father apologized profusely to his friend, paid for the Prairie Vista Automotive job, and told me I could drive when I could see. He also made it clear to me that he did not anticipate this being in the near future.

The unspoken agreement between me and the gang was that on spring nights when the weather was warm and our homework was more or less done we'd show up at the bottom of Lake Road on the beach where the bonfire pit was. I could have walked. It wasn't that far and I knew how to slide down the drainpipe and how to sneak back in through the screened-in porch, which was never locked. But it just wasn't considered cool to walk. I may as well have come on a bicycle. You had to come in a car, preferably your own. But if not, anyone's would do.

One night I was hoping that Patrick would show or maybe Vicky or Samantha Crawford or the Dworkin twins. Anybody who had their license and wheels. I was good as grounded without permission to drive and I had no idea when it would be granted. Miserable in my room, I went down to watch the stop sign on our corner for headlights. I told myself five cars and it would be for me. I got pretty good at seeing even the faintest glimmer of light in the stop sign and then I'd start my count. Sometimes there'd be a burst of them. Other times they would be few and far between. I could sit there in the dining room, looking down the driveway, and nobody knew what I was doing there. Nobody noticed, really.

One night nobody came for a long time and so I gave myself a few extra turns and then Margaret drove up. She had this neat red convertible with the hood down and her long black hair flapping in the breeze. I couldn't believe it when she drove up. I didn't particularly want to go with her, but on the other hand I wanted to get out of there. I dashed out the front door.

It was a warm spring night when the air felt fresh and green and everything was about ready to burst with buds and flowers. As I ran into the driveway, Margaret was waving at me. "Let's go," she said.

"Where'd you get this car?" I touched its shiny chrome, its red paint. The white leather inside smelled new. "Nice," I muttered, leaping in over the door without opening it.

"Oh, my dad," she said as she backed up quietly, then gunned it at the corner. "He promised me one when I got my license." She turned on the radio to a Beatles medley. They were very popular then and we turned it up high and sang, "I wanta hold your hand" and "Close your eyes and I'll kiss you." As we cruised toward the beach, Dion came on with "Runaway" and we shouted at the top of our lungs as we drove.

"Boy," I said, "you are so lucky." I thought about the family station wagon that sat idle in our garage. Even when my father gave me his permission, I'd never drive it again. I'd probably had those accidents because it was such a big lug of a car. "Your dad really gave you this?"

"Yes," she said with a strong voice of indignation. "He drove right down from Wisconsin and handed me the keys. Boy, did that piss my mom off." Then Margaret burned a little rubber as we zoomed into the beach parking lot, where big signs were posted everywhere that read NO PARKING AFTER DARK and BEACH PARKING ONLY DURING SEASON so that the police had some grounds for arresting us when we were going hot and heavy with our boyfriends in the middle of January.

Several cars were already assembled and I recognized most of them. Butch, Hawkeye, and JJ. The guys from Prairie Vista. They were there. Vicky's car was there and so were Lori's and Samantha's. I was a little pissed that no one but Margaret had picked me up. A bonfire was going and somebody had thought to bring beer. The cop cruiser usually came by every hour on the hour so we had a little while.

Patrick was lying in the sand, propped up on his elbow, a beer in hand. I was mad at him for not coming by for me so I played cool and ignored him. We'd already been going out for about a year or so. We'd gone to the sophomore hop the year before, which was the biggy, and we usually went to the movies on a weekend. Whenever there was something, it was just assumed we'd go together, though I'm not sure how it ever happened that we did. He never called me and I don't know that I called him. Now that we had cars we just showed up and then we'd go off together and neck in his car.

He saw me all right because I saw him perk up and laugh at something somebody said that wasn't so funny. He used to do that, laugh this big laugh when I was around so I'd notice him, but not really pay attention to me himself. I always had to go to him, it seemed, but I didn't care because it made him happy when I did. But tonight I didn't go.

"Hey," I said to Vicky, "what's the idea? Nobody came for me."

"We just figured Patrick would."

"Yeah, well, he didn't."

I turned to say something to him when I saw that Margaret had sidled up to where he was sitting. She stretched out beside him like a cat and Patrick grinned in the glow of the fire. When I went over to get a beer, he gave me a look like he couldn't help himself.

I stayed around for as long as I thought I could without all hell breaking loose when I got home. Margaret never moved but just stayed, joking with Patrick, and he kept sipping his beer, laughing at her jokes. Occasionally she tugged on his pants leg or tossed her pony-tail back as if she were swatting flies.

I sat down not far from them and Patrick kept giving me this dopey, hopeless look and I kept watching Margaret, who acted as if she didn't know who I was or that Patrick and I had been a thing for the better part of the past year. She just lay next to him as if this were her living room and she was stretched out on the sofa.

After about an hour I said I was going home. Patrick offered to drive me, but he made no move to get up. "Forget it," I said. Vicky said she'd take me, but she wasn't ready to go. I told them it was okay. I could walk. They'd all had a lot of beer, but they knew it was a fairly ridiculous thing I was suggesting I'd do, at that hour. They all told me to wait and someone would drive me home, but I was already heading toward the bluff.

They probably figured I'd take the road, which was the long way. I heard Patrick shout at me as I headed straight for the bluff. There seemed to be some discussion about whether or not to let me go because I heard an engine start, but I was already clawing my way up the bluff.

It was a steep incline of mud and rocks. I'd climbed up it before, but never at midnight, when I couldn't see. Still, it was the most direct route to my house and would shave half an hour off my walking time if I didn't kill myself. I reached for branches, found my footing in stones. Slowly I pulled myself up. Once I lost my footing and started a small landslide of pebbles, but in a few moments I was scaling the top without incident.

I took side roads to get home. I spotted a few cars I recognized on the main intersections, but I didn't want to see anybody. When I got home, the red car was sitting in my driveway. Patrick was with her and I suppose they were worried about me. I ducked around the rosebushes and sneaked in the back porch. I don't know how long they stayed there because whenever they pulled out, I was already asleep.

33

Outside tires screeched on the gravel and suddenly Nick was there in my driveway. He closed the car door, then just stood there for a long moment, taking in the view, smelling the coastal air. I opened the door, giving a wave. When he reached me, he held me to him, burying his head in my hair. Taking him by the hand, we walked around the house, stood at the bluff. "It's incredible, Tessie."

"If I sold this place, I'd be rich. The land alone is probably worth a million. But I'm never going to sell."

"Promise me you won't."

I crossed my heart.

Inside a fire blazed in the fireplace. I uncorked a bottle of good California Chardonnay as he wandered through the house. "I love this room," he said. "I love it here." He stood gazing at the view as I handed him a glass of wine.

"I knew I would."

He breathed a deep sigh as if he hadn't relaxed in a long time. Then we clicked our glasses together. "Can we take a walk? I feel like I've been cooped up. I could use the fresh air."

"Of course we can. We can do whatever you like." Putting our wineglasses on the coffee table, I took him by the arm and led him down the path of ice plants, through the grove of pines until we stood on the path the poet had carved through his own restless walks at the edge of the sea. Nick took a deep breath. "It's very dramatic, isn't it?"

Holding my hand, Nick followed the path. "I can see why you'd never want to leave."

I squeezed his hand, glad he could see that and wondering if it was still true. We made our way down the cliffs to the sea and walked the beach for a while, occasionally stopping to pick up a shell or a feather that struck our eye. We spoke very little, but I didn't mind the silence.

After we'd walked a ways, Nick paused and gazed up at my house. "Is it safe there?" he asked.

"Not particularly."

He laughed. "I didn't think so. It looks as if it could come tumbling down."

"It might," I said. "It could."

He put an arm tightly around my shoulder. "Be careful," he said. "I don't want anything bad to happen to you."

I took him by the hand, leading him up the path, back toward the house. "Nothing bad will."

When we got back to the house, I went to check on the bouillabaisse I'd made from whatever the local fishermen had caught that day. The kitchen was filled with the salty steam of fish and jazz was coming from my living room. Nick had put on a CD. Peter Duchin, Art Tatum? The music was dreamy, the way old jazz can be. It had been awhile since my house was filled with the smells of cooking and the sound of soft jazz. I peeked into the living room and saw Nick, sitting, glass of wine in hand, staring at the sea, a magazine open in his lap, as if he too belonged right there.

At dinner Nick ate a hearty bowl of bouillabaisse and drank down two glasses of Chardonnay. With a piece of bread he sopped up the juice on his plate. Then taking my hand, he led me into the living room, where the jazz played. It was Tatum, I decided. His head was tossed back. With one hand he tapped out the rhythm on my thigh.

Soon his fingers were moving up and down my leg. They were lifting my chin to his. His kiss was long and deep. "I've been wanting to do this for a long time," he said. His hands guided me down the hallway to my bedroom. He peeled off his shirt, his pants. He pulled my sweater over my head. Rising above me, he straddled my hips, hands on my nipples, eyes closed, body swaying. His hands were everywhere, his tongue coursed between my thighs. The hair on his back and shoulders was furry and thick as a beast's and I burrowed in. My fingers circled his nipples, reached down and held him. Everywhere his tongue went, he stayed for a long time. His body was firm yet soft at the same time.

When he entered me it was smooth and easy and he knew how to take his time. I felt as if I had taken a drug and was losing myself because I couldn't tell where his limbs ended and mine began. Suddenly I felt tired and I knew that I would sleep.

When I woke, it was just after midnight and the house smelled of fish and burning wood. The only sound was of waves crashing below. Moonlight shone in, splattering on the floor. Nick lay beside me, his eyes open, listening. When he saw I was awake, he reached up, stroking my face. "It's beautiful here." I rested my head on his belly. It had never seemed quite so beautiful to me before.

"I'm glad I'm here," he went on. "I've wanted to be with you for a long time. Maybe you've always been somewhere in my mind."

"I'm glad I'm with you too," I told him, rubbing my face on his chest. "You know almost everything about me."

"I'm with you because I want to be," he continued, still stroking my face, "but are you sure you know why you want me here? Are you sure you know why you're doing this?"

"Because I've grown fond of you," I teased, kissing his fingertips, his hands.

Nick turned over, resting his chin in his hands. The body that had seemed so large, almost overpowering to me just months ago now seemed gentle, tender. "I hope that's why. I hope that's so."

"Why else would it be?" I traced my finger along the line of his shoulder blade, down his spine in the moonlight.

"Because you want to get back at her?"

"Get back at her? Why? Why would I want that?"

"Oh, Tessie," he said with a sigh, "you know. You know why."

34

You never saw so many paper moons, all gold and cut out of cardboard, and roses, tissue-paper roses, perfumed, fluffed, tied with wire. We spent weeks making them, cutting the moons and twisting the roses until our thumbs got blisters. Painting the blue backdrop with the clouds. Boxes and boxes of them.

The gym, of course, would be transformed. It always was for junior prom. Not that I'd seen it before, but I'd heard. I'd heard how one day it smelled of sweat and basketballs, and the next of powder and eau de cologne. It was a vision we'd all conceived. We, the members of the junior prom committee. We'd eliminated Hawaiian theme (too much like the previous year, which was South Pacific). We'd thought about "Downtown," which was the big Petula Clark song that year, or "She Loves You."

Then somebody said why not "Moonlight and Roses." Yes, it was romantic, but then, we were romantic. We liked being romantic. We'd play songs like "Moon River" and "Paper Moon," silly romantic songs. The gym all decorated with paper roses and moons and the lights turned down low and the girls with their corsages and dresses, pumps and bags dyed to match.

It was, of course, what we dreamed of.

So we could just see it, the gang and me. And of course, we volunteered to decorate it. We who had practiced our pompon routines and our cheerleading and baton in this gym, yes, we would transform it into a different place. Another place altogether.

Of course I was going with Patrick. It was a fait accompli—an expression I didn't learn until college, but of course that was what was going to happen. No one doubted it, least of all me.

Still the phone didn't ring. I waited. It's not that it didn't ring, because it did. It rang all the time, off the hook, as Lily said. I had my own line now, not just for me, but for my brothers as well, but they'd make a phone call and it was "Meet me at the Idiot's Circle at five" or "See you at the field." Not like me, because I liked to talk and chatter and gab with the gang. If one of them didn't call every night or so, I was crushed, devastated.

But Patrick didn't call. I saw him at school and it wasn't like he was avoiding me. We chatted by my locker and walked up the hall and as far as I was concerned we were together. We were a couple, weren't we? Didn't we drive around in his car with his hand resting just below my breast? Didn't that count for something? So we were a couple; that's how I saw it. That's how everyone else saw it too.

Then Jim Richter called and asked me to the prom. Would you like to go with me to Moonlight and Roses? And of course I said no because I was going with Patrick.

"I don't think so" was Jim Richter's reply.

"What do you mean you don't think so?" I stammered.

"I think he's going with someone else."

Then I lost my cool because that couldn't be and I knew it was just an ugly rumor so I said, "Well, who might that be?" still trying to sound like I had a handle on exactly what was going on here.

And he said, "Well, I don't know . . . maybe I shouldn't say anything." And he hung up, just like that.

So I called Lori first and she hemmed and hawed, and then I called Maureen, and finally it was Vicky who told it to me straight because, she said, "Well, we just didn't know if you knew. We couldn't really tell what the story was because it seemed as if you didn't, but we thought maybe you were just trying—"

"Vicky, who is he going with?"

"Margaret."

"You're kidding. How could he? How could he do that to me?"

Vicky was silent. "I don't know. He just did. And she said yes."

"When did it happen?"

"Weeks ago."

I had my pride. I wasn't going to just lose it, not like that, not there on the phone. "Thank you for telling me. I appreciate it." Then I got off the phone. I shook, I cried, then I got my composure back and called Jim Richter.

"If you'd still like to take me, I'll go with you."

Jim Richter stood in the entranceway in his powder-blue suit, talking to my father. There was the dance to go to and then there was some late-night supper, and then a boat ride on the Chicago River, which my father hadn't known about, and I saw him blanch. "Oh, I don't know about that boat ride. How many in the boat, son?"

And Jim Richter said he didn't know, but that there were chaperons (which there weren't) and that I'd be home in the morning after a breakfast being held at some hotel, and it all seemed like so much and I wanted my father to say no to it all, but there I was in my rose-colored dress with pumps and bag dyed to match and I felt like a stupid flower and Jim stood there, a corsage in his hand because that was what the boys did, they brought the girls corsages, and I thought to myself, I don't want to do this, I don't want to go, not tonight, not to this prom. I want to put my feet up and read a good book or take a walk because I was sure to run into them and of course everyone knew.

We drove in silence, Jim Richter with his hand draped across the back of my seat, and I thought, Don't touch me, but of course he did. He let his moist hand graze my shoulder and I pulled away. All the cars were arriving as we pulled up. One after the other, cars pulled up with girls in satiny dresses—creamy blue and shiny pink, corsages that would leave elastic marks on their wrists, tied to their arms.

And the gym was transformed. Dark with evening-blue lights, the roses we'd made, the paper moons draped from overhead. On a platform the band played just like we knew it would—"Moon River." Dream maker, heartbreaker.

Jim Richter took my hand in his fleshy, sweaty palm and led me in and there they were, of course. I saw them. Margaret and Patrick, together, dancing. Close.

Drinks were being passed around. Boys had flasks under their coats and some had whiskey and some had gin and some had things I couldn't recall. Jim pressed me to him, made me dance with him, but every once in a while when a flask went around, I grabbed for it, took a long swig. I could see Patrick, his hand around hers. What happened? I wanted to ask him. Why did you do it?

But I knew why. Because for some reason she had to have what she didn't have. She had to have what was mine.

I drank from silvery flasks—scotch, gin. I didn't care. My mouth and tongue were warm, but my feet were numb, which was good because as we danced Jim Richter stepped on them.

And then we all piled into our cars and drove into town and had supper somewhere and then there was this boat, this boat on the river. By now we had all slipped out of our prom clothes into other things and I kept drinking from whatever flask and I saw the boat and I thought, I can't get on a boat on the river. So this is how it will end for me. Flailing arms, voices calling for help. But the boat moved easily from the dock and I drank from a bottle being passed around and the sky over the Chicago River was turning purplish, a lighter shade of purple, almost lavender and I felt Jim Richter slide his hand under my shirt, into my bra, pulling me to him, pulling me under him. I felt those hot, moist hands against my flesh and suddenly I knew I was going to be sick. I was going to throw up over the side, so I pushed his hands away and I shouted at him, shouted loud enough for everyone on the boat, all my classmates to hear, "How can you take advantage of a girl who's drunk?" I shouted it once, then twice, until Jim Richter shrank away and I turned and there was Patrick, his hand over my mouth to silence me, Patrick, leading me away to the side of the boat where I was sick.

"Tess," he said, "are you all right?"

"Get away from me," I told him. "I hate you. I hate all of you."

It was dawn when I walked in and my father was just getting up. "Squirrel," he called to me as I slipped in, "Squirrel, is that you?"

"It's me, Dad."

"Are you okay, sweetie?"

"I'm fine, Daddy. I'm just tired. I'm going to bed."

It was after the prom, just a couple of days or so later when Mom said, Take the car, Squirrel, take the car, and she handed me one of her lists, those long lists for the store. Sometimes she let me do the shopping for her and I liked to do it midweek when Dad was gone because I could buy a few extra things—things I knew he liked like root beer and popcorn we'd drink and pop the night when he got home. With the extra money she gave me I always picked up something special for my dad.

I liked the Indian Trail market with the giant Indian head on the front—a chief of some sort in full feathers, a tepee behind him (despite that fact that in Winonah there were no Indians who wore full feathers or lived in tepees. For tepees belonged to a nomadic tribe and the Potawatomi lived in lodges right in what is now downtown Winonah).

But still I liked the Indian Trail market with its wide aisles and everything you could imagine to eat, including lobsters in tanks and cereal from Switzerland, lemons from the South Pacific. All kinds of cheeses and peppers the color of the sky just before the sun goes down. All wrapped in plastic. Everything so orderly and neat that it just fit into my archival spirit, my love of objects and order. And I would almost always run into the mother of one of my friends, Mrs. Kahn or Mrs. LePoint, and she'd say to me, "Is that you? Tess, my God, you've gotten to be such a big girl. So pretty. I wouldn't have recognized you."

Some might comment that they never saw me since the swim club closed last summer. We belonged to the swim club and the synagogue. We were members of other things as well. My mother was active in the PTA and my father went to meetings of the Chamber of Commerce. We were citizens of the community we lived in and I loved that community. We belonged here. When I popped into Larsen's after school for gum, Mrs. Larsen knew my name. People knew who we were. That's how I'd define it best. People knew my name.

And my business. But in a good way, mostly. If you were sick, someone always brought you a casserole, a pot of soup. Neighbors were always stopping over to borrow things so that it was hard to know which cups belonged to whom or whose baseball bat we had in our garage or whose jacket had been left in the mud closet. It could be anyone's who lived within a ten-block radius or farther, just counting my friends and my brothers' friends who rode their bikes or cars to our house. A jacket could have been left by any one of a hundred people.

These were our friends, our neighbors, our community. The people we lived among, the people who knew us but didn't know our secrets. Or if they did, they didn't tell. At least no one told me.

The store was a mile, a mile and a half at most from the house, but I took my time driving. I still had that bad taste in my mouth from the prom and felt as if I had two heads. The car smelled of cigarettes and kids. I liked driving the car with the list in my hand, going to the store like a grown-up. I parked as I always did, got my cart, and slowly made my way through the wide, plentiful aisles. Aisles that smacked of the good fortune that had befallen the people of Winonah. We have done well, this store seemed to say. We are a success. I picked up coffee, broccoli, and potatoes quickly. I was on my way to cereal, then chicken breasts when I ran into Vicky's mom, Mrs. Walton.

"Tess, is that you? I don't recognize you anymore."

Mrs. Walton always embarrassed me, because she said it so loudly. I wanted to reply, But Mrs. Walton, I'm at your house every week, but I just said, "I've grown a lot this year."

"You all have. You girls are getting so big."

Perhaps it was then that I caught a glimpse of him out of the corner of my eye. Or perhaps not. Maybe I just remember it that way. But I slipped away from her, promised to be by to see Vicky soon. Already my hands gripped the cart too tightly, my list crumpled, sweaty in my palm. I made a right, then a left. Now the store was almost empty as I headed into its more remote wings—the bakery, the fish market.

Then I saw him, standing near aisle six, the dairy section. Right there on a Tuesday when he should have been no closer than Quincy. He had milk, juice, a package of hamburger in his hands. My father was shopping, picking up this and that at the store. But, of course, this made no sense since he wasn't due home till Thursday (he never got home before Thursday) and it was only Tuesday. And why was he shopping if I was the one doing the errands?

I stood there, motionless, watching my father select items from the shelf. He had no cart, but like a juggler was balancing them in his hands. It was odd to see my father picking cans off the shelf, reading labels. He took creamed corn. We never had creamed corn (or anything out of a can, for that matter) at home.

I didn't say hello. I backed up my cart and quickly slipped out of the store. When I got home, Lily yelled at me because I'd forgotten most of what I'd gone for. But I wouldn't go back to that store again.

35

All families have secrets, don't they? So why shouldn't mine have ours? Why shouldn't we keep things from one another? Even when you grow up within four walls with about as many people, you can't really know anyone for sure. Even families are built on fragments, the bits and pieces we show the world.

Still, it is a terrible thing to keep a secret inside. So far inside. Tucked deep like a tapeworm that works its way through you. Now I had to tell someone. And I knew who that would be. Once I knew I could hold on to it longer than before. Little Squirrel, guarding her nut.

I'm not sure when it was that my father became a man of alibis, of duplicity, a man who lived a double life. It never occurred to me that he was spending half the week with us as he always had and the other half across the railroad tracks, just a mile or so from where we lived. But it was a world away, really, where he went, a place where he could put his shoes on the coffee table and laugh out loud. Where he could sing as he put up drywall.

It has taken me a long time, but I can see it now. The disaster I feared had already happened. While I imagined him in the path of oncoming storms, racing tornados, dodging floods, the threat was in fact much closer and more real.

Sometimes I have these dreams in which my father is looming over my bed, larger than he was in life. He has come with a story or a song, something he has to tell me. I always wind up telling him the same thing. "It's all right, Dad. I already know."

"What're you going to do with your life, Trooper?" our father said to Jeb when he got home from Madison in June. Jeb was studying history and he unpacked his collection of books on the Crimean War, Central Asia, the Mongol empire.

"I'm going to figure out how the world works," Jeb replied without an ounce of irony, because that indeed was what he thought he would do—know how the world worked and then rule whatever corner of it that was allotted to him.

"He'll run for president, just like Abe Lincoln," Lily replied and Jeb nodded.

"I might. I just might."

That night Lily cooked Jeb's favorite dinner—a dish of juicy chicken and au gratin potatoes, green beans with almonds—and Jeb told us all about college. Art had a million questions. He wanted to know all about colleges. I waited a day or two. I waited for Jeb to unpack, unwind, settle back into being one of us again, part of the family. And I waited for Monday, when Dad set off on the road. I watched as Dad packed his car and we all waved good-bye. I was studying touch typing that summer and was working at the swim club. Jeb had a job with a law firm in town and Art was going to camp, but none of it had begun.

"Can we go somewhere today?" I asked Jeb.

"Like where?"

"McDonald's?"

We drove out along County Line and picked up a burger special and Jeb flirted a bit with this girl and that because he was now a very big man, strong, with nice skin, and our father's gray eyes. I sat silently, watching the girls come up, pat my brother on the arm. He turned to me and said, "You know, it's not bad, coming home."

I smiled and shrugged, but I felt shy, not like before when I always said what was on my mind and did what I wanted to do. Now it was as if there were a fence around me and somehow I was closed in. "You know, things have been a little strange since you left last spring."

"Oh, yeah?" Jeb took a bite from his burger. Some ketchup clung to his chin. "How so?"

He didn't seem to be listening to me or even wanting to be with me very much but I knew I had to go on. So I told him about prom and how Patrick went with Margaret and how I'd gotten drunk and this boy, well, nothing had happened, but this boy had tried to take advantage of me and I stood up on the boat and shouted at him, "How can you take advantage of a girl who's drunk?"

Jeb gave me a little punch in the arm and a "way to go," like brothers do, so I thought I could go on, I should go on, because he was the one person I could tell and I knew that Jeb more than anyone else would never, ever say a word. "But then a few days later this strange thing happened when I was at the market, you know, Indian Trail, Mom had given me a list of things to get. . . ."

Now he looked at me almost beady-eyed because he knew I was getting to the serious part, the real part, and something in his eyes told me that he wasn't going to be surprised with what I had to say, that whatever it was he already knew. And maybe he'd known for a long time, but I said it anyway. ". . . and Dad was there. He was buying things, but it was only a Tuesday and he shouldn't have been any closer than Quincy."

Jeb shook his head, then held up his hands as if warding off a blow. "I don't want to know about it," he said. "I don't want to hear about this, Tess."

"But what is it? What's going on with him?"

He finished his burger, crumpled up the paper. "Oh, Tess, don't make me be the one to tell you." He made a clean toss into the trash.

"But what about all his trips?"

Jeb shook his head. "Tessie, he hasn't been on the road for years."

I was silent for a moment. "Jeb, have you known for a long time?" My brother nodded his head ever so slightly. "Does Mom know?"

"Tessie." He looked me straight in the eye. "Everyone knows."

36

If a life is said to have a shape, then certain events form the structure of that shape. Francis Cantwell Eagger has come down to us as a man of contradictions—a gentle poet of letters who loved the rugged out-of-doors, a sensitive man known for his violent temper. What were the elements that shaped him? What made him the man he was? In the life of Francis Cantwell Eagger three factors can be viewed as defining. The first was a boyhood episode involving lightning, the second his flight to the West, and the third his parents' painful rejection when he turned to them for help.

Until he was thirteen, Eagger lived a life of privilege. His family was extremely wealthy (his mother was a Sutton and they lived on Sutton Place) and no advantage was denied him. He toured Europe, studied music, had his own horse. However, he was a lonely, introverted child and his parents were often away, leaving him and his younger brother with servants to fend for themselves. When he turned thirteen, he spent the summer at the family compound in Maine. One night he got up to go to the bathroom and a violent storm erupted. As Eagger returned to his bed, he heard a loud crash and saw a brilliant flash. Covering his ears with his hands, he crumpled to the floor. When he dared look, he saw that above his bed the wall was seared where lightning had struck and the impression of the lightning was branded into the wooden wall, making a letter "Z." (This episode is dealt with in his poem "Zorro," one of the few surviving poems from the lost manuscript that helps define his hero quest.)

Eagger was altered by this bolt of lightning. Life seemed unpredictable, random. Anything could happen at any moment. He lost interest in his studies and it was at this time in his life that he began to wander. He would walk all over Manhattan and once he walked to Westchester and back. His mother, who had never noticed him much when he was there, grew frantic when he would wander and this seemed to make him all the more determined to go further and further away from home. In the end he would flunk out of prep school after prep school and finally when he flunked out of Princeton, his parents sent him west. He was reluctant to go, but they gave him no choice. He either had to make good for himself or they would no longer pay his way. They set him up with a friend in the shipping business, but Eagger soon lost interest in it. Instead he attended classes at UCLA, where he met Jillian Palmer, the beautiful woman who would soon become his wife.

Eagger had fallen in love with the West as well and intended to make it his home. He would have even if he had not fallen in love with Jillian, for he had found his spiritual home in the rough, rocky Coast as had artists before him such as Robinson Jeffers, Henry Miller, and Ansel Adams. Jillian was brilliant, beautiful, ten years his senior, and divorced. He loved her passionate outbursts, her fitful intelligence. And he predicted, and he was correct, that his parents would disinherit him for marrying her.

The third and final formative event in Eagger's life (outside of the mysterious death of his eldest son, who died off the cliffs of the beloved seaside house Eagger had built for his family) was his parents' rejection of him. He tried for years to write them, to explain his love of Jillian, his marriage, his determination to be a writer on the West Coast. Finally when all else failed, and when little Thomas, their middle son, was stricken ill with tuberculosis, Eagger and Jillian drove across the country from San Francisco to beg his family for understanding and to help them in their financial woes.

Eagger writes in his poem "Dark Window" of what happened that day. He and Jillian returned to New York to the house on Sutton Place and as they walked up the front steps, he saw the curtains drawn, the house darkened to him. He and Jillian stoically got into their car and drove back to San Francisco. Francis Cantwell Eagger would mourn the loss of his family in his poems for the rest of his life, but he would never attempt to contact any of them again.

While Eagger was always an avid walker, he became obsessed with it upon returning from this journey. He walked for hours, sometimes days, with a pad and pencil. On his walks, he wrote down his impressions, jotted lines for poems, scribbled whatever popped into his head. Taking a walk with him was no pleasure because of these constant interruptions and in the end he walked alone. According to the letters of Francis Cantwell Eagger, a "desire path" is what hikers or walkers have worn thin through finding a better way, or a shortcut, to a desired place. From his poems we know that Eagger loved nature, that he was tormented in love, that he sought a better way. Once Eagger quipped in a letter to a friend that he preferred the dangers of nature to the threat of man and in his later years he grew more and more reclusive. In all of this, it is safe to say that he is the West Coast Robert Frost and indeed deserves his place in American literary history.

Bruno sat across from me at the kitchen table, pondering my slightest change in facial expression. "Bruno, this is fascinating. It really is very interesting." It seemed that Bruno had decided he could not write his doctoral dissertation without my help. So he brought to me page after page, note after note. Every word he wrote he ran by me.

He smiled at me, the smile of a child who has done something to please his parents. "Tell me. What do you like about it?"

"Oh, I don't know. I like the way it tells a story and that somehow the story it tells helps you understand the man." Bruno blinked, brushing his sandy hair out of his eyes. His hand trembled as it moved past his face. He seemed genuinely thrilled. I really didn't know what I liked about it until I said that to him. No one had asked me to read his doctoral dissertation before, and in a way it seemed rather boring, but interesting at the same time. "I like the way these events shaped this man's life. That's interesting."

He nodded, hanging on my every word.

I paused. "You must keep going," I told him. "I think it is very good."

"Oh, it means so much to me. That you like it. You know, Tess, I feel such an affinity for this man. In some ways our lives have been similar. I grew up in the East and didn't do very well in school—"

"And were you ever almost struck by lightning?" With a laugh Bruno shook his head no. "But you did have a falling-out with your family?" I asked a bit more gently for I could see where this conversation was heading.

Bruno nodded. "Yes, you know, my father was a minister and we didn't always see things eye to eye. I was seeing this girl, she was older. Anyway, my mother hated her and my father went along. When I moved in with the girl, we stopped talking. I felt they never approved of anything I did. We didn't talk for almost four years."

"How old are you now?"

"I'm twenty-six."

"So you must have been young when you had your falling-out."

"We only patched it up last year, but now we're good friends again."

"So are you writing this dissertation to find your father?"

Bruno thought about this for a moment, then shook his head. "To find myself," he said. "What about you, Tess? I don't know anything about you or your family."

"My mother lives in Chicago. My father died nine or ten years ago." Bruno gave me an odd look which I didn't understand at the time, but I know he was surprised that I couldn't recall the exact number of years. "He was an insurance salesman, on the road a fair amount. I have two brothers. We were an ordinary family. There was hardly anything unusual about us at all."

Nick phoned every day. It wasn't always easy with the time difference. Often he called collect from pay phones. He didn't want the calls to be on any of his accounts or on his calling card. But dutifully each week he sent me fifty dollars, which was what he assumed the calls were costing me. I was starting to think how we could live together, dividing our time between Illinois and the Coast, the best of both worlds. I started to have dreams of the future again.

Otherwise my life went as usual. Someone trashed the seashell house and Shana was beside herself. Vandals had gotten in during a few days when the house wasn't occupied and smashed the cowrie-shell mirror, shattered the scallop coffee table.

I had to deal with the owners, who threatened to sue us. I convinced them that it was an act of vandals and that the house was unoccupied at the time, but still there was much to do to straighten out the mess. During that time I became surrogate mother for a few weeks to two orphaned sea otter pups. And the National Registry of Historic Houses sent an inspector to look at the house.

I'd actually forgotten that I'd mailed in my application, but a very tall, thin woman knocked on my door one day and said she had come to inspect the house for the registry. She didn't say a word to me as she poked through rooms, stood across the street from the house, taking its picture. She wrote notes on a pad and after about an hour, she told me I'd receive a letter in a few months and that she thought it was a nice house, but she could not say if she would recommend it for the registry. I told her I wouldn't get my hopes up.

A few weeks later Ted returned with a story to tell—not a terribly pretty one. Sabe was into drugs and Ted had gotten out of there.

Soon both of my children became aware of the fact that I was accepting collect calls from gas stations and phone booths in the Midwest and they each asked me what I had going on. I told them what they had often told me. That it was my business and if and when I was ready to share it with them, I would.

Neither of them liked this answer. Jade asked me to go to lunch with her, where she pressed for details. She looked different than she had before going away. Her features were softer, her hair longer, no more purple spikes, though now she had a small gold nose ring. I confided in her as one might in a friend that I was seeing a man I'd known for almost my entire life, that his marriage was breaking up, and we hoped to find a way to be together.

Jade's jaw dropped when I told her this. "You aren't serious? That is so cool."

"I am serious," I said.

She gave me a little sock in the arm. "That's great, Mom."

They both got jobs. It was the law I laid down before I'd let either of them back in the house. Jade left her part-time position and went to work as a manager at a coffee-roasting factory. She came home smelling like the hills of Java. Ted got hooked up with an on-line company that sold space on the Web. He actually had a knack for this and began designing Web sites.

Then in the middle of the summer Nick called and said he could come out for a few days. He said to book us a room somewhere I liked to go and we'd have our first romantic getaway. I hesitated and he asked me what was wrong. "I can't do this," I told him. "Not while you're still living with her. Not while she doesn't know. I just can't do it behind her back."

"Tessie, I'm leaving her. Look, I was planning to tell her. I wanted her to know before I saw you, but she seems so fragile. Unstable, really. I don't know what it is, but it's as if she's transparent. She's not really there. She stares into space. Maybe she's on drugs. I feel as if I am living with a ghost, but I have to think of Danielle. I want to come and see you, and once I know what I'm going to do and when, then I'll tell her."

"It just doesn't seem right."

"Tess, she's going to know soon. Let me come and see you. I want to talk to you about it. Then we'll decide."

Along the coast the road dips and turns. Below Monterey the real cliffs begin. From the rocky points you can see terrifying vistas, the sea crashing against the shore. Nick had never seen this part of the coast and so I picked the Mermaid Inn down at Big Sur, though it was expensive. He said he didn't care what it cost. He just wanted to be with me. He flew into San Jose, where I picked him up, and we drove straight to the coast. He was stunned as the road curved and we followed the rocky coast down.

The Mermaid had a wooden mermaid over its entranceway. Our cabin had its own redwood hot tub with a special eucalyptus soap you could bathe in, a steambath, long paths lined with ice plants that led down to the ocean. First we took a long walk, climbing down the craggy pathways until we stood on a small, solitary beach. Seals and a pair of sea otters frolicked in the surf. Nick stood in the sand in his bare feet, just breathing in the air. "You're lucky, Tess," he told me, his arm firmly around my shoulder. "You got away."

"You've said that before. I know you think I did but I'm not really sure," I told him, "but, anyway, you could too."

"I'm going to." He squeezed my neck. "Just watch me."

When we got back to the room, Nick wanted to take a Jacuzzi bath. While the bath was getting ready, we ordered dinner in our room—seafood, salad, a bottle of California Chardonnay. Easing his way into the hot tub, Nick took a washcloth, dipped it in the eucalyptus suds, and began to wash me. He scrubbed the back of my neck and behind my ears. He let the washcloth dip under my arms, down my back. He brought it around in front of me, massaging beneath my breasts, along the ridges of my face. He covered me with suds and I lay back as the hot jets and the smell of eucalyptus and the motion of his hand on my skin made me drowsy.

I dropped my head against his chest as he reached down to my belly. I opened my thighs and he rubbed me between my legs. He moved his hand up and down, letting the washcloth reach farther and farther, coming back up slowly. Then he dipped back down again, rubbing me as I drifted, the air filled with the smell of redwood and eucalyptus.

Then we both got out, wrapped ourselves in the big terry-cloth robes, and made love slowly on the bed until we fell asleep. We woke when there was a knock at the door and a young waiter discreetly brought our dinner tray in, leaving it in the entranceway. Over dinner, we talked about Margaret and what we were going to do. "When are you going to tell her?" I asked.

"When I get back. We aren't even sleeping in the same room. We're hardly together."

"But still, I'd feel better—"

"It's not like you're taking me away from her. In most ways, except for Danielle, I'm already gone." I kissed him on the lips, and he kissed me back. "All right, if you'd feel better, I'll do it in a few weeks when the time seems right. Then we can be together."

"Yes, we can be together."

Then he lay back, staring at the ceiling. "You know, I've never done anything for myself. Everything has always been what other people—mainly my father—wanted me to do. Of course, he didn't want me to marry Margaret. He thought she was trash. Maybe I just did it to get back at him. Because I thought it was the way to have my own life. Anyway, it didn't work." He leaned over and pulled me to him. "I want something that's mine. My house, my work. Not what other people want me to have. Do you understand that, Tess?"

"Yes, I do understand."

"I know you do." He rested his face in my hair. "I know." In bed at night we made our plans. In October he would move out. He'd take a small apartment in town to be near Danielle. Then we'd decide what we were going to do. We'd figure out a way to divide our time. He'd help me refinance the Eagger house. I'd spend as much time in Illinois as I could. It all seemed fitting somehow. That after all these years I could finally go home.

"I've got this idea," he said. "We should plan to meet somewhere in town. At Starbucks or the bookstore. Run into one another as if we'd just met."

"Oh, we could do it in front of the Italian cookbooks."

"That's good," Nick said with a laugh, "I'll be working on my cooking anyway."

"People will see us; they'll think we've just met. So when we start to see one another, it won't be such a big deal."

"Yes, let's do that," he said. "Until then it will be our secret."

"Yes," I said, kissing him on the nose.

That night there was an angry storm at sea. Lightning forks shattered around us, thunder rolled like in some B-grade horror film. "I think a monster's going to walk in the door," I told him. Nick held me, stroking my hair. I told him about the little boy who got out of bed one night to go to the bathroom and lightning burned a "Z" over his bed. Like Zorro, I told him.

"What happened to the boy?" Nick wanted to know.

"He became a poet; I live in his house."

When we drove back up to my place the next day, the kids had made a dinner of spaghetti with broccoli and a green salad from our vegetable patch, which they'd neatly tended while I was away. They'd uncorked a wine bottle and set the table. I can't remember when they'd last done those things. Ted was dressed in a polo shirt and he shook Nick's hand. Jade did the same, looking him up and down the way she can do. But if I'd brought home a Martian, they would have approved. "Well, it's nice to meet you," Jade said so politely I almost didn't recognize her. "We've heard so much about you."

Over dinner Nick kept telling them how lucky they were to have me as their mother. He told them how in grammar school and high school I'd been such a popular girl. Their eyes widened in disbelief. I don't remember being that popular, but it was nice of him to tell the children that this was how he remembered me.

That night after we made love, I could just make out his face, those deep blue eyes. The house was quiet, only the katydids sang outside. They'd been brought out in the storm. From my bed we listened to the rise and fall of their song.

37

When early fall came, I was called back to Illinois in part because of my mother. Art told me she had left Post-its all over the apartment with our names, phone numbers, and birthdays written on them. But I was also drawn back, not only by Nick, but by something deeper in me than I can name. Even from California I could almost smell the crispness in the air, the scent of burning leaves. It had been so long since I'd seen the leaves turn, the seasons change.

If there is a place on the earth from where my life springs it is this place. This lake and this land, the golden light shining through the leaves as they turn, the hint of winter in the air, or the wetness of trails, the pull of the ground sucking down on your shoes and spitting you back again whole. I felt the pull of what I had known and what I had left behind. If longing has a tug, it is like that wet Illinois earth sucking on the soles of your feet.

I hopped into a cab at O'Hare and the driver, a West Indian man, asked me where I wanted to go. I hesitated because I wanted to go to Winonah, to find Nick and take him away with me. But we had both agreed that we had to be patient. We had to wait. He was sorting out what he needed to do with his marriage and Danielle. And I was still not about to rush into anything. Besides, my mother needed looking after.

The cab driver asked me again, but I gave him my mother's address on Astor Place in the city. As he drove along the expressway, giant murals of Chicago Bulls were everywhere. The faces of Michael Jordon, Scottie Pippin, Dennis Rodman covered the facades of giant buildings. The light was already waning and an orange sunset illuminated the buildings. I breathed in deeply as if a great adventure lay before me. On the dashboard the man had a photograph of four little girls with beaming faces. "Are those your daughters?" I asked him, thinking I could pass the time with idle talk.

"Yes," he muttered, "those are my little angels."

"They're beautiful," I said, looking at the four little girls staring at me with broad smiles.

"Yes." He nodded, not saying anything for a moment. "But they need their mother."

"She's not here?"

He shook his head and I noticed the heaviness in his shoulders. "She was killed. She went to work one day. Her girlfriends picked her up just like every day. And then they were all killed, just like that. Some guy ran right into them. He walked away with scratches." The man's voice was shaking and he seemed ready to burst into tears. "I don't know how we're going to make it without her. My little girls come to me and ask me to braid their hair. I don't know how to braid hair. How can you explain this? One day she is there. And then she is gone. Nothing will ever be the same. It makes me wonder. . . ."

He paused, unsure if he should go on.

"What does it make you wonder?"

"I don't know," he said. "I go to church and pray to God for strength and then my little girl comes in crying because there's no one to braid her hair and I just start to wonder." He shook his head, but didn't say another thing. We drove the rest of the way in the silence.

When he dropped me off, I gave him a big tip and he looked up at me with his watery eyes.

The smell off the lake was fishy and humid and it was already the start of Indian summer. Smelt fishermen lined the bicycle path along the beachfront. I didn't feel ready to go upstairs because I knew that once I went up, that's where I'd stay. Instead I dropped my bag off with my mother's doorman and ran through the underpass beneath the drive. I tried to shake off the image of those four little girls whose father did not know how to braid their hair. It sent a chill through me.

Along the shore the smelt fishermen sat with their pots, their sleeping bags, their small fires burning. Most would spend the night here. It was already growing dark and as I bent to look into the lake, I could see silver bodies, darting, rising to the surface, then racing back down again.

My mother's apartment stank of cigarettes and despair. Sour milk was in the fridge, along with too many cartons of leftover Chinese food. She sat in a housecoat in front of the television, remote in her hand. When I kissed her hello, she seemed bewildered, as if she didn't know why I was there. For two days I tidied up her apartment. I took her to the beauty parlor to get her hair washed and set, then to Bloomies for lunch. When she seemed better and her apartment was spic and span, I phoned Nick at his house. He picked up on the first ring as if he'd been expecting my call. I had already decided that if Margaret answered I'd hang up. "Thank God," he said, his voice sounding relieved. "I'm so glad to hear from you. How are you?"

"I'm fine, but I want to see you."

He told me he'd meet me the following night.

The next night Nick met me at a restaurant in the Loop. He wore a jacket and tie and swept me into his arms, held me to him. "God, Tessie, I've missed you." His hand slid to my back. We ate dinner slowly, talking about our plans. He had told Margaret he would be leaving.

"How did she take it?"

"She took it well. It hardly seemed to bother her at all."

"That's strange, isn't it?"

He shrugged. "Nothing surprises me."

After dinner Nick wanted to show me something. We got in his car, headed east, then south, past Buckingham Fountain, past the Field Museum until he came to Soldier Field. He drove around it once, twice. Soldier Field rose large and circular in the dark, right in the middle of the Outer Drive, like some Roman amphitheater.

Nick made the circle one more time, then pulled off into the parking lot. "Come on," he said, "I want to walk with you around here." We got out and stood in the empty lot, the huge round building looming before us. Nick stood, staring at the wall beyond, which was the field where the Chicago Bears played.

"I never saw my dad play here," he said. "But I'd always wanted to. I always wished I had."

"He wouldn't let you?"

"No." He laughed. "I wasn't born. I was born after his career was over. I saw videos and newsreels I saw him throw balls farther than anyone ever had, run faster, harder. Not bad for a Jewish boy. I went with him when he was inducted into the Hall of Fame. He cried like a baby. He used to tell me how people would shout his name, hissing over the s'es like a snake to cheer him on. He said how he loved the applause and he loved the crowds, but more than anything he loved the game. He would have played his whole life if his knees hadn't given out."

The thick, pale limestone of Soldier Field was illuminated by floodlights. Except for the whirr of traffic everything was quiet. "Sometimes I come here, just to try and imagine what it was like for him. The roar of the crowds, to be a hero like that. He did what he wanted to do and he did it well," Nick said. He pulled me to him and kissed me. "I'm going to do what I want to do as well." His hands groped under my shirt, touching the skin of my back, going up and down my ribs.

There was something monolithic, impenetrable about the walls of the stadium that rose before us. "My father never did what he wanted either. Something held him back," I said, wondering if this was the explanation for all that had transpired in my father's life. "It's good to do what you want."

Nick nodded silently. He led me to the car and we headed back past Buckingham Fountain, which was lit like a magic lantern, changing colors. He said, "My parents came here on their first date. They took off their shoes and jumped in the fountain." I tried to imagine my own parents barefoot and splashing in the ornate fountain. "You know," I said, "the lights and water are set from a computer in Atlanta."

"Really? How does that work?"

"I don't know. I just read it somewhere. I thought it was interesting that a fountain here would be controlled by something so far away."

"So, what's the point?" His lips were pursed and he had a scowl.

"There's no real point. I read it somewhere." I touched his arm. "What's wrong?"

"Nothing," he said. "I'm tired." But it seemed as if he was angry about something. As if he needed to tell somebody off. I watched the speedometer climb to 70, 75, 80 as he sped down the Outer Drive. His strength was focused on keeping the gas pedal down.

"Maybe we should slow down. We aren't in a hurry, are we?"

"I need to get home," he said. His face was filled with worry. "And I have things on my mind."

"What things?"

But he just shook his head. He turned off the Drive, cut through the side streets near where my mother lived. He was still driving too fast when we heard the thud. It had a dull, soft feel.

"What was that?" I asked.

He shook his head, sucked in his lip. He kept on driving. For a moment I thought he was leaving the scene of an accident, but he drove around the block. When we came around the corner, a small crowd had formed. I heard a woman crying. It's a child, I thought. He's killed a child.

Nick pulled over, got out of the car, and fell to his knees. A chocolate-colored cocker spaniel lay limp by the side of the road. Blood seeped from its mouth. The woman who cradled the dog was crying. "I am so sorry," he said, touching the dog, crying. "I am so sorry. . . . I thought it was a child. I thought I'd killed a child."

"Look what you've done," she said, shaking her dead dog. "You better be more careful," the woman screamed at him, "or next time it will be."

Tears streamed down her face. Her jacket was soaked in blood. Nick took out his wallet and tried to offer her money. "I don't want your money." She pushed him away. "You better watch out," the woman said, clutching her dog.

The Motel 6 by the highway just outside of Winonah had generic rooms—plaid bedspreads, scratchy sheets. The room smelled of smoke and stale air. When I pulled back the curtain, it had a view of the parking lot and the highway. Of course, I knew these rooms well. They were the motel rooms of my youth, the "acancy" I longed for. It was where I'd once felt the most at home, but as I opened the drawer the Bible was in, everything smelled tacky and sad.

When he had dropped me off the previous night, Nick and I had agreed to meet here. I wasn't sure I wanted to. The dead dog seemed like an omen; of what I did not know, but I thought that something bad was going to happen to me. Besides, this motel didn't seem like the place to consummate love. I wished there were a bed-and-breakfast in Winonah. Maybe I would open one.

I checked in early and had about two hours to kill until Nick left work. I phoned my mother to be sure she was all right and she was, though she kept asking when I'd be home. Then I called Vicky to say I was in town. I paced and wanted to smoke a cigarette, which I hadn't

done in years. I didn't think Nick would show up before seven and I
didn't want to sit in the room.

A bowling alley was next door so I went over and ordered a Diet
Coke. I was nursing it at the bar, the sound of smashing pins around
me, when Patrick walked in with a couple of guys and a bowling bag.
He spotted me right away. "Tess!" He gave the boys a high sign and
said he'd meet them in a few minutes. He sat down next to me and
ordered a beer. "What're you doing here?" He gave me a peck on the
cheek. "Oh, you don't have to tell me. I can guess."

"Can you?" I said.

"You know, it's a small town. Word gets around somehow."

"So what do you know?"

He paused, breathed into his beer, rubbed his hands up and down
the stem. "I know you've been seeing Nick. I'm not saying this
because I'm jealous or anything—though of course I am . . ." He gave
his funny little laugh, the one I'd always liked.

"I thought it was our secret."

"This is Winonah, Tess. People talk. In fact, Margaret's said
things. . . . Nick's a good guy, but I just don't see the two of you. I
don't get it."

I was wishing I'd stayed in my room and started feeling annoyed.
"There's nothing for you to get. It is what it is."

He raised his hands in surrender. "Okay, sure. Look, you can do
whatever you want." He finished his beer, got up from the bar stool.
"Of course, I wish it had been me, but it's not about that. I'd just be a
little careful."

"Because I might get hurt?"

"Because someone might get hurt," he said. Then he picked up his
bowling bag, making a face as if it were heavier than it really was, and
walked toward the lane where his friends were waiting. I finished sipping my Coke, watching Patrick's lane. When he got up, he gave me
a wink, hunched over the ball, and released it with a clear, even step,
a good follow-through. Pins clattered as they tumbled down.

When I got back to the motel, Nick was leaning against my door. He had that pinched look he'd had on his face the night before when he was driving too fast. "Where have you been?" he asked, an impatient edge to his voice.

"You couldn't have been here that long. I got restless."

"I got here early."

"I'm sorry. I couldn't stand waiting."

Then he seemed to soften. "I've just had so much going on." He kissed me. He ran his hands up and down my body. "Let's go inside." I pulled him toward the bed, but he kept kissing me, standing where he was like a wooden Indian. "What's wrong?" I finally asked him.

Then he sat down on the bed. Picking at threads in the bedspread, he told me, "I think she knows about you . . . about us."

"How does she know?"

"Well, she's asked. She suspects it. She's threatening me, threatening to take Danielle away."

"But she can't do that."

"She seems to think she can," he said wearily.

"You have your rights."

"I know, but she can make it difficult."

He hugged me and we lay back on the bed. But his kisses were small, just light brushes, and his hands moved as if they had somewhere else to be. He seemed to be listening to something I couldn't hear, his head cocked, the way he had the night we met and he hadn't liked the band.

It was as if a different person inhabited his skin. We made love the way you do when you've got an early-morning meeting or there's a bill you don't know how you'll pay. Afterward he said he couldn't stay. He wanted to, but it was too complicated.

"I thought you were going to spend the night," I said.

"I'm going to be spending lots of nights with you, but it can't be this one. I need to sort some things out. I'll call you in the morning."

"Please don't go."

He put his arms around me and he was trembling.

"Are you cold?" I tried wrapping the blanket over his shoulders.

But he shook his head. "I'm frightened, that's what I am. I don't even know why but I'm just afraid." Then he kissed me hard and walked to the door. "I'll call you in the morning," he said. The door slammed behind him. After he left, I wasn't sure what to do with myself. I didn't quite know why I was here. I thought about driving back into the city, but it was late. Instead I watched a pay movie on the TV that didn't hold my interest. Then I slept fitfully and woke up when it was still dark out. For a long time I just sat, waiting for it to get light outside. Sitting there in that motel room, I realized how stripped down I felt. How vulnerable. I hadn't felt that way in a long time and it made me somehow afraid as well.

At seven I went down to the coffee shop for a breakfast of cereal and decaf, which I carried back to my room because I didn't want to miss his call, but Nick didn't phone. Lying down on the bed, I waited until ten o'clock, afraid to leave my room, thinking I would hear from him. But I didn't.

By eleven I needed to get out. I couldn't stand sitting in the room, waiting. I got in the car and drove. Once again I thought of heading back to Chicago, which I knew I should do, but instead, I drove into Winonah. I drove through the downtown and cruised past Prairie Vista Automotive. I wanted to see if Nick was in his office. I drove around the block once or twice, thinking about stopping in, but thought the better of it.

Instead I decided to drive the old route I used to take to get to school. First I cut over to Mulberry and down past my house. From my house, I headed over to Laurel. Though I wanted to go straight toward the school, instead I went in the direction of the lake. I drove all the way until I pulled up slowly in front of Nick's house.

There were no cars in the driveway. The house looked empty, as if it were on the market. I pulled over, parking on the street across from the house. Walking up the gravel path, I stood for a moment at the front door. I knocked, but there was no answer. I knocked again. Then I smelled the smoke. I had no idea where it was coming from, but the air around the house had taken on a slightly acrid, smoky smell. Something was burning.

I tried the door but it was locked. Then I went around to the side of the house where the smell was stronger and my eyes began to water. In the kitchen I could see gray smoke billowing from a pot. There was a side door and when I pushed it, it opened. I ran into the kitchen, covering my face against the thick, noxious air, grabbed a dishrag, and pulled the pot off the fire. The bottom of the pot was charred with burned milk that I assumed Margaret had forgotten on the stove.

I took the pot, carried it to the sink, let the cold water pour inside. The pot sizzled and steamed. When it quieted down I found myself standing there in Margaret and Nick's kitchen, unsure of what to do. I opened windows to let the smoke seep out and clear the air. I wondered if I should leave a note to explain the burned pot and what I was doing inside their house. But what if someone was home? What if Margaret was asleep or passed out, drunk?

Walking down the corridor, I stood alone in their vast living room. The smell of smoke still hung heavily in the air. I called out several times, "Hello, is anyone home?" I knew I should go. I had put out that small flame and now I had no business being here, but for some reason I couldn't bring myself to leave. My heart pounded in my chest as I stood still. I was going to turn around and walk out, but I decided to make certain everything was all right.

I headed down a corridor to the wing where the bedrooms were. Peering into each bedroom and bathroom, I made certain that no one was home, no one was hurt. I had wandered through people's houses like this dozens of times on the job, examining closet space, testing

for the comfort of beds. I opened a closet in the hallway. The smell of
cedar and mothballs wafted my way. Winter clothes hung in there—
heavy woolens, parkas, lambskin coats. I closed it and continued down
the corridor, pausing at Danielle's room.

I saw that the room was oddly devoid of a child's things, as
Danielle seemed devoid of a child's spirit. The room even smelled
old, as if someone no longer young lived here. The bed was a spartan
cot with a gray comforter. A neat row of books, mainly mysteries—
Nancy Drew, Boxcar Children—lined the bookshelf, but looked as if
their spines had never been cracked. Two porcelain dolls and a stuffed
horse stood like sentinels on a shelf. The only sign of childhood was a
unicorn poster on her wall. If I could mother her, I thought, I'd buy
Danielle silly things—a Slinky, bandannas, pop-bead necklaces. But of
course she was their child, not mine, and I had managed my own mistakes with the two I had, though they were basically good kids. That
much I knew.

I needed to get away from this room, feeling as if I could stifle
here, as if someone had sucked the air out. I tiptoed down the hall,
heading farther into the west wing. The door was open; I wandered
in. I felt that pleasure Shana said she experienced having the keys to
other people's houses, thinking about what might be revealed there.

In the room Nick and Margaret still shared, I opened drawers,
rummaged through. I was looking for something, though I couldn't
say what. Opening Nick's first, I found boxer shorts, neatly pressed
and folded, T-shirts laundered a spotless white. The drawer smelled
faintly of Nick's sweat and his Paco Rabanne cologne.

In the dresser on the opposite side of the room, I found her things.
The top drawer contained blue silk underwear, a red teddy. The silk
lingerie slipped through my fingers. I fondled black panties with a red
trim. What could she possibly do in these? Nick had never mentioned
this side of their life together. Had they played games behind these
closed doors I didn't want to imagine? Was this the way she had
enticed and held him all these years? I did not want to contemplate it.

I moved swiftly through T-shirts, athletic clothes, cotton pajamas. Then I came to a bottom drawer, different from the others in its disarray. It was filled with odds and ends—old receipts, a school ring, miniature soap and shampoo bottles taken from hotel rooms, sewing kits, odd buttons, a box of old letters. But I did not reach for any of these. Instead my hand reached around, looking for something but I didn't know what. I dug in the back and something soft brushed against my hand.

Reaching for it, I pulled out what looked like a small animal, soft and furry. I turned it, staring, because it was something I had seen before but couldn't quite remember when. I stood in their bedroom holding a scarlet rabbit's foot on a key chain in my fist.

On the plush carpet I didn't hear the footsteps. I missed the slamming of the car door, the walk across the entranceway. Now Margaret stood glaring at me in her stiletto heels and toreador pants, her black hair wild with thick curls, where I expected to see twigs and leaves as if she had just barreled through the woods to get here. Her eyes were red with rage. "What are you doing here?" she shouted at me. "What are you doing in my house?"

"There was smoke," I told her. Margaret sniffed the air. "I wanted to be sure everyone was all right."

"But what are you doing here?" If she'd had a gun, I believe she would have shot me. Instead she just stood there, hands on her hips. Defiantly I stood before her and now I opened my palm slowly, letting the rabbit's foot roll onto my fingertips. "I came back for this."

She stared at it, then back at me. Perhaps from her look she had forgotten it was there. Or when I'd given it to her. Or that she'd claimed to have lost it so many years ago.

Then she said, "If it's yours, take it. Take it and get out of here."

38

Two days later Margaret left a message with my mother, saying that she wanted to see me. I phoned Nick to ask him what he thought I should do. "Call her," he said, his voice sounding relieved. "Maybe she wants to make peace."

"What do you mean?"

"I'm moving out next week. She seems ready to accept it."

"All right, I'll see her."

We met at the coffee shop in the newly refurbished mall off Main Street. It was a trendy little place with lots of espresso machines and steamed milk and housewives in workout suits with strollers. Margaret came in, wearing a jacket with padded shoulders, tight black jeans, and boots. She looked ready for Los Angeles, not Winonah, and it seemed to me that she was a woman whose experiences had never quite lived up to her expectations, though she'd come close.

We ordered our coffee, then sat down at a table by the window. "This is a little awkward, I know," Margaret said.

"Yes, I guess it is."

"Well, all's fair in love and war, isn't it? Anyway, Nick and I were probably not going to make it. I want you to know this, Tess. I don't blame you. I want you to remember that."

"You don't blame me," I said. "Well, I blame you."

She looked at me oddly. "Because I went with Patrick to the prom?"

"You must be kidding. No. Because my father had an affair with your mother; because you knew about it for years and you never told me."

"I was supposed to tell you?" Margaret looked at me, stunned. "Your parents never broke up; they stayed together. You had your family intact."

"Everything was ruined."

"Not like it was for me," she said cryptically.

"What do you mean?"

"Oh, it doesn't matter what I mean. It's the truth, that's all."

I took a sip of my coffee, but it was too hot and I burned my tongue. In the background a child cried as its mother spoke in harsh tones. "I'm sorry I went into your house the other day. I'm sorry I went through your things."

"It doesn't matter, Tess. I don't blame you for seeing Nick. For wanting to get back at me."

"I don't think that's what I've been trying to do."

"Oh, who knows what we've been trying to do. . . . Anyway, none of it matters now." She got an odd, distant look in her eyes, as if she saw someone she knew crossing the street. I looked behind me, but no one was there. Then she laughed that high-pitched laugh, but I just shook my head. I didn't know what the real joke was.

"Anyway, I was going to give it back to you. Here. I was going to give everything back to you. I brought you a few things I wanted you to have."

She handed me a thick brown envelope and nodded for me to open it. Inside was my old dog tag with my name on it that I'd been missing for years. The cardinal and bluejay feathers that had once been in my room were wrapped in a piece of yellowed newspaper. The Chicago Cubs T-shirt I'd lent her that night when we spun around in the rain was folded neatly and pressed.

"I was planning on giving you back the rabbit's foot anyway," she said. "You didn't need to take it."

"You kept all these things?" I asked, stunned.

She nodded slowly. Some were stolen from me. Some I'd lent her. What surprised me most was how much at that moment Margaret seemed to resemble me. How she saved things just like I did.

"I know you never liked me that much," Margaret said. "I know you hold things that happened in your life against me. But remember, Tessie, no matter what, we're blood sisters. We're bound for life."

39

The day it happened was an October afternoon when the sugar maples turn a blazing gold, like treasure from a pirate's chest. It was the kind of Indian summer day we'd once walked home from school in, dragging our heels, leaves crunching beneath them, the smell of burning in the air. We'd stop in the Episcopal churchyard and scoop up horse chestnuts in their thorny shells, stuffing them into our pockets until the light began to fade. Then we'd race home before our mothers came looking for us.

I had always loved those days of Indian summer. I'd dallied in them, been late, faced my mother's reprimands, all for the crunch of leaves and a pocket of thorny pods and that smell of burning. But that has all changed. Now, something in that time of year has been irrevocably taken from me.

In the brilliance of that afternoon an ordinary blue car pulled over to the side of the railroad crossing. No one really noticed the car or that Margaret was waiting inside. Later the neighbors said that they hadn't paid attention to how long she waited at the intersection not far from the Potomie River. It is just a small commuter stop where you can't even buy a ticket and there's hardly ever a stationmaster there.

It's a convenience stop, really, just a few blocks from the site of the Havenhill Summer Festival, that music event that draws conductors and orchestras from all over the world, that for two months a year puts Winonah on the map. In the summer you can see people from Chicago and as far north as Madison walking with their picnic baskets and blankets from the station along Dearborn Road to the old Potomie park.

As a girl, I'd lain in the grass at Havenhill for a Joan Baez concert or Crosby, Stills and Nash. Or listened to the Chicago Symphony with Ozawa conducting Beethoven's Ninth on the Fourth of July. I'd eat fried chicken and potato salad and make out under a blanket with some boy I hardly knew, whose name I cannot recall, let alone his face. Once I came home with mosquito bites all up and down my arm.

But the music season was long over and it wasn't the busiest intersection anyway so no one noticed the blue car. Nor did anyone notice the woman inside or what she was doing. Many women in Winonah pull over by the side of the railroad tracks to wait for their husbands to get off the commuter trains that take them into the city. No one paid any attention that it was too early for husbands to be coming back or that the woman in the blue car was waiting on the Milwaukee side of the tracks.

But the people who lived nearby would always remember the sound of metal, the shatter of breaking glass. Some rushed out, thinking the train had derailed. Others would report hearing screams, but hardly anyone on the train was hurt, though a few were tossed about by the sudden stop.

I wasn't there. I only know what I read in the newspapers and what people told me, the people I have known all my life. I only know what happened because I read about it and I can imagine it. But I do know what kind of day it was. It was one of those brilliant, golden days—the kind of day when Margaret Blair came to live in Winonah in the first place.

It was in October that Nick phoned and told me he'd moved out. "Tessie, would you come and help me get settled?" Though I had only been back a few weeks, I didn't hesitate. I flew back as soon as I could. Nick was moving into an apartment in a building he owned—the same building where Margaret and her mother had first lived.

I rented a car at the airport and drove right to Prairie Vista. Nick had already unpacked the little he'd brought with him. Just enough dishes and silverware, sheets and towels to get him through the next few months. Yet there was something cheery and hopeful about the almost barren apartment, and Nick looked as happy as I'd ever seen him when I rang the buzzer. I walked up the dreary stairwell, and he greeted me at the top. "Come check out my new bachelor pad," he said. It was a convenience, he explained, just across the street from the office. "I'll just be here a month or two," he assured me.

Nick had decided he would sell the big house by the lake. He didn't need it, he said. "Besides," he told me, "it was never really mine. Not really."

He'd buy Margaret and Danielle a town house and he'd take an apartment for himself in the city. I noticed, I couldn't help but notice, that when he said this, he made no mention of our being together. But he was distracted and kept saying it was just a temporary move into the apartment across from the repair shop.

Besides, the neighborhood had changed over the years. It had changed so much that residents complained that the repair shop shouldn't be there anymore and if it wasn't the business of one of the town's most celebrated residents, they would have forced it out, though some of the newcomers didn't know who Cy Schoenfield, the great quarterback, was. Or if they did, they didn't care.

Nick had furnished the apartment with furniture loans from friends and a mattress from Dial-a-Bed. It was just for now, he kept saying. I helped him shove a dresser against the wall. Put the bed so that it faced the sunny windows. After we moved the bed, we made love, on top of the sheets, the sun pouring in. Afterward we just lay there. It was a warm, lazy afternoon and I thought we would stay there forever. I was pretty clear about what I was going to do and Nick and I had been lying in bed discussing it. If there had ever been a moment of decision in my life, it was now. In a month or so I would come home for an extended stay. If all went well, by next spring I'd put my house on the market. "I want you to be with me," Nick said, stroking my head. "We're going to make that happen. . . ."

"And I want to be with you," I said at last. Just then the phone rang. We both stared at it.

Nick hesitated to pick it up. Then he reasoned, "It could be Danielle." But it was Margaret, calling to say that Clarice had had some kind of an attack. "What kind of attack?" I heard Nick say.

Nothing too serious, Margaret said. They didn't know for sure. She just had a spell, a kind of fainting, but the doctors wanted to make certain it wasn't her heart, so she was in the hospital out in Crestwood and Margaret needed to get there. "Could you be sure to meet Danielle when she comes home from school?" Margaret said.

Nick said he would be there and wait until she came home. And then she added, "Say hi to Tess for me."

Nick looked at the phone oddly. When he hung up, he seemed perplexed. "She told me to say hello to you." Before he went home to meet Danielle after she got out of school, he told me to come with him. "She knows about you. I think she's all right about it."

When we got to the house, Danielle gave me that cold stare she'd given me the first time I'd come there, carrying Vicky's dog after we'd been stuck in the ravines. But she gave her father a hug. "Daddy, you're home." She said it in such a way that I knew she was thinking he'd come home to stay. "Where's Mummy?" she asked, looking around, almost looking through me, as if I weren't standing there. Nick told her that her mother had to go do something and she'd be back later. Danielle went and did her homework while Nick defrosted a pizza. I wanted to make them a proper dinner, but he said it would be too strange if I cooked in their kitchen.

"Yes, I suppose you're right."

We ate pepperoni and cheese pizza with a small salad and Cokes in front of the television. After dinner Danielle showed Nick her home-work and he patted her on the shoulder because she had gotten all her math right, which was not her strongest subject, he told me. Danielle blushed and seemed to smile and that gave me the hope that she might warm up to me with time. Then he put on some Coltrane and asked Danielle what she wanted to do until bedtime. I could see that already he was getting anxious because Margaret was taking so long. He kept glancing at the clock over the mantel. "I wish your mother would call," he said at one point.

"Me too," Danielle said. "Let's play Scrabble until she gets here."

We played for a while. I had terrible letters. Useless consonants like "V" and "W" and two "O"s. There was little I could do on the board, though Danielle was very good and she had also drawn good letters. She put down "parrot" and "compass", but the best I could do was "who" and "vow." Nick was distracted as he played and he kept asking Danielle for help. He looked at the clock from time to time and Danielle kept asking when her mother was coming home.

Finally Nick got up and went into the kitchen to phone the hospital in Crestwood. I could see that he was concerned about Clarice. I followed him in, ostensibly to get something to drink, and saw his face turn pale, his hand tremble as he held the phone. He asked for patient information; Clarice Blair was not in the hospital. Nor had she been there that day. He asked over and over again, "Are you sure? Can you check again?"

Then he phoned Winonah General. Then he called Clarice at her house in Crestwood. When she answered, Nick told me later, he knew. "You aren't sick?" he said to her.

"No," she answered, "never felt better. Why?"

When he got off the phone, he called the police. Already Danielle was hollering from the living room for him to come and finish the game, but Nick just shook his head. He put his hand over the phone, shouting, "Tell her I'll be right there." When he told them that he thought his wife was missing, the police suggested he come down to the station.

When he asked why, the pitch of his voice rising, they told him there had been an incident on the railroad tracks. It was an express train, the police told him. There weren't many of those a day so she must have planned it well. Later a neighbor said that she thought she'd seen Margaret's car parked down the street, waiting until Nick arrived at the house. The last thing Margaret did was make sure that Danielle would not come home to an empty house.

I tried to hide how stunned I was. How was this possible? I found myself shaking as he told me and then went into the bathroom and sobbed, not wanting Danielle to see me. Before Nick went to identify the body, Danielle threw her arms around his neck, demanding to know where he was going.

"I'm going to get Mommy," he told her. Then he asked me to walk him to the car. "Would you stay here with Danielle," he said, "until I get home?"

"Of course I will," I said, leaning into the car.

Then he put his head on the steering wheel and began weeping, sobbing like a baby. I reached across, stroking his hair. Finally he composed himself. "How could she do this?" he said. "How could she leave a child behind?"

When he drove off, I turned and saw Danielle staring at me from the picture window of the house. When I came inside, she just stood there, glaring at me with her cold, dark eyes. "Do you want to read a book?" I asked her. "Would you like to play another game? We could play Monopoly," I said, "or Clue. I could make us some cocoa."

But she stood there in her little pink bathrobe, silent and morose, and I stared at this poor, motherless child who was just a decade old, the same age I'd been when I met her mother, and my heart went out to her. I could see how Margaret could do this to herself, but how could she do this to her child? When my children were small and my marriage was breaking up, I felt at times as if I could just jump off the bluffs, do myself in. But how could I leave my children behind? Now, gazing at Danielle, I thought I would raise her as my own. I could love her and my love would soften her, somehow take away her edges, make her want to curl up and read a book, listen to a story. Take the dolls down from her shelves. I'd bring her a pet, I thought. A puppy dog that she could love.

But Danielle kept looking at me in the oddest way. Then she said, "I'm not stupid, you know."

"Oh, I know you aren't stupid, Danielle."

"I know that something is wrong. My mother has never done this before. She has never not come home."

"You're right. Something is wrong. Your father has gone to find out what it is. Do you want to wait up for him? Do you want to play a game?" I just looked at her, not sure of what to say. I kept thinking she would burst out crying. I didn't expect she would rush into my arms, but I thought she might let me comfort her somehow. Instead she kept her icy stare on me. "We could do something," I told her, "to pass the time until your father gets back."

But she stood up abruptly. "I don't want you," she shouted at me. "I want my mother."

She stomped off to her room as I sat in the living room, folding my face into my hands where I wept silently. At the same time I was listening, ready to rush to her side, but I didn't hear a sound. After a few moments I went to check on her. Her light was off and she was turned to the wall. When I touched her, she was sobbing. "Danielle," I said.

"Get away from me," she cried.

"I'll be in the living room," I said, "if you want me."

I went back to the sofa where I stretched out, listening for her. I must have drifted off because when I awoke, there was a knock at the door. I thought it would be Nick, but instead there was a man I'd never seen before. A woman stood behind him in the shadows. Though her hair had turned gray and she seemed wraithlike in the shadows, I recognized her.

"Hello, Clarice," I said. "It's Tess. Tess Winterstone." I hadn't seen her since my father's funeral. I was surprised she'd had the nerve to show up, but she had. She'd stood at the back and hadn't gone to the graveside, though Art tells me fresh flowers come to my father's grave on the first of every month.

"I thought you might be here, Tess," Clarice said. "Nick told me to come and look after Danielle. He has things to tend to, arrangements to make."

"Well, I could stay," I offered, "and wait for him." Somehow I felt that if I went now, I wouldn't be coming back. I felt as if I had to hold on.

"He asked that we stay with Danielle. He said he'd call you in the morning."

I nodded. "All right, Clarice. I'll go."

"Well, Tess, I suppose you got what you wanted, didn't you? I suppose it's only fair. That we should both lose what matters most to us. That it should end this way." Clarice spoke in a bitter, unforgiving voice.

"I didn't have anything to do with this, Clarice, and I certainly didn't want it to happen."

Clarice was hidden in the shadows behind the light, where I could hardly see her. I couldn't make out her features. She was a thin, ghostly figure in the darkness. Deep, hiccuping sobs came from somewhere in her chest. She doubled over, as if she were in terrible pain, howling like an animal, and the man who'd come with her held her up. I went into the kitchen and wrote a note to Nick. I told him how sorry I was and that I would be at Vicky's.

I gave him her number and said I wanted to be there for him and for Danielle. Folding the note three times, I stuck it under the coffee-pot, where I was sure he'd see it in the morning. I told Clarice I was very sorry and she looked at me as if I were a stranger to her, not a girl she'd once begged to stay to play with her daughter.

When I left, they shut the door and pulled down all the blinds so that the house was cloaked in faint, shadowy light. I watched the house for a few moments. Then I got into my rental car and drove down the road toward the railroad trestle, made a left, and drove until I saw the police cars and the wreck.

She had killed herself just beyond the place where I liked to wander when I was a girl. At the place where the town divides itself in two, where the rich live on one side and the poor on the other. Just beyond the underpass where I used to say good-bye to her and she'd go her way and I'd go mine.

———

That night I waited at Vicky's for Nick to call, but he never did. Vicky had already heard, as had the rest of the town. "It's a very tragic thing" was all Vicky said, "especially for the child." There was something in her voice, I could tell, that was blaming me. Even though she didn't say it, even though she didn't even imply it, somehow it was my fault. Though I had never so much as shoplifted a candy bar as a kid, I felt like a criminal now. I had brought this on and even as Vicky poured me a drink, then said good night, I knew something about my friendship with her—and everyone else in this town—had been altered.

In the morning when I still hadn't heard from Nick, I called the house. Danielle answered the phone and surprised me by sounding so grown up that for a moment I took her to be her mother. "Could I speak with Nick, please?"

"He doesn't want to talk to anyone," she said.

"Danielle," I said softly, "I'm so sorry about your mom. It's me, Tess. Tell him I'm on the phone, tell him I need to talk to him."

But she'd already hung up.

After lunch I drove over to pay a condolence call. Cars lined the driveway. When I walked in, Nick saw me, but there was a blank look to his eyes.

"She didn't seem to even care when I told her I was moving out. She didn't blink an eye. I can't imagine what would have made her do that. I really can't," he said.

Then he told me what I hadn't known. Margaret left no letter, but she had a cryptic note in her bag when she died. He reached into his pocket, pulled it out. It read: *I waited as long as I could.* "Waited for what?" he asked me, tears in his eyes. "Waited for whom? What would make her do such a thing?" he said, now breaking down in sobs.

"I don't know." I shook my head. "I have no idea. I just know that I want to be there for you."

"Then leave me alone for now," he said. "Let me call you after the funeral."

The funeral was held the next day at Our Lady of the Meadows, a Catholic church in Prairie Vista. I bought a black dress and sat in the back. I was ashamed and tears rolled down my cheeks. This was all my fault. I'd brought ruin on all these people. At the funeral, Danielle stared straight ahead with cold, dark eyes. I kept thinking I'd see her break down and weep, but she just stared.

Once Danielle turned and looked at the crowd that stood behind her in the church and for a moment her eyes landed on me. But there was a blankness to her stare. Nick cried on the coffin. He wept and broke down and he had to be pulled away. I stood at a distance, watching him. In the end Margaret was buried in Winonah in the cemetery near the lake, the place where she'd always wanted to be.

That afternoon I joined the mourners back at his house and Nick took me aside. "I care for you, Tess. I really do. But I'm going to need some time. Go home and in a few weeks I'll come out and see you."

"But I don't want to go home. This town is my home too. I want to be with you."

He shook his head. "Not now."

When I returned to Vicky's that evening, she was waiting up for me, reading the *Winonah Weekly*. Her slender white fingers held the paper and I thought how she did have beautiful hands, how it was right that people should pay to admire them. She passed me the newspaper. "Here. It's all here."

The article gave the details of Margaret's death, said that Margaret Blair Schoenfield's car had stopped on the railroad tracks at a well-lit crossing. It was assumed to be a suicide and that she was despondent over her failed marriage to the son of a former football star. She was survived by one child, age ten, and her husband, from whom she was estranged. I read that the engineer said he saw her coming only at the very last moment, as if she'd appeared out of nowhere, and then it was too late. He wasn't even traveling fast because he was coming into the station, though it was not a scheduled stop. She just drove on the tracks and stayed there, he said. She didn't move.

"May I keep this?" I asked Vicky after I'd read it through.

"Of course you can." Vicky tore it out of the *Winonah Weekly* for me. "Still saving things. You haven't changed much, have you?" She handed me the clipping and I folded it neatly, then tucked it inside my wallet.

That night I went to Paradise and Patrick was there. He sat down beside me and had a beer. "I saw you at the funeral," he said.

I nodded, sipping my beer. "I feel terrible . . ." Patrick reached across, clutching my fingers. "But I saw Margaret just last week. She acted as if everything was fine. As if there were no bad feelings." Tears started to come to my eyes; in fact, I did not understand what had happened or why. I tried to reconstruct what had happened when I'd seen Margaret that day for coffee.

What had I missed? Some gesture, some word I hadn't quite gotten at the time? Of course it was strange that she'd given me those items that she'd saved over the years. But her manner was so natural, almost breezy. Now as I sat there, with Patrick's fingers wrapped around mine, I was certain there was something I'd overlooked, something I just hadn't seen.

"Tess, there was always something off about her. I don't know what it was. Maybe this doesn't have anything to do with you."

I just shook my head. "How could it not?"

"I don't know," Patrick said, "but maybe it doesn't."

Just then the door opened and Nick walked in with a crowd of friends. They were all quiet and subdued. When Nick saw me, he gave me a little nod, but he didn't come my way. "Just give him some time," Patrick said. "He'll come around. He doesn't know what hit him."

"Thanks." I patted Patrick on the hand. "That's good advice."

"Don't blame yourself, Tess," Patrick said.

When Patrick left, I stayed at the bar drinking my beer. I ordered another, but felt strange sitting there alone. I looked over at Nick, who sat with his friends, and gave him a little smile. At last he got up and came over to the bar and sat down beside me. His movements were wooden, like those of an actor uncomfortable in his role.

"Tess," Nick said at last. "I don't know how to say this, but I can't see you for a while. I feel sickened by everything. I don't know that I'll ever feel any differently."

"But it will pass," I told him. I hesitated, but then I said, "We can be together now if we want." I spoke softly, just loud enough for him to hear me. "There's nothing to keep us apart."

"Yes, there is," he said, shaking his head.

"Who? What?" I asked him, my voice quivering.

I was sure he was going to say Danielle, but instead he said, "Margaret will keep us apart. That's who."

40

Because I keep everything, and I always have, I knew just where I'd find the yearbooks. They were in the back of the old storage closet off the garage. When I got home, I dug them out and propped them up on the table in the breakfast nook. Then I went to the index and found where her name was listed.

I spent the next few days in my breakfast nook, where Francis Eagger drank himself to death, staring at the pictures of Margaret Blair. In fact she was not in many pictures. Though it wasn't easy in our high school to avoid being in the yearbook, she had managed fairly well. But in the few I found of her, Margaret seemed to be gazing down, the way she used to when she lived above Santini's Liquor in Prairie Vista. She stood in the back row, off to one side, her long black hair tumbling around her face. Was she hiding? Didn't she want to be seen?

In some she was just a blur, as if she had moved at the moment the picture was being snapped. This wouldn't surprise me at all. Because there was something about her even then that could never be pinned down, that was always trying to get away.

Margaret, frozen in time. She wouldn't wear reading glasses or see her hair turn gray. She wouldn't get those little wrinkles I was starting to get around the mouth, those furrows on the brow that Jade said came from frowning in your sleep. You look angry, Jade tells me, when you sleep. Margaret would just stay right there, the way she was.

Turning to the back of the yearbook I read what had been inscribed: "To Tess from Margaret, don't read what I've written in the corner." She had dog-eared a corner of the page. I opened this and read, "Only rats look in corners."

When the kids got home from work that night, Jade took one look at me. "What is it, Mom? What's wrong? You look terrible."

Then I told them about Margaret. It all poured out.

"What was it?" Ted asked. "What did it say?"

"It said that she'd waited as long as she could."

"What did she mean by that?"

"I don't know. Maybe she was waiting for Nick to come back to her. I don't know."

Jade was very upset. "Mom," she said, "what're you going to do?"

"I don't know," I told them, "be patient. Wait." A chill passed through me as I said that. Wait for how long? Wasn't that just what Margaret had tried to do?

"God," Ted said, "did she kill herself because of you?"

Jade motioned for him to be quiet, but that was the truth of it, wasn't it? She'd killed herself because of me. "Yes," I said, "I believe she did. And she left behind her child."

I stayed up that night, drinking. It wasn't something I normally did, but I could not sleep. I longed for Nick, but made a promise to myself that I would not call. I'd hear from him when he was ready. And with time I felt certain he would be.

But finally I couldn't stand it any longer. I had to hear his voice. In the morning when I picked up the phone to dial, my neighbor Betsy was on the line. She was talking to a doctor's office, setting up an appointment. I didn't want to listen, but I did. Infertility. She had tried everything to have a child.

The next day when I saw Betsy, I gave her a wave. I thought perhaps I'd have her over for coffee someday.

Later that night when I couldn't sleep, I poured myself a brandy. Then I picked up the phone and called Nick. I let it ring three, four times. Night after night I phoned, thinking he would be waiting by the phone, that he would know it was me.

But he never answered. I left messages, but he never called me back. I found I still could not sleep. I wondered where he was, what he was doing. I had dreams of him at night, of his hands on my body, of his body looming above mine. I found myself raw and exposed as I hadn't been since I was a child.

Once I phoned and Danielle answered. I heard her voice on the other end, insistent, almost in a rage. "Who's there," she shouted into the phone and I hung up.

In the paths in the hills above my house wildflowers grow. At certain times of the year after heavy rains the hills are carpeted in small blue and white flowers, thick patches of yellow, tiny shades of rose. It was that time of year now. I thought if I forced myself to get up early and go for a run, I'd be able to sleep at night. I began getting up before seven and heading into the hills. I'd run several miles, making a loop that brought me home. Each day I ran farther and farther, as if I had to get away. Morning after morning I would be gone an hour, then two. The path I took was paved, but it quickly turned to dirt. Wildflowers lined the path. Trees dropped back after the first mile or so. Higher up, the landscape turned to desert; scrub pine, thistle weed grew in abundance. I ran until I couldn't see the highway or any houses. Sometimes I thought I could just keep going and never stop.

One morning, the air was brisk, the ground firm beneath my feet. I ran for a mile or so, then higher. At the point where I should have turned back, I kept going, my body unwilling to return. I was soaring. I was flying and climbing as if I could just keep going. As if there was nothing to stop me.

In the hills the day was warmer and sweat dripped, evaporating as soon as it hit the air. So this was what it felt like to be free, to be a bird. My body flying through the air. My body flying like the wind. I went up higher into the hills, way above Salinas, behind my heels was a trail of dust. I kicked up the dirt as I climbed into the scrub pine, the desolate places where nothing will grow.

I was high above the ocean and I couldn't even tell it was an ocean anymore. It was as if the sky started just there at the shore, which was now the horizon. I didn't hear a thing except my heart and my feet pounding. My breathing was a steady pant and sweat poured down me, my T-shirt clung to my breasts. If someone wanted to rape me, I always told myself as I ran up here, he'd have to catch me first. So far no one had tried. I never saw anybody up here. There used to be a guy who trained in these hills but I hadn't seen him in a long time and any-way, we didn't run at the same time of the day. I was running on straight to a grove of pines, like nothing would stop me or could stop me, and then I saw her.

Those yellow eyes fixed on me. A dead stare. It took everything in me to stop. Stop cold. I thought my heart would burst. I'd die right there. It is a fitting end, I thought. Looking her in the eyes. Our eyes fixed on each other. She was in a branch, a low branch, and poised. Ten yards farther and she would have pounced on my neck. Now it's this standoff, I think, and if I move, I'm dinner. Or maybe I'm dinner no matter what I do. I'm a dead woman right here. I'm going to be eaten alive and they'll only know it's me from the dental records if they find my teeth. One of us has got to move and I know it won't be me.

Then I saw it. Her shoulder twitched. Just a tiny twitch but enough to tell me she was ready to make her move. She jumped down and all those yellow muscles rippled and her flesh moved like sound waves, like foam rubber. Muscles moving and with a thud and four rising waves of dust, she hit the ground, her yellow eyes never off me.

My heart pounded in my chest. Hairs bristled on my arms and I couldn't catch my breath. I stood there, staring straight at her as she stared at me. I vowed I would not be the first to move. Then suddenly, with all those powerful yellow muscles rippling, she turned and walked away.

I arrived home, panting, hot, dripping wet. Though I'd walked the last half mile home, my heart was still pounding, my hands shaking as I opened the mailbox. There was the usual assortment of junk mail, bills I couldn't pay, solicitations from organizations that I made nominal contributions to. Walking into the kitchen, I threw the mail down on the counter and poured myself a glass of herbal ice tea. I downed the tea, pressed an ice cube to my temple. Then I opened a drawer to look for some Tylenol.

There in the drawer where I kept recipes and over-the-counter drugs was the envelope Margaret had given me the last time I saw her—the one that contained my old dog tag, bird feathers, and the Chicago Cubs T-shirt. I sat down in the breakfast nook with my herbal tea and opened the envelope once more, spreading the items in front of me.

I kept the feathers in front of me, moved the dog tag and T-shirt to the side. The clipping the feathers were wrapped in was from an old Kenosha newspaper, dated some forty years ago. It was yellow and tattered, almost crumbling in my hands. I hadn't noticed it when Margaret first gave me the envelope, but now I unfolded and read it. On the back was an advertisement for soap. A notice about a missing dog. On the other side were obituaries. One was for a schoolteacher from Milwaukee who had been a believer in equal education. The other was for a Wisconsin man who had jumped or fallen to his death off a railroad bridge when he was forty-nine years old. Then it gave the funeral arrangements, and that was all.

I was puzzling over this clipping, wondering if there was any reason why it had been placed among my things, when there was a knock at the door. I stuffed everything back in the envelope and stuck it in the kitchen drawer by the sink, which was already filled with recipes and flyers for men who wanted to help me plant shrubs. Bruno stood in my doorway, staring at me, dripping wet. "Tess," he said, "are you all right?"

"I'm fine."

"Well, you look like you've seen a ghost."

"Just a cougar," I said.

"Are you sure you're all right?" He looked genuinely concerned.

"I'm fine," I told him. Suddenly I wanted to cradle him in my arms, hold him as if he were my child and not someone else's.

"Look," he said, waving a sheet of paper in my face, "I found it, I found it."

"Come in, Bruno. I really should shower." I reached for a kitchen towel and began wiping myself off.

"The poem, 'Desire Paths.' It was in some old papers, some drafts. I found it in the Santa Cruz library. Now I have the whole poem."

He handed it to me and I read it.

DESIRE PATHS
From the unfinished manuscript of Francis Cantwell Eagger

> *Along the wind-racked bluffs*
> *We have made our way*
> *To the edge and back again*
> *So many times*

That we have made a path,
Worn down weeds and shrubs.
We tried other routes
Through sharper rocks and
Steeper climbs
But this trail was the best by far
We forged the way
Of our longing.
Desire paths, these are called
Because this was the way we had to come
As if no other path presented itself
To the edge of this raw world
Where there is nothing left to do
But look down, then walk away.

"It's beautiful, Bruno," I said. "It's actually a very beautiful poem." And in truth it was the first poem by Francis Eagger that truly moved me. "It's great for your dissertation, isn't it?"

"Oh, yes," he said. "And I'm going to write some journal articles. This will help me get a job."

Holding the poem in my hands, I read it again. The way of our longing. Then I sat down in the breakfast nook and wept. I lay my head on the table and cried and cried. Bruno sat beside me, trying to comfort me.

"Tess, what is it? You can talk to me."

My body shook and I could not stop. "I think I've killed someone," I said. "I think I'm the reason that someone is dead."

"Are you sure . . ."

And then I told him about Margaret and Nick and how she had died. Then Bruno reached out for me and pulled me in. He held me tightly and I was amazed at the strength in his arms. It was the hug of a man, not a boy, but there was nothing improper in it. He held me for a very long time, then he pulled away, looking me square in the eyes. "Tess," he said, "you are also the reason someone is alive."

"I am?" I said, wiping my eyes.

"Yes," he said. "You saved me."

"I did?"

He nodded solemnly. "You don't even know it," he said, "but you did."

That night strange dreams overwhelmed me. I woke up shaking, feeling alone. I dreamed of sleepers in pods, wrapped in sheets, unable to extricate themselves. I dreamed of Jade as a little girl, going off to star in a Broadway show. I wanted to accompany her, but I was dressed in a nightgown and a robe. But the strangest dreams were always those of the two men. One was dark and clever, the other blond and simple. One was good and the other evil, but I was never sure which one it was. You'd think the clever one would be evil, the simple man good, but there was something in his simpleness that stifled me, something in the other's cleverness that uplifted me. I woke, knowing that I knew nothing of myself and never would.

After I had my coffee and sat in the breakfast nook for a while, it occurred to me that somehow these dreams were not my own. They belonged to someone else—to the troubled poet who lived here before me. Surely these haunted dreams were not mine.

Night after night I stayed up drinking. I couldn't sleep and the quiet of the house unsettled me. The children came and went but mostly they were gone. When they were away, I drank to try and sleep, then fell into a sleep that brought no rest. Nothing could save me. I tried to conjure Bruno's hug, but it too was slipping away. Nick wasn't returning my calls and Margaret was dead and I was lost as surely as if I'd wandered off into the wilderness alone.

I couldn't stand being alone in the house so I headed out into the pitch darkness along the cliffs where the poet who had drunk himself to death had lost his own son. I found the desire paths the poet had made and trudged along, finding my way. Branches cut against my face. A razor-sharp thorn tore at my sleeve. I could feel blood trickling down my arm, but I kept going. It was the blackest of nights and all I could do was follow the roar of the sea.

I walked until I came to the edge with the sea crashing below me. It was high tide and the beach was almost gone. It would be so easy to slip, to fall. Everyone would think it was an accident. They would say I had been despondent, but they'd never be sure, the way they had never been sure with Francis Cantwell Eagger's son. Or with that Wisconsin man in the clipping Margaret had given me. Not like with Margaret. They were sure about her. If I slipped and fell here, no one would know if it was what I'd intended. It would remain a big question, something people—my children, my brothers, Nick, the neighbors, even Betsy—would talk about for years to come.

My own thoughts frightened me. I'd never quite had these thoughts before. I had to fight them, fight them back. I took a deep breath. The air smelled fresh, almost lemony with the scent of eucalyptus. Then I saw it, halfway down the bluff. The hunchback tree from Francis Eagger's poem, bent over, its arms offering protection. The tree bent back in the wind. It was the one Bruno had been looking for. It had probably fallen down the cliff due to erosion. Now I stepped away. I eased my way back from the cliffs and, following the paths Francis Eagger had shaped in his own despair, made my way home.

The next night the phone rang and it was Nick. He had some business to finish up in San Francisco and he wanted to talk to me. "Tess," he said, "I'll be there next week. I think I owe you an explanation."

41

The following Friday Nick drove down to meet me at Half Moon Bay. We met at a Thai restaurant and sat in a corner booth on red vinyl seats where it was dark and rather quiet. Large tropical fish swam in tanks above our heads. No one bothered us. He looked tired and haggard. His face seemed jowly and he was not the same boisterous man I had known. In fact he slumped and seemed old. We ordered drinks, but Nick said he wasn't hungry. "I don't have much of an appetite these days."

I nodded. "I can imagine. How are things? How's Danielle?"

"Not so good. She's silent, then she blows up. I don't know what I'm going to do."

"She blows up? How?"

"She hits people. For no reason." Nick shook his head back and forth like a man who had reached the end of his rope.

"She needs a mother."

"She had a mother," Nick said, the bitterness unmistakable in his voice. "I will never understand this." He reached across the table for my hands. "Tessie, I wanted things to be different. I didn't want it to work out this way. I don't know why she did this. I don't know why it happened. I just know that at least for now we can't be together. I'm not going to be able to look at you and not think of her." He turned my hands in his. "I can't look at your face and not see Margaret's. Do you understand?"

"Yes, I understand. Maybe she wanted it that way. Maybe she did it on purpose." I was angry and wished I hadn't said what I just did.

"I don't know why she did it. She seemed to take it all in stride. She didn't want to stay married any more than I did. I don't know what it was. Honestly it's a mystery to us all. I never thought she'd leave Danielle; that's the part that makes no sense. But somehow I don't think it was about us. Not entirely anyway."

"Then what was it about?"

He shook his head again and he looked pathetic and small. "I keep thinking about the note. What was she waiting for or who? What did it mean? That she'd waited as long as she could?"

"Maybe it will be better in time," I said, wrapping my fingers more tightly around his.

"Maybe," he said, but he did not sound convinced.

"I was thinking I could move home, be near you and Danielle."

Nick raised his hands. "Oh, no, don't do that. Not on my account."

We were silent for a moment and I understood that it was no use. It was over. He planned to go on with his life and I was to go on with mine and that was how it was to be.

I signaled the waitress for the check. As we waited for it to come, I said, "Nick, may I ask you something?"

"Of course you can."

"Did Margaret ever talk to you about her father? She used to talk to me about him. She always seemed to be waiting for him to come and get her."

"She certainly wasn't waiting for him." Nick looked perplexed. "I was sure you knew. He died when she was a little girl."

"He did? She told me he was in Wisconsin." I couldn't bear to contemplate where all those gifts had come from. The clothes, the car.

"I don't think she was waiting. He was dead a long time before she ever moved to Winonah."

"But she told me . . ."

Nick downed his beer and kissed me lightly on the cheek. I couldn't let him go so easily. I reached up, my hands searching his face. My lips reached for his. If I could only, like some skilled fishermen, pull him in gently, bring him back to where we had been, but he was like someone with no memory of anything before. His eyes were red and watery. "I've got to go," he said. "I'll always care for you, Tess."

Standing up, he reached across, placing his hand on my cheek, and I let my face rest in it for a moment. Then when I looked up, he was gone.

Over the next few days, the mail built up, one letter after the next. I opened a few bills, then put them away. The creditors could take my house. I didn't care. I sat reading the complete works of Francis Cantwell Eagger. I felt I owed it to this house before I put it on the market to know the work of the man who lived here.

The children were away. Ted had gone back to Sabe. Jade was with her dad in San Francisco, looking for more substantial work. I found myself with nothing to do. Nowhere that I had to be. It was good because I seemed to be so tired. I had never felt so tired and thought this would be a good time to sleep. I slept perhaps for a day or so. I lost track of the time, just slipping in and out of bed to go to the bathroom, to get a bite to eat.

At first I had cereal, big bowls of it, until I ran out of milk. Then I ate carrots, small salads, crackers. Dishes piled up in the sink. The bed went unmade. I sat up in my pajamas in bed, reading. I read through and through the collected works of Francis Cantwell Eagger. Once in a while I'd check the refrigerator. I should eat something, I'd tell myself. I knew I should eat. I even had a memory of eating. Certain foods came to me, like fried chicken, olives, ice cream, but when I opened the refrigerator nothing appealed to me, nothing made sense. There were eggs, bread, beans, onions, jam, but I had no desire to combine these ingredients—to make a sandwich, a bowl of soup.

I had tea, cups of it, and when I ran out of tea, I sipped water with lemon. I stopped answering the phone or the door. There was no one I wanted to talk to, no one I wanted to see. I don't remember eating, though I do remember drinking at night, long sips of brandy. I drank until I was drowsy. Some nights I walked the cliffs, half inebriated. I am becoming the poet whose house I inhabit, I said to myself one night as I fell asleep in my chair, the Winonah centennial blanket draped over me. All day long and sometimes all night I read his work, one poem after the other, even the half-baked poems that somehow contained my own sorry dreams.

The days folded one into the next. Sometimes I slept when it was light out; often at night I read, then slept with my light on. I had lost track of time, the hours. I was sure there were things I was supposed to do, but I couldn't seem to remember what they were or why I had to do them. I was so tired. I couldn't seem to sleep enough, but I'd sleep, wake up tired, then sleep again.

One afternoon there was a knock at the door. I ignored it, went back to sleep. But the knocking kept coming. It was an insistent, almost angry knock. Betsy, my neighbor, stood there in blue jeans, a sweater, her dog on a leash. Betsy, infertile, in a second dead-end marriage, her pathetic life conveyed to me over crossed wires, held the door back and stared at me as if she'd expected to find someone else. I thought she was going to complain about the crossed wires or hand me a piece of my junk mail she had received. Instead she looked shocked to see me. "Your daughter phoned me," she said. "She's worried about you. She says you haven't been answering your phone." Then she looked me up and down again. "Are you all right?"

"I'm fine," I said, "I've just been very tired." But Betsy kept looking at me with concern.

"You don't look fine," she said.

"No, really, I am."

She tied the dog up. I noticed that it was an obedient dog. When she told it to sit, it just sat. Then she came inside. She saw the mess. "Are you ill?"

"I don't know. I don't think so."

I know a lot about you, I wanted to tell her. You can't have children, you give friends poor advice, your marriage is floundering. "You should eat something," she said. "I'm going to call your daughter and tell her to come. I'll stay here for a few hours while you rest."

"I'm not very hungry," I told her. "I think I want to go to bed."

"All right," Betsy said, "I'm going to help you to bed, then I'll wait until your daughter gets here." Betsy took me by the arm, led me back to my room. As I crawled into bed, I got a glimpse of myself in the mirror on the bathroom wall. I didn't quite recognize the person who stood there. I was dirty. My hair clung to my head. Dark circles like saucers lay beneath my eyes. I looked like a shell of my former self. How long had I been alone? Three or four days? A week? I couldn't recall.

Now as I crawled between the sheets, I was so tired. I couldn't remember ever being so tired. I was vaguely aware of time passing, the light moving across the wall of the room. Somewhere in the house, appliances whirred. It was a strange sleep, like on an airplane, when you are aware of everything around you, yet you are sleeping. I heard the sound of the dryer, clothes being tossed around. Somewhere a dog barked and I knew it was Betsy's dog.

When I woke again, it was dark and Jade was sitting in a chair beside me. She was staring at me in such a concerned way that I thought perhaps I was in a hospital until I heard the surf pounding below. "Mom," she said, "what's become of you?"

"I'm not really sure."

She put on the small light by the bed stand. It was just five in the morning, but she had me sit up. "When did you eat last?"

I shook my head. "I don't know, really. I was so tired."

Jade pulled the covers back and led me into the kitchen, where all the dishes had been washed, the counters wiped clean. She made me eat some soup that sat bubbling on the stove. Then Jade ran a hot bath with orange-scented bubbles. As the tub filled, I sat beside it. "Now, I'm going to help you take off your things." My daughter undressed me, dropping my pajamas into the hamper, helping me slip my panties off. When I stood naked in front of her, Jade took me by the arm, easing me into the tub. Then Jade sat at the side of the tub with a glass of ice water and a sponge.

The ice water she made me sip was so cold and the bath so hot.

The blood coursed through my body again. As I lay there, I saw Jade go into my room, rip the sheets off the bed, bundle them up, put fresh ones on. I heard her fluffing pillows, shaking out comforters. Then she came back and knelt beside me. With a sponge she had me bend forward as she rubbed my back, my neck. She ran the sponge across my breasts, over my belly, down my thighs. She put shampoo on her hands, scrubbed my head. I was docile as a baby in her hands as my daughter made me sparkling clean.

"Now, let's get out of the bath," she said. I rose up naked, dripping wet, and Jade wrapped me in a towel, white and fluffy. The towel was warm and I knew she had just gotten it from the dryer. It felt so good to be wrapped in that warm towel. As I sat on the lid of the toilet, Jade combed and blew my hair dry. Then she helped me into fresh pajamas. "When did you have the time to do all this wash?"

"Betsy did it," Jade said.

"Betsy?" I asked.

"She cleaned your whole house, Mom."

When I was spruced up and dry, she put me back into the bed of fresh sheets and I slept again. When I woke, it was still dark and I was ravenous, ready for something to eat. Suddenly I wanted soup, a big pot of lentil soup, and I wanted to make it myself from scratch, never mind that it would take hours to cook. I had a good recipe somewhere in a drawer and I tiptoed into the kitchen to find it.

The kitchen floor was cold and I was barefoot as I stood rifling through the drawer where I kept all my recipes in a folder. I pulled out the folder and on top of it lay the envelope that contained the things Margaret gave me the last time I saw her. I took everything out, dumped it on the counter. Once again I gazed at the clipping of the man who had killed himself forty years before.

I stood in the breakfast nook staring at it, as I had several times before. Then for some reason I thought of the clipping of Margaret's death that I had taken from Vicky's copy of the *Winonah Weekly*. Digging into my errand bag, I found my wallet and inside was the article, still neatly folded where it had been since I put it there on the day of the funeral.

Now I was less hungry than I'd been. Forgetting my plans to make soup from scratch, I lay the two pieces of paper side by side. I looked from one clipping to the next. I knew that there was something in these two articles, written some forty years apart, some clue I'd overlooked. No names were the same, no details of the two suicides, yet I kept going from one article to the next.

It was a puzzle I was trying to solve and suddenly it became clear to me. I remember when the children had these activity books they did in the car—find the telephone in the tree, find the tiger in the closet. You scan the picture until you see, hidden in the intricate, leafy branches, the telephone, or in the clutter of an unkempt closet, a tiger. And of course once you've seen it you wonder what took you so long and you will always see it each time you look at that picture again.

I went over each detail in the two clippings. The places were different, as were the names. The years were different. Nothing appeared to be the same. There seemed to be no overlaps, but then I saw the dates of both deaths—October 12—and realized that Margaret had killed herself on the same day as this man, whose name I now noticed was Martin Burton. He had her initials and they had both died at the age of forty-nine. I sat thinking about what this meant.

I don't know why it had eluded me for so long, but at last I understood. The sun was rising as I gazed out across the Pacific, looking through my favorite grove of trees. Margaret wanted me to have this clipping. She knew I kept things. That was why she had given it to me.

It struck me with a clarity that stunned me and never would have occurred to me otherwise. She had planned it. She had planned it all along. And, the meaning of her note now made explicit, she had waited as long as she could. Margaret had known for years what she was going to do. And when and where.

I made my way back to bed, crawled into the sheets, and slept until late morning. When I woke the room was filled with light and Jade had a fresh pot of coffee brewing. She also had a pile of a week's worth of mail. Catalogs, junk, bills. On the machine, solicitations, messages from Shana, from Ted and Jade. I was tossing most of the mail away, but Jade retrieved the letter from the trash. Buried somewhere at the bottom of the pile of mail she found the letter from the National Registry of Historic Houses.

Jade opened the letter and informed me that my house had qualified, which meant I couldn't change the outside and that it had to have all the proper protections for historic houses under the law of the United States.

The first phone call I made with this news was to John Martelli. He was cool with me on the phone, but he said he'd look into the status of my policy, and a week later he wrote to say that all pertinent riders, including the act-of-God rider, had come through and that as a national monument my house, henceforth, would be fully insured.

"Thank you, John, thank you for all your help."

"It was my pleasure, Tess. I wanted to help you."

I hesitated, but then I said, "Perhaps you'd like to have coffee sometime?" It wasn't that I imagined anything would happen between me and John Martelli, but it seemed like a step back into the world.

"Yes," he said, "I'd like that."

I'd never expected they'd give it to me, but there it was. The premium was higher than I would have liked, but not beyond what I could afford, and I decided to open my bed-and-breakfast. I applied for a loan at the bank and, with Shana's underwriting, I got the money I needed to buy the fluffy green towels, the little bars of soap. I bought nightstands and fake little Tiffany lamps with green glass shades, cozy hassocks. I had the original poems of Francis Eagger, which Bruno had given me, framed. On the walls I hung photographs Francis Eagger had taken of the cliffs he loved so well.

In the library I made out a special place on the shelves for his work. I had a sign made that read THE EAGGER HOUSE BED-AND-BREAKFAST: GUESTS WELCOME. And a brochure printed up that Bruno helped me write:

Come stay in the home that the inspirational poet, Francis Cantwell Eagger, built stone by stone. Experience the house and read his poems. Walk the cliffs, enjoy the marine life below. Make this your weekend getaway or your stop as you head somewhere else.

Come walk with me and I will take you to the path we have carved for ourselves along the sea.—"Desire Paths"

Bruno, who understood now that this was the only way to keep my house, came and helped. I was surprised that he was good with his hands. He nailed up shelves, helped me repaper Jade's room. Jade was glum about all of this, but with a little work we fixed up the old wood-shed and it became a perfect getaway room for her and she actually grew to like it. Ted helped convert the room over the garage into an extra bedroom and he said he'd live there when there were no guests.

Jade and Bruno would sit up late after a day spent working on the house. I'd hear their voices reading poems of the windswept shores, the rocky coasts, poems of trees and animals. Sometimes they'd whisper down below and I wondered what they were doing, but I stayed in my room. One night I heard Jade's door close and it did not open again.

In the morning Bruno was sitting at my spot in the breakfast nook, in his workshirt without his glasses, a sheepish grin on his face, poring over the morning paper. "Good morning, Tess," he said. "Would you like some coffee?"

Slipping into the breakfast nook, I said, "Yes, thank you, Bruno, I would."

In silence Bruno poured me a coffee. "How do you take it?"

"A little milk."

He poured a little milk for me. The coffee was strong but very good. A few moments later Jade came in, showered, her hair damp. She wore a baggy shirt, jeans, but there was a freshness to her face I hadn't seen in a long time. I wanted to reach out and hug her. They both looked hungry to me so I said, "Would you guys like me to scramble you some eggs?"

They nodded and I cracked into a bowl a half-dozen eggs, sprinkled in some cheese and herbs. Diced tomato and onion. I heated olive oil in the skillet and stir-fried the vegetables, poured in the eggs. I made a hearty omelette. I hadn't eaten an omelette like that in years. I watched them gobble it down, their intimacy barely hidden in their silence. "So why don't we all have dinner tonight?" I said. "Help me map out the future."

That night over dinner, Jade made the decision that she would bake for me. She found an interesting recipe for muffins with coconut and chocolate chips and cranberries that sounded terrible, but turned out quite delicious, and these we named Cantwell muffins; she baked scones and coffee cakes and we bought an espresso machine. The house was now filled with the smells of cooking and the sound of young people, but I was haunted by something I could not quite name.

I kept thinking Nick would call. That he would seek me out. How could he not want me when at last he could have me? Or perhaps that was just the point and I'd missed it all along. Perhaps that was what made him stay with Margaret all those years. The fact that he could not have her. No one could.

A few nights later I invited the children out to dinner. I felt there was a reason to celebrate, though I wasn't quite sure what it was. The end of something; the beginning of something else. We went to a trendy new place with lots of hanging plants and polyurethaned tables that was supposed to serve good burgers and vegetarian dishes. Bruno joined us and, just after we ordered, I noticed a family that came in.

They were a fairly large group, at least six or seven of them, and they were seated at the round table next to ours. They were rowdy, laughing, having a good time, but the odd part was I recognized them all. I knew them from somewhere. Even as we ordered and had our drinks, I couldn't help staring. I had seen them all somewhere before.

Even as the kids talked on and went up to the salad bar, I was still trying to decide who these people were. Were my kids friends with their kids? Had I rented them a house? Then I knew. I realized they were the other Winterstones. The family whose pictures I had inadvertently picked up when I went to get the photos of the reunion. I could still see the pictures of the empty room, the Formica table, the chairs, the open suitcase. Pictures of them moving into a simple apartment, laughing around a table with beers and Chinese food. And now here they were intact, eating dinner beside us, ordering hamburgers and onion rings.

I had to resist the urge to go up to them. To say, "I'm also a Winterstone. I'm the person who took your pictures once accidentally. I know something about you that you don't know. I know that you are happy; that you are whole."

But I didn't begrudge them a thing. Instead I joked with Ted about the company he was starting to form and listened as Bruno told Jade in detail about his discovery of the "Desire Paths" poem. As I sat there with Ted, Jade, and Bruno, his hand lightly resting on Jade's knee, surrounded by my children, I thought, This is my family, not the one I was born into, but they are what I have now. The family I have made.

42

It's an odd thing because I live so far away from where it all began and think there are a million things I could have done differently—we all could have done differently—and then maybe we could have saved somebody's life. But whose life would we have saved? That dour child who lives in a big house by the lake alone with her father now, or the child her mother once was who spun with me in the rain?

Or my father, who was a good storyteller and a charming man, but a liar all the same. I forgave him long ago. Or at least I've made my peace with him. I've come to pity Margaret because she waited all those years for a father who would never come. I wished she'd had another father; if only she hadn't wanted mine. I can still see him, dipping into those dark shadows under the railroad trestle and coming out into the sun. Then putting the radio on, singing out loud. His fingers tapping on the wheel.

I've stopped calling Nick. He doesn't return my calls. With time he might come around, but I'm not waiting. I'm going about my business. I'm going to open my B-and-B next season and the kids have agreed, all things being equal, it's probably the best thing. There'll be all kinds of people coming in and out, interesting people from other places. The place won't have this dank, empty feel much longer.

But then something frightens me and I'm not quite sure what it is. I feel it in the air around me. And then I know. I am afraid because Margaret could just show up again, right here. I think of how Margaret was always showing up at our houses, uninvited, searching for what she had lost long ago and would never replace. And though I know this is impossible, it feels as if I am expecting her.

Just the other day I rented the seashell house to a young couple from the Midwest who came highly recommended. They kept oohhing and aahhing and laughing over the accoutrements of the house—the mirror framed in cowrie shells, the shell-shaped sofa—and when I agreed with them that it was an eclectic place, they just started laughing again. Eclectic, they said, then started to laugh. Everything is funny when you are young and in love.

Afterward when I got home, things didn't seem quite where I'd left them. A sweater I hadn't remembered wearing was draped over a chair. A book I wasn't reading was off the shelf. But more than these small things (for Jade could easily go rummaging through my things), the house felt as if someone had been there.

I needed to be outside. I took my usual walk along the dunes, the Poet's Walk, I've come to call it (I've even made a little sign), the path he blazed with his grief, strolling among the ice plants, up and down the cliffs. I peered down at the hunchback tree that had inspired some of Francis Eagger's poems, still struggling to grow on the bluff it had slipped down, that same bluff that would eventually erode its way to my house. But hopefully that was years or decades from now.

I was glad to be outside, collecting pine cones and shells. The air was fresh and I roamed for a long time. The roar of the surf was soothing and I followed the paths along the cliffs. I found a red feather, which I kept. I wandered until the sun began to set. Then a chill came into the air as the wind from the ocean picked up. I was starting to shiver and I had no choice but to turn around and go home.

When I got back, it was just after dusk and I couldn't get warm. I sat up in an armchair in the living room near the hearth, though it had no fire. In a few months I'd rarely be alone in this house. Soon it would be filled with guests, strangers stopping on their way somewhere else. People with their own stories to tell about what has happened in their lives.

I was still cold so I grabbed the Winonah centennial blanket from the back of the chair and tossed it over my legs. The high school, "Home of the Winonah Wildcats," and the train station rested across my lap. Here I was, once more, ensconced in the past. It was time, I thought, to put it away. I took the blanket, folded it, placed it on the top of the linen closet.

Someday I would take it down again, but for now I tucked the blanket in the back of the closet and grabbed a plain down comforter—one that cats had slept on and children had napped in. I wrapped it around my legs until the chill was gone.

Acknowledgments

I want to thank Caroline Leavitt and Larry O'Connor for their excellent critical advice. I also want to thank Julie and Ruediger Flik and Sarah Lawrence College for travel grants that enabled me to do research in California and Illinois, and Mary Jane Roberts and Jerry Evans, who shared their home and their knowledge of California insurance law. I want to thank the friends of my youth for all we've shared, Ellen Levine and Diana Finch for their invaluable input and support, and my editor, Diane Higgins at Picador, for her focused attention. And my daughter, Kate, who traveled the road with me.